The daughter of a Norwegian Viking and a Finnish Moomin, Karina Halle grew up in Vancouver, Canada with trolls and eternal darkness on the brain. This soon turned into a love of all things that go bump in the night and a rather sadistic appreciation for freaking people out. Like many of the flawed characters she writes about, Karina never knew where to find herself and has dabbled in acting, make-up artistry, film production, screenwriting, photography, travel writing and music journalism. She eventually found herself in the pages of the very novels she wrote (if only she had looked there to begin with).

Karina holds a screenwriting degree from Vancouver Film School and a Bachelor of Journalism from TRU. Her travel writing, music reviews/interviews and photography has appeared in publications such as *Consequence of Sound, Mxdwn* and *GoNomad Travel* Guides. She currently lives on an island off the coast of British Colombia with her husband and her rescue pup, preparing for the zombie apocalypse.

To discover more about Karina visit www.authorkarinahalle.com, find her on Facebook, and follow her on Twitter @MetalBlonde.

Why you should lose yourself in a Karina Halle novel:

'Karina Halle has done it again with this violently beautiful tale of love, pain, revenge, and loss, that will rip you apart, piece by piece, and put you back together again' S. L. Jennings

'A story that just about jumps from the pages directly onto the big screen. Fans of suspense and twisted romance will be overjoyed with Halle's talent' *Romantic Times*

'I'm officially addicted to Karina Halle's writing, but I don't plan on seeking a cure for this obsession anytime soon' Chelsea M. Cameron, *New York Times* bestselling author

'I knew from the moment I began chapter one that Karina and I are kindred ⸻⸻⸻⸻⸻ ⸻⸻lling author

D0279855

By Karina Halle and published by Headline Eternal

KARINA HALLE

Bold Tricks

headline
ETERNAL

First published as an ebook in Great Britain in 2013
by HEADLINE ETERNAL
An imprint of HEADLINE PUBLISHING GROUP

First published in paperback in Great Britain in 2014
by HEADLINE ETERNAL
An imprint of HEADLINE PUBLISHING GROUP

1

Cataloguing in Publication Data is available from the British Library

ISBN 978 1 4722 1170 5

Printed and bound in Great Britain by CPI Group (UK) Ltd, Croydon, CR0 4YY

Headline's policy is to use papers that are natural, renewable and recyclable
products and made from wood grown in well managed forests and other controlled
sources. The logging and manufacturing processes are expected to conform to the
environmental regulations of the country of origin.

HEADLINE PUBLISHING GROUP
An Hachette UK Company
338 Euston Road
London NW1 3BH

www.headlineeternal.com
www.headline.co.uk
www.hachette.co.uk

To my future—Scott MacKenzie

ACKNOWLEDGMENTS

Typing "The End" on *Bold Tricks* was a surreal experience for me. It was the first series I've written to be completed in its entirety, and by the time the epilogue came rolling around, I was a complete and utter mess. I've loved these characters like no other and to say good-bye... well, that was extremely hard. So, I have to thank Ellie, Camden, and Javier (and Gus!) for being so complicated and fun to work with. I know, these people are creations from the dark recesses of my head, but honestly, I feel like they're out there somewhere, living their lives. I hope I did your stories justice. You certainly made 2013 such a wonderful rush, and you changed my life in a big way.

Scott MacKenzie, your unfailing support and belief in me is the reason I could even complete these books to begin with. Thank you from the bottom of my heart. I love you.

Brucey Poo... you're one tough puppy. Thank you for somewhat understanding when Mommy had to go write and didn't have time to play with you. Your ability to lie on the couch for hours has been very helpful. Also, big thanks to Dana Hicks!

My family: Tuuli, Sven, Kris...thank you. You've all helped in your own ways, my mother especially in taking care of the dog and the house when I was too busy under deadline to even bathe myself. Though, next time, please leave fewer notes. And to the MacKenzies, particularly Wendy and Jill for your tireless purchasing of my books, thank you for being awesome!

Kelly St-Laurent: your help in brainstorming for *Bold Tricks* gave me the right framework to lay down the beams. Thank you for believing in me.

My beta readers: Megan "Po Po" Simpson, Nina "Cries for Camden" Decker, Laura "Soulless" Moore, Claire "Mrs. Gus" Contreras, Kayla "Team Jumper" Veres, Lucia "Javi Hater" Valovčíková, Barbie "Art Vandelay" Bohrman, Chelsea "Not Married to Kirk" Cameron, Kara "Partner-in-Crime" Malinczak, Emily "Skulls" Franke, Amanda "Vegas Princess" Polito, Robin "Ticket Ripper" Prete, Shawna "Boom" Vitale, Jamie "Pusher" Sager Hall, Boobie Snickle Tush, Kirsten "Camden Lover" Papi, Brenna "Team Psycho" Weidner, Fluffy Dippen Face, Stephanie Sandra "Happy Valentine's Day" Brown, Megan "Take No Prisoner" Ward O'Connell.

So many authors to thank, all for their support and belief in my work: SL Jennings, Madeline Sheehan, MJ Abraham, Courtney Cole, KT Grant, EL Montes, Gail McHugh, CC Brown, JA Huss, JD Salsbury, Ashley Wilcox, Joanna Wylde, Janine Olsson, Kenya Wright, RL Griffin, SL Scott, KA Tucker, Jenn Cooksey, Carey

Heywood, Jesse Lane, Misty Provencher, Rachel "Team Camden" Wade, Lori Otto, Melissa Brown, Kimberly Stedronsky, Venessa Kimble, Ella Fox, LH Cosway, Rebecca Espinoza, Stephanie Lawton, Trevi Truitt, Elle Chardou, Jasinda Wilder, Michelle Valentine, and many, many others.

Bloggers make the writing world go round: Maryse's Book Blog, Autumn Review, Reading in Winter, Ginger Reads, Book Hookers, Angie's Dreamy Reads, Aestas, Natasha Book Junkie, My Secret Romance, The Demon Librarian, True Story Book Blog, Books Babes and Cheap Cabernet, Flirt and Dirty Girls, Under the Covers, Group Therapy Book Club, The Romance Cover, Xpresso Reads, The Book Bellas, The Reading Vixens, Hook Me Up Book Blog, A Love Affair with Books, and the list goes on...

Then there's the team at Grand Central Publishing/Forever Romance: my lovely editor, Latoya Smith, the enthusiastic publicist Julie Paulauski, plus everyone else who has come on board TAT train. And of course, my favorite, Naj Qamber, for her wonderful covers.

Can't go without showing my gratitude to my superhero agent, Scott Waxman, and his team at Waxman Leavell, plus Samantha Howard and Mary Cummings. Farley Chase and Kate Abnerstein, you also rock my socks.

Last but not least, the readers, the fans, and everyone in Halle's Harlots. I would not be HERE writing this right now if it weren't for YOU. Love you all long time.

Bold
Tricks

PROLOGUE

THE GIRL WOKE up screaming.

The pain that had engulfed her the night before hadn't subsided while she lay unconscious, lulled to sleep by the drugs the doctors had given her. The pain wrapped around her legs, defying the morphine that seeped through her young veins.

She tried to sit up in her hospital bed and look around the dark room. There was no one there, not even her parents. She started to shake and cry, not understanding what had happened to her, not able to deal with the agony that had taken over.

She was alone and forever damaged.

Finally one of the night-shift nurses appeared at the door and came running over to her.

"What is it, Ellie?" the nurse asked, but the girl couldn't speak. Her sobs were too powerful. She could only shake her head and moan pitifully, tears streaming down her face.

The nurse knew. She quickly administered more

drugs through the IV drip that went into the girl's arm. The girl had been horribly burned on her leg, one of the worst instances the nurse had ever seen. The doctors had done what they could, but without insurance, her parents were unable to pay for any reconstructive surgery. A skin graft could have saved the girl from having horrible scars in the future.

Her parents weren't even around. They had been sitting in the waiting room for most of the day, but at night they'd gone elsewhere, leaving the girl alone in the hospital. The nurse was extremely suspicious of them—everything from the furtive way they kept leaving the building to the way they explained what had happened to the girl.

Though it was believable that the girl came from the type of low-income family that would allow her to search for car parts on a nearby trash heap, the whole story about accidentally spilling battery acid on her leg didn't ring true. The nurse thought it sounded like her parents were probably running a meth lab instead. Even worse, they could have been neglecting or abusing the girl. There was definitely something wrong with the story, but the girl had been in so much pain that neither the doctors nor the nurses could find out what her version of events was.

Except now. The girl's sobs were subsiding as the morphine began to take effect, working quickly in her eleven-year-old system. The nurse watched her carefully, debating whether or not she should try to ask her. This was a job for Child Services, not for her, but there was something about the girl she wanted to protect. It was like she could see that the child was already damaged before the burns on her leg had happened.

"Ellie," she said gently, smoothing back the girl's fine blond hair. She was going to grow up to be a stunning woman, already showing promise in the usually awkward preteen phase. That made the nurse feel even more sickened for her, knowing her beauty would be marred by the scars that would come.

The girl opened her wide brown eyes and looked up at the nurse. Her face was wet from tears and she looked scared despite the subsiding pain.

"Ellie," the nurse went on, "are you able to tell me what happened to you?"

The girl blinked, unsure of what to do or say. She could barely remember what had happened herself but knew that what had happened was wrong. And even though her parents hadn't told her yet to keep quiet about Travis Raines, the bad man whose house her mother had made her break into, she knew all too well to keep her mouth shut. She was the daughter of con artists, after all, and truth was never an option.

Still, there was a part of her that wanted to tell the nurse what had happened. She wanted to get the Travis man in trouble. She wanted him to be put away for what he had done to her.

"I...I don't remember," the girl said, so terribly afraid she'd tell the truth.

The nurse studied her. "Do you remember looking for car parts?"

Car parts? The girl had no idea what her parents had told the doctors. The confusion came across her face, just long enough for the nurse to pick up on it.

"Ellie, what is the last thing you remember?" the

nurse asked quickly. "How did you burn your leg? Did your parents do this to you?"

The girl's face fell as she tried to figure out what to do.

"What the hell do you think you're doing?" Amelie Watt yelled, appearing at the doorway.

The girl cringed at the sound of her mother's voice. In her increasingly delirious state, she was worried that she may have done something to anger her.

Amelie marched into the hospital room, her eyes blazing at the nurse.

"Why are you questioning my daughter?" she yelled, furious, her arms waving. "That isn't your right."

The nurse stepped back from the girl but refused to apologize. "I'm concerned about her."

"Your only concern is to make my daughter better." Amelie crossed her arms, head held high. She was a striking woman with exotic Eastern European features: high cheekbones, a strong jaw, and dark, sloe eyes. She gave off the impression that she wasn't afraid, but she couldn't hide the tremor in her voice. "Why are you waking her up in the middle of the night anyway? Let my poor baby sleep."

The nurse raised her brows. "Your baby was crying in the middle of the night, screaming from the pain. I was the only one around." She let those last words sink in like daggers.

Amelie sucked in her breath and shook her head. "Don't you dare question my parenting skills. We had to leave to get some sleep at home. It's the only way we can be there for her."

The nurse stared back at Amelie, wondering if she should push it further. She glanced at the girl, who was staring at her mother with a mix of admiration and fear. Perhaps there was no use digging around here. If the girl really was being abused or neglected, Child Services would find out about it. They'd already been notified anyway. The Watts could deal with them in the morning.

Finally the nurse sighed and said, "You've got five minutes before I'll need you to leave the room. She'll need to sleep and the drugs will keep the pain at bay."

Amelie narrowed her eyes and then looked to her daughter. The nurse left the room, closing the door behind her.

Amelie relaxed visibly once she heard the door shut. She came closer to her daughter and placed a hand on Ellie's thin, tanned arm, wincing at the sight of the IV going into it.

"Baby," she whispered. "What did you tell them?"

By now the girl was slowly losing consciousness, eased into a comfortable state by the morphine. She licked her lips and said what she knew her mother wanted to hear. "I didn't tell them anything, Mama."

Amelie gave her a pained smile. "That's my baby girl. When you're feeling better, we'll let you know what to say. For now, tell them that you were looking for car parts at the dump and that is the last thing you remember. You got it? The last thing you remember."

"But..." the girl started. "But the man. Travis." Amelie shuddered at the sound of his name. "He needs to be punished. He needs to go to jail."

"He will be punished one day, baby," her mother said. "One day, he will pay. But that's not your job. We'll take care of it. I promise."

Her mother stayed with her, holding her hand.

I'll make him pay, the girl thought. Then she fell asleep.

CHAPTER ONE

THE STORM RAGED on and inside I was screaming.

I was sitting in a stolen Jeep with no roof, parked on the side of a dirt road beneath a wavering canopy that occasionally let a spattering of rain pelt me in the face. Despite the warmth of the tropical night, I was cold and soaked to the bone in my muddy evening gown. On one side of me was Camden McQueen; on the other was Javier Bernal. One more light than dark; one more dark than light. Both men had come for me. Both men had loved me. And both of them I had seriously underestimated.

There really wasn't much time to sit around and try to get my head on straight. But after everything that had happened—after Javier had manipulated me into coming with him to Mexico; after he'd tried to convince me to kill Travis, his cartel rival; after that went horribly wrong and we had to go on the run in an explosion of gunfire—I knew a panic attack was just waiting to devour me, to incapacitate me, to take me out of the

game. I could feel the fear buzzing through my veins,
threatening to tear me up from the inside out. The fear
of losing everything—Gus, my mother, my revenge,
my purpose. I feared Javier and what he might do to
Camden. I feared Camden and the way he'd changed
toward me. I feared myself and the things I might do to
try to make sense of it all.

We had only been in the Jeep for about ten minutes,
heading back to Veracruz, when I'd told Javier to park the
car so I could have a moment. He reluctantly complied,
finding an area beneath some massive trees that shook
from the howling winds. Both men were staring at me,
and I could only look down at my hands as I rubbed them
up and down against the mud on my dress, the coldness
seeping into my palms. They both knew me, knew my
attacks, and that alone had me screaming internally, wanting to run. I couldn't even look at them. I couldn't even
accept the situation. Javier and Camden. The three of us
having to work together, let alone sit in a Jeep together
without them killing each other. And I was in the middle.

My mind raced back to our escape. *My mother.*
Dear god, my mother. I really never thought I'd see her
again, let alone at a drug lord's party, but there she'd
been, serving motherfucking champagne. She was
working for Travis of all people, the man who poured
acid down my leg when I was just eleven years old, the
same man who my mother wanted to rob that night in
Mississippi. What the hell had happened to her? After
everything we had gone through as a family, after all
the pain I'd suffered, the inquests from authorities, the
move to Palm Valley to stay with Uncle Jim, and her

eventual abandonment of me, why was she here with him now? And where was my father?

I swallowed, my throat feeling thick, and debated asking Javier. He had known this all along, knew where they were. He'd even wanted me to kill them for some sick, divine purpose based on that damaged moral code of his. This whole time he'd known and he was using me.

I couldn't even be angry at him over that, though. I should have known better, I should have expected this. I was so damn angry at myself for falling for his old tricks, for slipping into a past that would have been better left buried. I listened to his sweet, sweet lies, and I believed them, like the naïve girl I used to be. I hated myself for losing my faith in Camden and putting it in Javier instead, and hated myself even more for the damage I had caused. That was another reason I couldn't look at him. Every time I looked at Camden, I saw the ways he'd changed. He was stronger, tougher, and more ruthless. He was also hurt, scarred deep inside by what I'd done. He now had the kind of scars that even his skilled hands couldn't transform.

"Are you okay?" Camden asked, his voice low. My knee was touching his knee. My other knee was touching Javier's. I could feel them on either side of me, hear their breathing, both their bodies tense and rigid as we sat there in the darkness. This was so awkward. So fucking awkward.

And from the looks of it, with Gus and my parents in the clutches of Travis Raines, my cover being blown, the three of us having to make our way through Mexico together, awkward was the least of my problems.

I nodded, still looking at my hands, even though I wasn't okay. None of us were.

Javier sighed loudly. Something about his manner made me look over. Somehow it was easier to look at him, maybe because I didn't feel guilt when I did.

"What?" I asked. I pressed my fingers into my thighs to keep my nerves from misfiring.

He tilted his head toward me, and though the only light came from the glow of the Jeep's dashboard and the far-off flashes of lightning in the sky, I could see the gleam in his eyes. Unreadable, as always.

"I'm just wondering how long we're going to sit here in a fucking tropical storm," he said simply, a false smile spread across his face. "That's all."

Camden sat up straighter. "At least the rain should wash all that blood off your face."

Javier's eyes flicked over to him. "Are you sure you want me to help you get your fat Gus back? Because I think I'm the one doing you both a favor. Aside from saving your behinds, of course. I don't recall either of you thanking me yet."

I exhaled through my nose. "Just give me a few minutes. I need to figure out the plan."

Javier let out a dry laugh, rain running off the tip of his nose, and eyed me incredulously. "The plan? You're not in charge of the plan, angel. If you want my help, then you're doing it my way."

"Fuck that," Camden spat out.

I finally had to look at him. His eyes were raging beneath his glasses that reflected the dull glow from the car, and he was gripping the door handle like he was about to break it in two. Oh god, I didn't need this. But then again, it was partly my fault. Maybe I did need this. I deserved it.

"Camden," I said, trying to placate him with my eyes, "please, let's just . . . let's just stay calm and think."

"I am calm," Javier answered as Camden opened his mouth. "I need to go find my sister, Violetta. That's my goal first and foremost. Then I'll help you get to Travis and Gus."

"And my mother?" I filled in, daring him to be honest.

He gave me a short nod, though he was looking off toward the dark road. "Yes . . . and your mother."

Now was the time to ask him. Better now than never.

I took in a deep breath. "Where's my father? I didn't see him at the party."

He raised a brow and looked over my head at Camden. Why, I had no fucking idea. I turned to look at Camden, but he was staring back at Javier like he didn't even know who he was.

"Javier," I repeated. "Where is my father?"

He frowned at Camden and looked back at me. His face went stony. "The man you call your father is dead."

Every limb on me froze. My lungs sucked in warm air and raindrops.

"Dead?" I asked, feeling like I was choking.

Dead.

My father was dead?

No.

Javier's eyes softened, but only for a moment. "I didn't know until I got here."

I let it soak into my bones. My father was dead.

The good parent.

The weak one.

Dead.

With my mother working for Travis, I truly was an orphan now.

"Oh god," I said, finally finding enough air. I leaned forward, trying to ward off another panic attack, and Camden's warm hand met the small of my back, just enough to let me know he was there. His touch somehow strengthened me. "Oh god."

"I'm sorry," Javier said.

It took a few moments before I realized what he'd said.

I immediately whipped my head toward him. "No you're not," I seethed. "You wanted me to kill them. You sick fucking bastard, you wanted me to kill my own parents. You brought me here for that. You are not fucking sorry!"

Javier stared at me impassively, his features forever reptilian, smooth and calculating. No emotion. No anything. How could I have ever thought there was something warm inside him?

"You're right," he said, turning his attention back to the empty road. "I'm not sorry. I'm glad he's dead. He deserves it for what he did to you. But I am sorry you feel this way, right now."

"Like I wouldn't have felt worse if *I* killed them?"

He shrugged. "Obviously now I know how that would have played out. Apparently you don't hold the same grudges that I do."

I felt like elbowing him in the nose again, seeing it break over and over. But Javier was one of those men who could take the pain and make it work for him. He had too much of an advantage over us at the moment, and he *liked* it when I hated him. Maybe more than when I loved him.

"How did he die?" I asked, grinding my teeth.

"I don't know," he said. "All I know is that there is one less person to hurt you."

"You are so fucked up," Camden muttered, his hand pressing against my back.

Javier merely grinned at that, his teeth white in the darkness, taking no offense at all. "Whatever I am, you need me more than I need you. And because of that, you'll do as I say."

"Sounds like a deal with the devil," I told him.

"My, my, angel, how quickly you've changed your tune now that this tattooed ape is back in your life." He eyed Camden. "You know, just because you're here now doesn't mean you've won anything."

"I only came to get Ellie back," he said, his voice quiet but full of animosity. I knew that Camden was keeping himself on a very tight leash. I also knew that when he didn't—well, I didn't have to look long at Javier's bruised and bloodied face to know what happens.

"Oh, of course," Javier said with deliberation. "But is she really back?"

"Javier, shut the fuck up," I said. "If you've got a plan then tell us what the plan is, because the longer we sit here arguing, the farther Gus gets away from us."

He slowly looked back to me. "That has been my point all along. Are you able to think now? Is your little attack over? Because I know what worked last time you—"

"Get on with it," I cut in. Neither Camden nor I needed him to finish his sentence. The last time I had a panic attack around Javier, we ended up having sex in an orange grove. I was vulnerable, driven by lust, desperate for closure, and lured back into my own past. I had a million excuses for why I'd fucked him, but what bothered me the most was that at the heart of them all, I did it because I'd wanted to. I'd needed to. Now, looking at him, knowing how much he had and hadn't changed, I hated myself for being so weak, hated my body for betraying me so easily.

He held my gaze and I knew in the dimness he could make out the raw anger in my eyes. He was thinking, wondering how much more he could toy with me. He now had the ability to get a rise out of both Camden and me anytime he wanted. He was a man with too much ammo, but perhaps he'd always been that way. He stockpiled it like a squirrel gathering acorns for winter.

He shifted the Jeep with a lurch, causing me to fall into Camden, and pulled the vehicle back onto the dirt road, the rain whipping us as it continued to fall in heavy drops. We sped in the direction of Veracruz, where the city lights were casting a dull orange glow on the bottoms of the storm clouds.

"The first step is to get rid of this car," Javier said, his mouth set in a grim line. "They'll be looking for it."

"There's always Jose," Camden said.

I looked at him incredulously. "You have Jose?"

He gave me a small smile. "The car's a bit battered,

but yeah I have Jose. It brought me and Gus down here. All your stuff is still in the trunk."

Thank god, because all my other stuff was in the hotel room that I wouldn't be returning to. The only thing I had on me was what fit into my clutch purse: Eleanor Willis's passport (which was pretty much useless now since Travis knew it was a fake), some makeup, a few pesos, and that was it.

"Right," Javier scoffed. "I'm sure the car isn't wanted by a few people either."

"You mean other than you?" I asked.

He grunted. "The past is the past. We're better off getting something more inconspicuous, don't you agree?"

"We're getting my stuff out of the car, at least," I told Javier. "You can add that to your plan."

He made another disagreeable sound but didn't argue. "Fine. Get your stuff. Get a new car. Head to Mexico City to check on Violetta."

I frowned at the mention of his sister. "Check on?"

He nodded. "I'll tell her to get out of town, go to Marguerite's or Alana's in Jalisco."

"And she'll listen to you?"

He bit his lip for a second. "She knows what happened to Beatriz. She'll listen."

"Who is Beatriz?" Camden asked.

Javier shot him a look as he brought the Jeep onto the main highway. "None of your fucking business."

"It's one of his sisters," I quickly told Camden. "Travis murdered her."

"Of course he did," Camden said with a sigh, leaning back into the seat. I finally had the strength to watch him for a few moments. The wind was ruffling up his dark hair, his glasses reflecting the lights of the few cars on the highway that were braving the storm. His jaw was strong, lips full but held together tightly. I knew he was tormented but I didn't know by whom. Was it Javier?

Or was it me?

He took his glasses off and wiped the rain off of them with the sleeve of the tuxedo he had gotten for Travis's party. It took effort, his brilliant blue eyes wincing with pain. His shoulder was still messed up from being shot.

"Do you have any more of your painkillers?" I asked him.

He closed his eyes and nodded while he slipped his glasses back on. "Now's not the time. I'll deal."

"Well you certainly dealt with Javier's face," I said. It slipped out before I had a chance to take it back. I wasn't about to start provoking the monster, but it was easier said than done.

And provoke him I did.

Javier's grip on the wheel tightened and he slammed on the brakes so hard that we went skidding across the highway. I screamed, the tires squealing beneath us, as we came to a shuddering stop on the shoulder and he shifted into park.

"Jesus!" Camden yelled. "Are you trying to kill us?"

Javier immediately whipped out his gun so it was in front of my face and pointed at Camden.

"No. Now I'm trying to kill you," Javier sneered, staring down the barrel of the gun.

"Then fucking do it," Camden said, his eyes blazing, meeting the challenge.

"You shouldn't tempt me," Javier countered.

My eyes darted between the two of them and the
gun. It wavered slightly, betraying Javier's smooth exte-
rior. He was damn angry, angry enough to do something stupid. He didn't need Camden egging him on.

I raised my hands slowly, careful not to touch the
gun that was inches away. I spoke carefully, trying to
keep my voice from shaking. "Please, please, Javier,
Camden, let's just...let's just calm down."

"Shut up," Javier said, his eyes flitting to me and
back to Camden. "This is all your fault."

"How is this my fault?" I exclaimed and then realized it was. I needed to keep my mouth shut. We all did.
I looked between the two of them and said, "Okay, I'm
sorry. It is my fault. Obviously we're not getting anywhere if we can't get along."

Javier's grip tightened on the gun. "This isn't a
matter of getting *along*, angel." He licked his lips and
nodded at Camden. "Tell me, Camden, how did you
manage to escape from your ex-wife and the mighty
Vincent Madano?"

Camden frowned at him, his jaw tensing. "How do
you know about that?"

Javier grinned. "I read it in the newspaper like
everyone else."

"Bullshit."

"I have to say, I'm impressed," Javier went on. "Vincent Madano is not a man you can just mess up and
walk away."

"How well do you really know them?" I asked Javier, remembering that Camden had said something about it all being a setup, that Sophia and her brothers and possibly Javier were all in on it. The exchange, the kidnapping—it was all for show. All to get me away from Camden and maybe to put Camden in danger.

It must have been driving Javier crazy to have Camden here with us. Camden could not be caught that easily.

"I know them well enough," Javier said. He loosed his grip on the gun, shook the rain off of it, and put it back in his waistband. I exhaled in relief. "But I suppose that's neither here nor there at this point."

I was sure that Camden wouldn't let it go that easily. Just how deeply was Javier tied to his ex-wife and her brothers and why? But Camden only gave Javier a final glare before turning his attention back to the darkened farmland we had stopped beside.

"Let's just get Gus back," he said and pressed his lips together as if to prevent himself from saying something else.

Javier watched him for a few moments before putting the Jeep back into drive and returning us to the highway.

We sat in unbearable silence as we made our way into Veracruz, yet it was safer than saying anything. I felt as if we were a word away from incinerating one another. Camden only spoke up to give directions to where he had ditched Jose.

Unfortunately it was a bit too close to Travis's compound for comfort. We pulled down a quiet residential street only a few blocks away, the leafy trees blowing wildly in the wind, the rain having thankfully dropped off. The sound of helicopters buzzed in the distance.

Javier eyed the sky and I asked, "Are those his or news choppers?"

He nodded slightly. "They're his. The news wouldn't dare cover this."

"Turn right down here," Camden told him, and we came down another street, this one more narrow, with the trees blocking out the streetlights that were few and far between. This was still a well-to-do area, though the houses were smaller and spaced farther apart, all behind tall gates and walls. I did note that it was a dead-end road, which meant there was only one way out if something were to happen to us. We couldn't be too careful, not with the choppers circling in the distance, their spotlights occasionally lighting up the sky.

"There she is," Camden said, pointing to the end of the street where jungle seemed to have taken over and there were no streetlights. I could barely make out the shape of the car in the darkness.

"She?" Javier asked, eyebrow cocked. "Its name is Jose."

Camden shrugged. "Guess she's a cross-dresser."

Javier sighed, shaking his head in disgust, and pulled the Jeep up to it. "Let's make this fast."

We hopped out and it was only now that we were closer that I saw what Camden meant by "battered."

"Holy shit, Camden!" I cried out at the sight of the poor vehicle.

"What the hell did you do to my car?" Javier yelled, his hands thrown up in the air.

The GTO had the paint scraped off all along one side, the windows on the driver's side were all shot out, the driver's-side mirror was missing, and the front was totally crunched up, with only the right headlight intact.

"*Your* car?" I asked Javier once I managed to look away from poor Jose. "What happened to the past being the past?"

"Now's not the time to argue semantics," Camden interrupted us. "She's broken but she's a survivor." He fished the keys out of his suit jacket and tossed them at me. "Just like you."

I caught them and he held my eyes for a moment before walking past me back to the Jeep.

Javier scoffed, though I didn't know if it was for the state of the car or Camden's comment, and made his way to the trunk. He bumped it with his fist. "Come on, let's get her open."

I was about to hurry over to him when Camden suddenly said, "Fuck."

I spun around and looked at him. He was frozen in the act of taking off his jacket, his good arm free, his head cocked upward, eyes searching the sky. The sound of the choppers had gotten louder, and over the tips of the waving trees I could see the spotlight in the sky, the blades whirring.

"Yeah, no kidding fuck," I said. I turned to Javier and quickly ran over to him, trying to get my keys into the trunk of the car. I kept fumbling, missing the lock just as the wind blew my hair back and we were lit up by the spotlight, the helicopter coming closer. We were in their sights, no doubt about that. We had been spotted.

"Hurry up!" Javier yelled at me before ripping the keys out of my hands.

Camden hit the side of the Jeep with his fist. "There's no time!" he yelled. "We have to go!"

"No!" I yelled back as Javier got the trunk open. "Not without my stuff!"

Suddenly the ground in front of Camden started exploding with bullets as a steady stream of them came off the approaching chopper. We all cried out, dirt flying everywhere.

Javier quickly slammed the trunk shut. "Then we're taking Jose. Get the fuck in!"

He went for the driver's seat as Camden came running over, taking my hand and pulling me to the passenger's side. He shoved me into the backseat, telling me to lie down, and barely got in the car himself before Javier was gunning the engine and driving the car backward. I could feel the wheels spinning for grip beneath my head and tried to sit up just as the sound of more bullets filled the air. I was tossed back down as Javier put the pedal to the floor and turned the wheel, the sheer power of the rear wheels grinding until we did a 180 and were facing the right way. The chopper was now directly above us, and I could feel the wind its blades created flowing through the smashed windows, the spotlight blinding me.

"Hang on," Javier said. "This is going to get ugly before it gets better."

He pressed down on the gas again and the car roared

loudly before it lurched forward and we were all pinned back to our seats from the force. This is exactly why I loved this car. I just hoped it was stronger than it looked at the moment.

We raced down the street, the chopper in hot pursuit, the whir of blades and bullets gaining on us. I leaned forward between the seats, reaching for the glove compartment, waving my hand at it when I couldn't reach. "My gun, give me my gun!"

Camden gave me an odd look but opened the compartment and handed me the gun that was thankfully still in there. It wasn't my Colt .45—that was in the trunk still—but it would do.

"What are you doing?" Camden yelled as I quickly checked the clip and slammed it back in.

"She's being a good girl," Javier said just as the trunk was bombarded with bullets, sounding like metal fireworks being set off. "Fuck!" he yelled and swerved, trying to lose them, as I attempted to lean out of his window. I wedged myself up against the back of his seat and faced behind us. The wind whipped my hair around, the spotlight blinding me, but I managed to keep the gun aimed upward at the helicopter. I had no idea if this would work like it did in the movies, but I figured it was better than just sitting in the backseat and doing nothing.

Only problem was, Javier kept swerving and throwing me off balance and the chopper kept moving out of my sights. You'd think that would mean that their bullets weren't any closer to hitting us, but that wasn't quite the case. One hit the trunk again, a dangerously close call, just as Javier brought the car spinning around the corner and onto another road.

"Where do I shoot?" I screamed above the noise. "The fuel tank?"

"Shoot the fucking person who's shooting at us!"

"Right," I muttered. All I could see against the light was the outline of the chopper, not anyone inside. Still, there was a faint red glow whenever the gun went off, so I just aimed there, firing off a few rounds and hoping they went somewhere.

Suddenly the windshield in the back of the car was hit and I screamed as it exploded into a million shards of glass. Obviously I hadn't hit the gunman yet.

"Keep shooting!" Javier yelled as he brought the car around onto another street. We were leaving the hidden, residential hills of the wealthy and coming into the more open and busier suburbs of Veracruz. It was well lit and now there was traffic we had to contend with.

The chopper ducked down lower and sped up as we slowed to navigate around the cars on the road. The sound of horns, irate yells from drivers, and screeching tires filled the air. I took aim once more and fired again and again, hoping it would hit at least the windshield. But the helicopter came closer, the wind from the rotors shaking my arms like jelly, its landing skids almost coming down on top of us until Javier swerved the car to the left and the chopper had to rise quickly to get above a tall semi-truck in its path. I took the time to grab my arm with my other hand, trying to steady myself, to ignore the cramp in my lower back, the pressure of the door frame against my shoulder.

Come on, Ellie, I told myself as the helicopter came back again, much faster now and much lower, as if it didn't give a fuck anymore.

"Drive faster!" I yelled but wasn't sure Javier could hear me over the noise. I took in a deep breath, trying to see past the hair flying in front of my face, and started firing.

I fired and fired but it just came closer and closer.

And then there was a dull click.

There were no more bullets left in my gun.

And my other clip was in the glove compartment.

We were fucking screwed.

CHAPTER TWO

"SHIT, SHIT, SHIT!" I yelled at the gun, trying to figure out if I had enough time to duck back into the car to get the extra round. The helicopter was close enough now that I could see the guy with the semiautomatic leaning out of the door, one of his feet on the landing skids, the gun aimed directly at me.

A shot rang out through the air, blasting my ears.

The man with the gun wavered from his position, the gun slipping out of his hands first before he fell over and smashed onto the street below him, the cars behind us trying to drive around his body.

What the hell?

I turned my head and looked over the hood of Jose. Camden was leaning out of his window, a gun in his hand, aimed at the chopper.

"Nice shot!" I yelled at him, feeling a surge of giddiness and adrenaline run through me. I think I was grinning.

He gave me a look that was as blasé as it could be

when he was hanging outside of a speeding muscle car having just shot a man in a helicopter. Then with stark determination he aimed again and shattered the chopper's window. Within seconds the helicopter started to tilt off to the side before going into a tailspin and crashing onto the shoulder of the road.

My mouth dropped open, eyes wide as hell, as the helicopter erupted into a giant fireball that lit up the street, nearly engulfing the passing cars around it. Though we were still speeding away, I could feel the blast of heat on my face.

I looked back at Camden incredulously. Where the hell had this man learned to shoot?

He gave me a weary smile. "I have steady hands." Then he disappeared inside the car.

I slipped back in as well, my heart racing a mile a minute as I found the security of the backseat. That was a rush greater than a thousand cons. I'm not sure why I expected Javier to say something encouraging, but he just glared at me in the mirror and said, "Took you long enough."

"You should thank your ass that she's a good shot," Camden said quickly. I guess from his perspective, Javier couldn't really tell whose gun took down the helicopter, and Camden was making it look like it was all my doing. I felt simultaneously touched and ashamed. He was trying to make me look better than I really was.

Javier grunted and kept Jose swerving in and out of the cars on the road.

"Now what?" I asked.

"There will be more helicopters where that came

from," Javier answered. "We're going to have to avoid the highways now."

"Can we switch cars?" Camden asked.

"No time," Javier said, not looking at him. I watched his grip on the steering wheel, the pronounced ridge of his knuckles. He was gripping it hard; he was rattled to the bone over what had just happened. I wasn't sure if that should make me feel better or not. "We're not stopping until we have to."

It was about three in the morning when we finally *had* to stop. Jose ran out of gas right outside the city limits of Apizaco, not too far from Mexico City. Luckily we were able to pull up to a small albeit rundown motel to shelter us until the nearest gas station opened in the morning.

"Are you sure it's even open?" I asked Javier as we climbed out of the car, legs stiff and tired from the voyage. Taking the back roads and staying off the major highways meant it took us much longer than it should have, though I was appreciating the fact that we had arrived close to our destination and still in one piece.

He jerked his head at the motel. "They'll take our money."

It was a row of rooms all facing a dirt parking lot. It reminded me a lot of Shady Acres, the motel where Camden and I had met Uncle Jim just before he set me up and Javier shot him in the head. I tried to control the wave of anger and sorrow that was rollicking through me. I couldn't keep dwelling on the past, things that would drown me if I let them. I couldn't succumb to it now, not in this situation, not with the murderer right beside me. The very murderer I'd been blind enough to sleep with—as if the sex erased all past sins, as if it smoothed over the lies our relationship had been built on.

Crickets filled the night air as Javier went toward the small house behind the motel, probably to go wake up whoever was in charge of the place. There were no other cars in the parking lot, and from the look of the dilapidated grounds they probably didn't have much business. I supposed the fact that it was the middle of the night and Camden and I were dressed as if we were attending the Oscars wouldn't faze them either.

I looked at Camden as Javier disappeared around the corner. "How's your shoulder? Ready for those pills?"

He grimaced. "We'll see."

I took a step toward him, feeling entranced by his presence so close to me. This was the first instance we'd been alone all night, and after the escape from Travis's and the consequent car chase, he was looking larger than life. His tuxedo tie had come undone, his white shirt unbuttoned a bit, just enough to show off his tats, which looked dark in the dim light.

"Can I see?" I asked, reaching for his jacket. I wasn't a nurse by any means, but I still wanted to help. He'd gotten fucking shot trying to reach me.

He shrank back slightly, something I pretended didn't hurt like hell, but in the end relented and let me help him get his jacket off. His shoulder was completely soaked through with blood.

"Jesus, Camden," I couldn't help but exclaim. "We need to get your bandages changed."

I carefully pulled the rest of his arm through the jacket.

"Don't worry about it," he said.

"What do you mean, 'don't worry about it'?"

He gave me a leveling gaze. "It's not your problem. It's mine. I can take care of myself."

"I know you can but—"

"Ellie, I think you need to stay with Javier tonight."

My lungs felt as if they were suddenly full of glass.

"What?" I managed to get out.

He rubbed his lips with the back of his hand and brought his gaze over to the motel. "I don't know about you, but I don't trust that fucking bastard for a second."

"And I do?" I asked incredulously.

He smirked, only for a second. "Well, it's hard to say."

"Camden, the minute he discovered the tracking device on my necklace—"

"Oh, so that's what happened? I finally find you after all this fucking time, tell you what you're up against and try to save you with the tracking device, and somehow Gus and I end up tracking Javier instead."

I inhaled quickly through my nose, trying to keep from panicking. "I didn't set you up. He found out! You have to believe me."

He sighed and looked back at me, but all I could see were the lights of the motel in the reflection of his glasses. "I believe you, Ellie. I believe you."

"But you think I should stay with him?"

"If you don't trust him either, then you know we can't leave him alone. We'll wake up and the car will be

gone with all your stuff. He'll abandon us. I don't care
what he says. There is no way that he needs us to do
what he wants. He's got connections, he's got his cartel...We're just being allowed to tag along and I don't
know why."

I almost stamped my foot. "But I can't stay with him!"

"Obviously if I do, one of us will end up dead. At
least for you it's as natural as wiping your ass."

I glared at him. "Why are you doing this?"

He shook his head, as if to himself, and kicked a
stone that went skidding across the dry soil of the lot.
"I'm doing what needs to be done. It doesn't mean you
have to sleep with him, Ellie. Just keep an eye on him.
I'll be stationed outside the door anyway."

I walked over to him and placed my hands on his
firm chest. "I want to stay with you." I bit the bullet. I
didn't care.

He peered at me, his Adam's apple bobbing as he
swallowed hard. He opened his beautiful mouth, about
to say something, then abruptly closed it for a few
moments. "He's coming."

I stepped back and took my hands off him.

Javier appeared around the corner and came marching to us with a smile on his face. "Well, I got us our
rooms. *Uno*, *dos*, and *tres*." He gestured to the first
three to our left.

Ugh. Sharing a room with Javier would be a night-
mare at this point, but Camden did have a point. I
didn't trust Javier and knew he was capable of screw-
ing us over at the first opportunity. Staying in separate
bedrooms this early in the game would be the perfect

opportunity for him to up and leave us. Javier's alliance only extended to his sister, not to Gus, and the fact that he was even agreeing to help us at all said a lot. Unfortunately, I didn't know exactly *what* it said.

"I'm staying with you," I quickly said to Javier. I didn't bother putting on an act, smiling or acting coy. He'd see straight through me anyway. He always did.

He raised his brow. "Is that right, angel? And to what do I owe your angelic company?"

"Because you're both the same," Camden filled in. He stepped forward and quickly swiped a key out of Javier's hand. "You're meant for each other." He took off for his room, his back straight and proud. My heart both lurched and ached at his words, how badly he was brushing me off, how ill he thought of me.

Javier was surprised and loving it. He turned to me, mouth slightly agape. "Wow. Something tells me he was trying to be insulting."

I couldn't even fake a smile. "Which one is our room?" I asked, feeling sick as the words came out.

He grinned at me, all snake, no conscience. "Whichever one I choose, angel. Have you got all your belongings?"

Normally I would have brought out everything from the trunk, but there were an awful lot of lives in there, an awful lot of stuff. With me keeping an eye on Javier all night, it was probably safe.

I shook my head. "It's fine."

He smiled again, especially as Camden shut the door to room number one.

"Let's take *numero tres, sí*?" Javier asked. "More privacy." He grabbed my hand and led me toward it, though there was nothing gentle or warm in his touch. Just like that, those days were over. I was back to dealing with the spurned Javier, the hunter and the sadist.

He opened the door and flicked on the lights. A few cockroaches skittered underneath the bed, and moths darted to the threadbare light fixture hanging from the ceiling. The room was as run-down as I'd ever seen, and for one twisted second I was glad I wasn't sleeping there alone. In the next second, though, I was reminded that the company of insects was preferable to his.

He closed the door behind us and put his hand at my neck, holding me there, and leaned into my ear. "Do you want top or bottom?"

I stiffened for a moment, then rammed my elbow back into his gut. "Fuck you."

He let go of me and coughed loudly, still trying to smile. "You should be glad I'm giving you the option, angel."

"You're a sick pig."

He straightened up and shrugged. "It's what you liked until about, oh, twelve hours ago. Tell me, angel, what is it about that boy that makes you forget who you really are? Is it the tattoos, because you know I have those." He quickly shed his linen shirt and stood bare-chested before me, the tattoo of his mother's name on his inner arm. He turned around slowly, making sure I saw the large cross going down his spine. "Or is it those horrible glasses of his? You know, I can look like a fucking idiot if I really wanted to."

I narrowed my eyes, keeping far away from him like wary prey. "He sees the good in me."

He laughed. "The good. Of course. The good. So, is that why you're spending the night with me? Because I looked into that boy's eyes tonight and there was no good in there left for you."

My gaze locked with his, a war without further words. His eyes shone yellow-green in the light, looking more inhuman by the moment. Deep in his insanity, he was making some sense. That's what I hated most about Javier, that there was always a kernel of truth to his words, a truth that made you fall for the lies.

I sucked back my breath and nodded at the sagging bed. "You better get a good night's sleep." Then I grabbed one of the pillows and the top sheet and brought it over to the thin Mexican rug that ran along the foot of it.

"You're serious?" he asked as I started making my bed on the floor.

"Good night," I told him, lying down on top of the sheet. I didn't trust the cleanliness of the floor and it was too hot to have a sheet on top of me anyway. I rolled over so I was facing away from him. He was still standing near the bed.

"Come now," Javier said. "Sharing a bed with me isn't that bad. You've been doing it for the last week. Is the inevitable sex too distracting?"

I ground my teeth together but didn't say a word.

Suddenly he dropped to the ground on top of me, flipping me over so I was on my back, pinning both of my arms to the ground, his face just inches from mine. Wild strands of his hair partially obscured his feverish eyes.

"I'll scream," I said hoarsely, fear pulsing through my veins.

He grinned. "You know I love that."

Then he lowered his lips to mine, his warm and salty taste engulfing me. I did my best to keep my lips shut, to wriggle my mouth out of the way.

"Oh, angel," he murmured near my lips. "Stop the act. We both know you want this."

"Don't you fucking dare," I grunted, "or I will make you pay."

He chuckled and lifted his head, peering down at me curiously, still keeping a death grip on my arms. "You're not thinking straight. You've got everything backward, you know?"

"I'm thinking just fine." I stared right back at him, refusing to be intimidated, even though he was straddling me on the floor of our hotel room. "You're backward."

He gave a subtle shake of his head. "How quickly you change your tune, how easily you are manipulated. You think that just because Camden came for you that it means he knows what's best for you?"

"I know what's best," I said, trying to keep my voice steady.

"You don't," he said, "and you never did. You keep trying to be good, to be this person that you're not, and you think the minute someone tries to convince you, tells you something that you want to hear, that they must speak the truth." He ran his fingers down the side of my face, gently at first before pressing them in harder near my mouth. "So beautiful, so naïve. You know, even though he is here it doesn't mean you're obligated to be with him. It doesn't mean you owe him anything. You never asked him to come after you." He traced my rigid lips with his forefinger. "It isn't too late, you know. I can forgive your lies, your... lack of loyalty. I can forget that you ever conspired with him. We can do this, just the two of us."

"Do what?" I asked once he removed his fingers.

His smile was lopsided. It would have looked cute on anyone else, but the depravity in his eyes soiled it. "Rule the world. Don't you remember? I'll be the king and you'll be my queen." He leaned in closer and closed his eyes, whispering, "Travis is in our reach. We are so close now. You are so close to getting your revenge."

"No," I said. "I only want Gus back. You can have Travis."

His eyes fluttered even though they were shut, as if he was having trouble comprehending what I was saying. "Of course, your Gus. And your mother too, I suppose."

I swallowed with effort, stifled again by the memory of seeing her at the party. "Yes, my mother. I'm just here for them. That's the only reason I'm going after Travis."

He opened his eyes, narrowing them slightly. "I figured as much. You know, you'll change your mind when you see Travis again. And I'll be the one handing you the gun to finish the job. Then you'll have your people back. And then, with his blood on your hands, you'll finally have your peace. Don't forget what you were prepared to do earlier. Don't pretend like you weren't going to drop that poison into his meal. Don't act like you weren't fully prepared to kill the very man that ruined our lives."

"Our lives?"

He blinked a few times. "Your pain has been my pain."

"I call bullshit on that."

"And I call bullshit on you. You know what you mean to me, angel. You know the lengths that I'll go to, all to make sure you get justice."

I took in a deep breath, so conscious of how close his face was to mine, so mindful of his lips that looked ready to come crashing onto mine again. I had to say what I needed to say and had to say it right. Being straight was the only way out.

"Javier. I appreciate you saving us. And I do want to get your sister someplace safe. And if you can really help me get Gus back, then I owe you everything in the world. But what we shared, what we had, is over." I swallowed hard but kept my voice steady. "It was over the moment I found out your true intentions. It was over the moment I realized I was being manipulated like some fucking puppet on a string. And it was over when I realized you and I are as toxic as the poison you put in my necklace. That has always been the truth and that will *never* change. The us that was is gone. This is the new us. We can help each other and if we can't, then we shouldn't be in each other's lives. If you're going to have your own agenda and your own plan other than helping me get to Gus, then we should part ways, right now, tonight, and never look back at each other.

Never look for each other. Move on and forget. Do you understand?"

My heart was beating so hard I could feel it in my lips, in my fingers. I had no idea how he was going to take this.

He stared at me stone-faced, as if he didn't even hear me. He clicked his tongue against the roof of his mouth and looked up at the ceiling. "I think I understand. Yes, I think I hear you." He cleared his throat and straightened up, still straddling me, but at least my face was free from his lips and grasp. His eyes still focused upward and he said, "Angel, angel, angel," while shaking his head back and forth. "I thought I knew you. I only knew the...*fetus*...compared to the woman you could be." He looked at me sharply. "What a fucking disappointment you are."

Then he quickly got up and marched over to the bathroom, slamming the door behind him. I sat up, rubbing at my face. He hadn't hurt me, but his touch still lingered like an aftertaste. The thing was, a part of me still wanted that revenge on Travis. But now that it was Javier's idea, I wasn't about to give him credit. Javier had the advantage when it came to tricks, to contacts, to the plan. But I felt like I had the emotional upper hand. I didn't know how long it would last and I didn't know what kind of man it would make him—this would be the second time I'd spurned him, after all. He was a loose cannon, a wild card, and it was the moment I underestimated him that he'd totally pull the rug out from under us.

I thought back to Camden, wondering if he was in

his room or outside the door like he'd said. I know it shouldn't have, but it hurt like hell that he'd asked me to stay with Javier. I wanted Camden to be protective, to be my shield, especially now when I needed him the most. Instead, he was distant and becoming more distant by the moment. I knew he'd never let anything happen to me, that he would do his best to make sure I was alive, that he'd help me get Gus back, that he'd return me to California all in one piece. I just didn't know how deep his wounds went either. When he was gone, Javier had been the person I relied on, whether that was a smart decision or not. But now with Camden in the picture, I felt myself naturally gravitate toward him.

Screw Javier and what he thought of my nature. My real nature, my real self, wanted that person to believe in me, to see the good, ignore the bad, and make me feel like I had a future. Camden was my future—though now that he was closer than ever, I felt that future being taken away from me. All because I made a foolish mistake. All because I had no faith.

The fact was, when I really looked at it, when I really searched deep inside, I knew I was still in love with Camden. It was a love I'd had to bury for the last few weeks, a love I thought I could never have, that I'd never deserve. But I felt it, hidden underneath the layers, like the center of the sun. It was blinding when you had a glimpse of it, but it was enough that you knew it was there, shining down on you. I'd let myself get burned if I could.

Yet now that everything had changed between us, that he knew I'd been with Javier, that I'd been sleeping with him…I wasn't sure how we could recover from that. I could argue my side until I was blue in the face, keep telling him it never meant anything. But he wouldn't believe that and even I knew that was a bit of a lie, because Javier did mean something. Just for those moments where I could fool myself into thinking it meant more than it did, it still meant *something*. That was what I was having the hardest time wrapping my head around. How could I ever explain that my body got what it needed at the time but my heart was fooled? That my heart had belonged to Camden, even if just the memory of a man I never thought would come for me? What man would ever understand that? Camden was noble, but he was still a man with insecurities like everyone else. He'd go out of his way to make sure I was okay, but I was afraid he'd never let his own heart get over it. I was so fucking afraid that he'd never let himself love me again.

I felt shredded up inside and my own heart was afraid to repair itself.

I sighed and looked down at my dress. It was dirty, brown from mud, and I quickly shimmied out of it and into a pair of jeans and a T-shirt I'd brought out of one of the spare bags from the trunk before Javier came out of the bathroom. I was tempted to go out to Camden, but even then I wouldn't know what to say. And he was right. Someone had to make sure that Javier wasn't about to screw us over, especially now that I'd slighted him. He was extra volatile.

I was sitting cross-legged on the makeshift bed when Javier came out of the bathroom, ruffling his now-wet hair with a towel. A shower would have been nice considering I had dried patches of dirt on my arms, but I'd get by without it. I couldn't risk leaving Javier alone right now.

"You're still here?" he asked, tossing the towel across the room. He walked barefoot, just a towel around his waist, to the bed. "I would have thought you'd left after what you'd said to me."

"Sorry, you're stuck with me," I told him, turning my head away before he dropped his towel like I knew he would.

"Or perhaps you're the one stuck with me," he said. He climbed in under the shawl-like blanket I'd left on the bed and rolled over to his side.

"You're not going to turn off the light?" I asked.

He laughed quietly, facing the wall. "Believe me, angel, you don't want to see what comes out in the dark."

I gradually lay back down, keeping my arms close to my chest. Within moments he was snoring and I did my best to stay awake. Even with the light on, it wasn't too long before I fell asleep.

*　　*　　*

I was awakened the next morning by Camden's warm and strong hands on my face. I smiled into his touch that I knew without question, still half-asleep and delirious with dreams.

"See, she's alive," Javier's voice broke through the clouds. I blinked a few times and looked beyond Camden's chiseled face. Javier was standing behind

Camden's crouched body, fully clothed and ready to face the day.

"Then why is she on the floor?" Camden asked, looking behind him in annoyance.

Javier turned around and left my vision. "Because she wanted to sleep there."

Camden looked back at me, shaking his head as Javier left the room. "Asshole. Like he couldn't have taken the floor himself." But I could tell he was relieved that I hadn't shared Javier's bed. I was relieved too. I had fallen asleep and slept all the way through the night. I was still exhausted and groggy-headed, though, but I felt more prepared to face the day, to face North America's largest metropolis, Mexico City.

"What time is it?" I groaned, wishing Camden would keep his hands on me for as long as he could. My eyes drifted over to his shoulder where the blood had dried and I winced at the sight.

"It's eight," Camden said. "We slept in a bit."

"Your shoulder."

He eyed it. "Yeah. I took the pills last night, okay, Nurse Ellie? New bandage, too, from Jose's first aid kit. I'll be okay. Need a change of clothes though."

I smiled despite myself, feeling strength returning, and slowly sat up. He grabbed underneath my arms and pulled me to my feet. There was a second or two where he was holding on to me, my chest against his chest, my head positioned just below his lips. I stared forward at his battered collar, at the bright tattoos—snake heads—that were coming through. I breathed in deeply, taking in his familiar smell and making it my fuel.

Don't ever leave my side again, I thought. I wanted to say, *I missed you. I still love you.*

I looked up at his eyes, hoping he could see far enough in, see how I was really feeling.

I love you.

The feeling was hitting me like a jackhammer, vicious and quick. But he had no idea. He stared back at me, eyes so perfect, so blue. Then he cleared his throat and looked away. "Are you ready to go?"

I took a second to compose myself and shot him a weak smile. "I just need to use the bathroom. I'll be quick."

Within minutes I was slipping a bra on underneath my T-shirt and heading out to Jose. The poor car looked even worse in the daylight. I was amazed it had even gotten us this far.

Javier was standing by the driver's-side door and noted my expression. "At least the car will blend in with the city. Every car looks like this. Such a shame."

I made my way to the trunk. "We should at least put on new plates." I opened it, throwing in my overnight bag, and started rifling through the large ziplock bag where I kept all the spare plates. There were about ten of them and two of them were foreign, one from British Columbia in Canada and the other from Baja California in Mexico. I took the Mexican plate out and waved it at them.

"This should help a bit," I said and fished out my screwdriver from my spare toolkit. Man, it was nice to have my stuff again. I quickly took off the old Cali plates and put the new ones on, already feeling the heat of the morning sun beating down on me. With any luck, Jose would blend in with any old Mexican car now.

I brought out a pair of black shit-kicker boots that were extra wide at the top and had a leather belt around them that I'd added. They were perfect for stuffing in a gun and strapping a knife to you. I brought out my Colt from the box in the trunk and shoved it down my right boot, making sure it was secure. It looked awfully pretty next to the cherry blossoms on my shin.

I straightened up and looked over the trunk at Camden. "Hey, where did you get the gun you were using last night?"

"Gus," he said, and my heart was immediately crushed at the thought of him. He'd come all this way with Camden for me and could very well have been tortured, if not dead, by now. Every second we spent trying to get to Javier's sister, the farther Gus slipped away. But we needed Javier's help, his knowledge of Travis, of the cartels, of Mexico. We had to help him before he could help us, even though I had a feeling all of us were equally wanted now.

I looked over at Camden and Javier, the wheels in my head turning.

"Javier," I said, "do you think we need to change our appearances?" As it was I had a blond wig in the trunk, too, and brought it out before he could say anything. I plopped it on my head and turned to look at them.

With Javier on one side of the car and Camden on the other, they both looked at me, speechless. I guess with the blond hair I looked to Camden like I did in high school and I looked to Javier like I did when we were living together.

"Take it off," they both said in unison, then exchanged furtive glances with each other.

All right, so no disguises. I took the wig off, my scalp already sweating from it, and threw it back in the trunk. I was okay with being who I was.

Camden pulled his seat forward and let me squeeze into the back of the car. I hated being back there. I missed being in the front, I missed fucking driving, but knew Camden would feel slighted if I asked to change places, and that was the last thing I wanted him to feel. More than he already did, anyway.

Javier pulled out of the dusty motel parking lot and drove steadily until we reached the first gas station. After we filled up, it was only about two hours before we reached the city.

I wasn't prepared for the sprawl. I mean, I knew how large Mexico City was, especially since it was one of the largest cities in the world. I knew how far it was spread out, how many people lived there. But I still wasn't prepared to see block after block of shanty houses juxtaposed with cathedrals, food vendors, and gated mansions reaching as far as the eye could see. There was no land, just houses. Just cars. Just people. No wonder Javier vetoed our disguises—if you couldn't get lost in Mexico City, you couldn't get lost anywhere.

"Do you even know where to find your sister?" I asked him as he took the car down a busy thoroughfare off one of the many intersecting highways. Traffic was thick enough to cut with a butter knife yet everyone was driving horrifyingly fast. The humanity was spilling out of the city's pores, leaking everywhere, poor beggars sitting roadside and skinny-limbed children playing in black exhaust. Everything was alive. Everything was dirty.

"Of course I know where to find her," he snapped. "She's family."

I bit my lip, feeling slightly chagrined, then said, "When was the last time you were here?"

He didn't say anything for a few moments, just laid on the horn at a dusty BMW that had cut him off with no apology. "Violetta doesn't live in the slums. She lives like she should. I'll find her soon."

Camden looked back at me and I raised my brows. I wasn't going to argue with Javier about his sister. It just all seemed a bit impossible, especially without GPS.

"Camden could use his GPS," I offered and was immediately shut down with an icy glare in the rear-view mirror.

"Camden can go fuck himself," Javier said, still looking at me. Camden didn't bother reacting, only looked back out the window at the never-ending hills of buildings. There were a few skyscrapers in the middle of the city, but beyond that it was just house after house after house. Shack after shack after shack. It took a lot of effort to keep another panic attack from coming on, that's how *engulfing* the city was. It went on forever, yet made you feel like you were trapped in a box.

We drove for quite a bit, never really making it anywhere, before Javier begrudgingly told Camden to enter "301-1250 Calle Burnaby" into the GPS on his phone. To his credit, Camden did it without saying anything, though it was at least another forty-five minutes before we got to the place.

Javier might have said that his sister didn't live in the slums, but she was at least surrounded by the slums. Or maybe that was the case everywhere in Mexico City. Her apartment building was whitewashed and fairly clean-looking, with underground parking and a concierge-type person I could see lurking behind the barred windows of the lobby. But on either side of the building were slum houses, mostly one story, some two, rising up around it like weeds.

We managed to find parking across the street. Javier got out of the car and glanced at us.

"You wait here."

"No fucking way," Camden said, quickly getting out from his side. I followed, joining him on the broken sidewalk. "We're going with you."

Javier waved at us dismissively and kept walking across the road. Camden and I waited until it was safe— the drivers here were crazy—before trotting after him.

"So mistrusting," Javier muttered to himself as we approached the building.

"How can we be so sure that your sister isn't part of your little plan?" Camden asked.

Javier shot him an exasperated look. "She is the plan. Get her safe, get her out of Travis's way."

"And then you're going to help us out of the goodness of your heart."

He looked the building up and down, rubbing his hands together. "You're not the only one who wants Travis dead. I've wanted this for a long time."

"For revenge or so you can take over his cartel?" Camden asked.

Javier eyed him and smiled, teeth white against his bronzed skin. "Who says I can't have both?"

"Even though it's the same cartel that murdered your parents?" I dared to ask.

"There's always room for improvement," he said.

He went up to the building's entrance and I was impressed to see it had a buzzer system. His finger trailed along the buttons until it paused at #301 BERNAL. His shoulders rose and fell as if he were steadying himself before he held down the button. I knew—back in the day, anyway—that Javier was fond of his sisters and had taken it upon himself to care for them financially after his parents had been murdered by a rival cartel, the same cartel that Travis was now a part of, the same cartel that Javier suddenly had his sights on. Or maybe it wasn't so sudden after all.

We waited for a few anxious moments, the ringing repeating until we heard a faint yet demanding *"Hola?"* over the intercom.

He shook his head and looked at us. "She shouldn't even be answering this right now; I could be anyone." Then he faced back to the intercom and said, *"Violetta, es Javier."* There was a longer pause and he added, *"Tu hermano."*

"Javier?" she asked. *"Qué … ?"*

He quickly asked her to let him upstairs and after a few more heavy pauses the door buzzed open. He grabbed it and swung it open for us, then marched inside the cool building, his dusty yet sharp shoes echoing on the tile floor, and nodded quickly at the concierge who only briefly looked up from his newspaper, not even batting his eye at Camden's bloodstained shirt. We walked past the elevator and went for the stairs, running up the flights until we got to the third floor.

We walked swiftly and quietly down the hall, stopping in front of 301.

Javier knocked quickly and took a step back from the door as it promptly swung open.

We were greeted by a large gun aimed at his head.

CHAPTER THREE

I AUTOMATICALLY THREW up my hands, though Javier barely even flinched. A slender young woman stood on the other side of the door, a large Beretta in her hands aimed right at him. Her eyes hadn't even left his face to take me and Camden in, but one look at those golden-green eyes of hers and it wasn't hard to see she was related to Javier.

"Violetta," Javier said calmly. He rattled off a question to her in Spanish with that smooth voice of his. Her gun never wavered; if anything, her eyes narrowed even more. Finally she looked over his shoulder and spotted me and Camden. She frowned, lowered the gun, and then jerked her head to follow her into the apartment.

Camden and I eyed each other nervously. I don't know what I was expecting, but I certainly wasn't expecting this, particularly from someone who had to be in her late teens, early twenties. Then again, I guess I was handling guns at a young age too.

We walked into her apartment and Camden slowly

closed the door behind us. It was quite large, considering how much space seemed to be an issue in this city, with a terracotta-tiled floor, blue-and-white porcelain accents in the kitchen, and large windows that looked out onto a sea of roofs. There was a room off to the side, and I caught sight of a rumpled bed and a large balcony beyond that. There were hair appliances and makeup and clothes strewn all over the place, cementing the fact that Violetta may have had a gun in her hands, but she was still a young woman.

She spun around in the middle of the room and suddenly slapped Javier clear across his face. I couldn't help but suck in my breath, afraid of what Javier might do. But he merely took it as she started to rant at him in rapid-fire Spanish, throwing up her hands and launching what must have been a million obscenities.

Violetta really was a very beautiful woman, slim-limbed and around my height, 5′6″, with thick and long, golden-highlighted hair, dark olive skin and full lips, and slightly slanted yellow-green eyes. She was wearing a summery dress that was cut short and had applied her makeup with a heavy hand.

When she was finally done, Javier retorted with a sentence or two, still succinct in his own language, and it wasn't until I picked up on the words *Eden White* that Violetta looked toward me.

She frowned and pointed my way, looking askance at Javier. "Eden?"

"Ellie," he corrected her with a grim smile. "Her real name is Ellie. And she doesn't speak Spanish, not that much, anyway."

She stepped slowly toward me, her flip-flops smacking against the tiles, and though I was very conscious of the gun in her hands, I stood my ground and looked her in the eye.

She smiled, playful and deceptive all at once. "So you are the famous Eden. You're the one who broke my brother's heart all those years ago."

It took everything I had to keep from rolling my eyes. Of course I had been painted the villain. Of course Javier never bothered to fill his sister in on the fact that he was cheating on me with at least one woman he'd later ended up beheading.

"I guess it depends on what side you hear," I answered.

She smirked and took another step forward. I caught a whiff of her perfume, freesia and linen. Fresh. Out of place in this smog-filled supercity.

"You know, for the longest time I swore I'd kill you if I ever saw you," she said slowly, her accent barely audible. "I wanted to make you suffer for the pain you caused my brother. But now I'm older. And I see how Javi is. The only thing I want to do is shake your hand."

She put hers out for me to shake, and I did so, surprised at the strength of her grip. She smiled and jerked it up and down. "I'm Violetta Bernal."

"Ellie Watt," I said, returning her smile. I nodded over my shoulder at Camden, who was still by the door. "That's Camden McQueen."

Violetta looked at him, her eyes widening appreciatively. "Hello, Camden McQueen." Then they went over to his shoulder. "What happened to your arm?"

"Got shot by the *policía*," he said with a grin, and I felt a weird prickle surge through me. He sounded almost as if he was flirting with her. I couldn't help but look over at Javier to see how he felt about all of this. He was watching the three of us carefully; his brow was furrowed and he was slowly running the back of his hand underneath the scruff of his jaw, calculating something.

"Let me get you something," she said brightly and took off to her room. Through the doorway I could see a flurry of clothes being tossed across the room and within seconds she'd come back out with a large, plain black T-shirt. She placed it in his hands.

"Here," she said. "Some guy left it here. I won't be calling him again anyway, so it's yours."

"Thank you," he said genuinely, flashing her his drop-dead gorgeous dimples. Damn, and I thought those were reserved especially for me. "Do you have a washroom I can change in? *Baño?*"

She smiled and pointed down the hall to a door. Once he disappeared, she put her gun down on the mantel and placed her hands on her hips. "Is he your boyfriend? Or are you still with this guy?" She jerked her head at Javier.

I swallowed hard and said, "Neither."

"Good, I guess," she said. "Do you know what this asshole has done? Nothing. Nothing at all! He's been promising to send me money every month and the last check I got from him was, oh, two years ago!"

I glanced at Javier in shock. He was red in the face, sweating a bit at the temples, but not arguing with her.

She looked at him too. "Well, so what was your excuse, hey, brother?"

He rubbed his lips together, eying the both of us, before saying, "I was busy. I tried."

She snorted and walked over to the kitchen, her little ass sashaying. *"Puta, cabrón,"* she swore. She opened up her fridge. "Do you want a glass of water? A beer?"

It was just before noon, and I definitely needed my head on straight, but I still said, *"Cerveza, por favor."*

"Make that two," Camden said, coming out of the bathroom. He was looking much better, his hair slicked back with water, his biceps bulging from the shirt that was a bit too snug on him. That, combined with his black dress shoes and tuxedo pants, made him look dapper. Well, with a shitload of tats and Clark Kent glasses.

"We don't have time for beer," Javier said angrily, watching as she brought me and Camden a Modelo each. He fastened his eyes on me. "You haven't forgotten about Gus, have you?"

I felt the sting from that and glared back at him while Violetta asked, "Who is Gus?"

"A family friend of mine," I answered, eyes still on Javier. "Actually, more family than my own family. Travis has him. He kidnapped him in front of Javier."

She looked at him. "This is true?"

Javier ran a hand through his hair and turned to look out the window. "Someone took him. I'm assuming it was Travis, since my own fucking men turned on me just seconds before."

"So is that why you're here?" she asked, cocking her head to the side. "To warn me about this Travis?"

He kept staring out the window, at the rows and rows of houses, the layer of muddy smog that blocked us from blue sky. "There is no 'this' Travis, Violetta. He's not a made-up character. He's real. And he will be coming for you."

Her smile faltered for a second before she noticed I was observing her; then it was full of false bravado. "I know all about Travis. I've been watching the news."

"This made the news?" Camden asked, stepping forward. His arm brushed against mine and I tried to ward my mind against the warmth of our contact. "I thought he owned half of Veracruz."

"Of course it did," she said, smiling her bright teeth at him. "I'm sure in Veracruz you wouldn't hear anything, but this is a different state. People here don't look too kindly on the Zetas and their new leader. It's been playing all morning, how an unknown cartel attempted to assassinate him at his own party. Most people have been celebrating."

"Did they mention how one of his helicopters was shot down?" Camden asked eagerly.

"Most people?" I asked at the same time.

She gave us both a placating smile. "I never heard anything about a helicopter. But yes, Ellie, most people. This is a big city, right here, bingo, in the middle of the country. There are ties to *all* the cartels here. The Zetas definitely have a presence, it's just not the most ... popular one. I have a few friends in the Zetas right now."

Javier moved so fast that all I could see was a blur of menace and stealth. He grabbed Violetta by the chin and forced her backward until she was pressed against the door. Camden immediately went for him, but I grabbed Camden quickly and pulled him back. This wasn't his place to interfere.

Javier started swearing at her in Spanish. I picked up a few words, but anyone could have figured out what he was so riled up about: the fact that she was fraternizing with members of the same cartel that had her parents and sister killed. For the first time I saw fear in Violetta's eyes, shame and anguish. I reached forward and touched Javier lightly on the shoulder.

"Hey," I said gently, heart racing knowing he might turn on me at any moment. "You're here for her."

He squeezed her face harder, and Violetta's eyes looked to me. In this moment of fear, she finally looked her age.

"Javier," I warned.

He loosened his grip and lowered his head, hair hanging around his face. He grunted, trying to control himself. Finally he let go of her completely and stormed straight to the bathroom, where he slammed the door shut.

Violetta rubbed at her jaw, her chest heaving, eyes on the bathroom door. "What is wrong with him?"

How well do you actually know your brother? I couldn't help but think. I gave her a sympathetic smile. "He thinks you're in a lot of danger. He's worried."

"Does he really think Travis would go after me?"

No way to say this delicately. "He went after your sister."

She ran her tongue over her teeth. "Beatriz was wrapped up with the wrong people. I'm not."

"You're friends with the cartel that murdered her and your parents," Camden said, playing devil's advocate.

She cocked her penciled brow at him. "Oh, do tell me what else you know, you American boy."

I placed my hand on her arm. "I think Javier has a right to be worried. We need you to leave the city."

She gave me a dirty look and shrugged out of my grasp. "This is my home. I will do no such thing."

Javier came out of the bathroom, looking slightly more collected. I'd rarely seen him so short-tempered and never expected it with his own sister. But he'd always described Violetta as the youngest, the bratty one, and I could definitely see that youngest sibling/oldest sibling dynamic coming out. It was a bit weird, actually, to see someone as lethal as Javier interacting with someone younger than him, someone who had the power to bring him down and get under his skin. He cared about Violetta a great deal, that much I could tell.

"Ellie is right," he said, his voice measured. "That's why I came. You have to leave, today."

She rolled her eyes, shook her head, and did all the things a girl her age would do when asked to leave the life she'd built on her own. "I don't think so. No."

"Violetta," Javier said slowly, coming up to her. His eyes were locked on hers. "Please. This isn't an option. You have to go stay with Marguerite or Alana."

She laughed, loud and dry. "Are you serious? *¡Dios mía!* You have no idea, do you, Javier? I haven't spoken to those witches for the last eight months."

"They are your sisters."

"And you're my brother!" she suddenly screamed.

Her face contorted, all control, all the facade disappearing in one second. "You're my brother and I haven't heard from you for years! Years! You just left us, all of us! Once Beatriz was gone, it's like you thought the rest of us died too!"

She pushed him back with one hand, snatched my beer from me with the other, and stormed off to the bedroom, slamming the door behind her. So much dramatic door-slamming already.

Javier looked pale. I almost felt sorry for him until I remembered he'd been lying to me about sending money to his sisters. How much was the price of his rise to the top? How much money had he kept to himself to ensure he could pay off the right people? Not family, not the people who needed it, but the people who could help him with his single-minded goal?

He rubbed his ashen lips together and went to the fridge to bring out a bottle of water. He drank it down in one go and tossed it in the sink when he was done. The air was thick with tension and humidity, and I felt awkward, unsure of what to do or say. One glance at Camden let me know that I wasn't alone. I hadn't been prepared to be brought into family drama. Then again, neither of us had been prepared for anything, really. Except, apparently, for Camden when he shot down that helicopter. He did that with such ease that it floored me and seriously had me hot and bothered every time I thought about it, no matter how inappropriate the circumstance.

And yeah, standing in my ex-lover's sister's apartment was a pretty inappropriate circumstance. I bit my lip and looked away from Camden. Getting turned on wasn't going to help me at the moment, and his tight T-shirt was only making it worse.

I slowly went to Violetta's door and rapped on it gently.

"Violetta?" I asked. I waited, hearing her stirring inside. I didn't expect her to want to talk to me and I wasn't sure why I cared so much about getting her safe. If anything, she seemed slightly untrustworthy, thanks to her casual ties to Los Zetas. Well, that and the fact that she was related to Javier.

Suddenly her door flew open and I jumped out of the way as she marched past me to the front door.

"I'm starving," she announced, taking her gun and stuffing it in her purse. "Which one of you people is going to buy me lunch?"

We all looked at Javier.

He grunted and went for the door, holding it open for us. "Okay, but we aren't going far and we are going to talk about this, Violetta."

She rolled her eyes and we followed her out.

Luckily the café she was thinking of was only three blocks away. The air had somehow grown more oppressive while we'd been inside, or maybe it was that I felt heavier after meeting Violetta. I could see this wasn't going to be easy for Javier, and unfortunately if it wasn't easy, it wasn't quick, and if it wasn't quick, I was further from getting to Gus.

Though I tried to prevent my brain from going there, I had to wonder what Travis was doing to him right now. There was a cartel leader in the Baja who was infamous for drowning people in vats of acid. I wondered if Travis would do anything so depraved; maybe my leg was just his first little taste. When I had looked at that man, I couldn't see any trace of humanity in him. He was a shell, a mask, the devil disguised as *El Hombre Blanco*. Now he had Gus, and he had my mother, and the idea of rescuing them seemed more and more impossible.

"Hey," Camden said to me, voice lowered, as we walked down the cracked pavement, Javier and Violetta ahead of us. He put his warm hand on the small of my back, and I felt both strong and weak at the same time. "How're you holding up?"

I looked up at him, squinting against the sun that fought valiantly through the smog. "I'm holding up."

He shot me a smile. "We'll get to him, don't worry."

He could read me like a book.

"It's just every second that we're here…" I started.

"We'll get him," he said more grimly, then removed his hand. I couldn't tell who the "him" was in that sentence—Gus, Javier, or Travis? I think if it were up to Camden, he'd get them all in some shape or form.

The café was a busy place, noisy and dark and thick with cigarette smoke. Javier was looking paranoid as he scoped the room, and I couldn't really blame him. But everyone in the café was drinking copious amounts of beer and coffee, ordinary citizens of Mexico City, minding their own business, not even pausing to look up at us.

We were able to squeeze into a small booth near the back, the Bernals on one side of the booth, Camden and me on the other. Violetta immediately brought out a pack of cigarettes and lit one up.

"You smoke?" Javier asked her, looking disgusted.

She laughed. "When did you become so lame? Aren't you running a small cartel at the moment?"

His eyes widened then darted around the café, but she patted his hand and said, "This place is cool, it's cool." Then she blew smoke in his face and smiled. "Cool."

She turned to us and said, "So can one of you tell me what's really going on here?"

"It's as he says—he just wants you safe," I said, avoiding Javier's eyes. Last thing I wanted was for him to think I was vouching for him.

"*Sí*," she said, taking another puff. Her eyes darted to him, then to Camden and then back to me. "But why are you here?" She nodded at Camden. "And why is he here?"

Oh boy. Javier's eyes narrowed slightly, daring me to tell the truth.

So I did. I took in a deep breath and launched into it. "It's a long story, longer than what I'll tell you. Basically, I knew Camden back in high school and recently returned home to Palm Valley in California. He ran a tattoo shop there, was stuck laundering money for his ex-wife's brothers, who have some sort of gang in Cali running guns or pot or whatever. He wanted me to help him escape with the money. I did. Meanwhile, your brother shows up with a fifty-thousand-dollar price tag on my head. Goes to Camden. Camden tells me. We go on the run. Javier nearly finds us. Then he bribes my Uncle Jim with the money. My uncle almost turns me over to him, ducks out at the last minute. Javier shoots him in the head."

This whole time Violetta had been watching me with her mouth slightly open, forgetting her cigarette existed, the ash piling up on the end. Javier looked stone-faced, not even caring what I was telling her— which, of course, was the truth.

I went on, my voice strained by the memories. "After he killed Jim, he contacted us and told me that either I'd go with him or he'd hurt Camden's son, Ben, and his ex-wife. Camden and I went back to Palm Valley and the exchange was made. I went with Javier, Camden got his son and ex back, plus the money your brother was originally offering people. Only Camden discovered that everything had been a setup. His ex had gone willingly with Javier. She and her brothers planned to take the fifty grand from him afterward, and I'm guessing right now that, Javier, you had everything to do with it. That in the end, Camden would never have gotten very far."

He stared right back at me, unflinching. Camden, on the other hand, was growing tense beside me. I didn't need to look at him to know his eyes were shooting daggers at Javier, that his strong hands were gripping the edge of the table.

"Anyway," I said, and brushed the sweat off the back of my neck. Fuck, it was hot in here. "Javier's plan at first was to get me to kill Travis, which I was willing to do...well, I was willing to help him kill him. We ended up here. Then I find out it wasn't just Travis, but it was my parents too. That they'd been working with Travis and Javier knew this. I was supposed to be his fucking assassin."

Violetta puffed nervously on her cigarette and looked to Javier. "This true? You wanted her to kill her own parents?"

Javier swallowed hard but didn't say anything.

"I'm afraid your brother is sick in the head," I told her, half apologetic.

She snorted. "This much I know."

Javier cleared his throat. "Ellie"—he spoke softly and folded his hands on the table—"you're neglecting to tell her the part where I rescued both you and Camden at Travis's party, saving you from certain death."

Yes. That part.

I smiled weakly. "I almost forgot. That was after you let them take Gus."

"Gus isn't my problem. I never asked for him and Camden to come down here."

Violetta nodded to Camden. "And why did you come down here?"

"Why do you think?" Camden asked, his voice clipped.

"To get the girl?" She smiled at the two of us. "Which would be very romantic if it weren't for my brother sitting right here, correct?"

Romantic. I looked at Camden, feeling my face growing hot. I *did* find it romantic, actually. I found it sexy. I found it brave, honest, noble, and borderline crazy. I found Camden's devotion to me filled my soul with a warmth I'd never, ever felt before. Just like he had when we were bullied teens, he understood me in ways no one else did.

But how could it be romantic when I could see the

hurt and anger in his eyes, his disappointment in me and what I'd done to him? How easily I tossed away his accountability? This wasn't romantic anymore; this was tragic, and it was all my fault.

I didn't need to say that to Violetta though. She only stubbed out her smoke on the table and said, "Oh, but I forgot, you aren't *with* him."

Camden looked at me sharply.

She went on. "And you're not with my brother. And yet here you all are. Together."

"He's helping us get Gus back," I said.

She looked at him. "So you keep saying. And me. I'm assuming Javi was too afraid to come and get me on his own."

Javier sighed and leaned back in the booth. Though her cigarette was out, there was still a layer of smoke that hung above our heads in the muggy air, the overhead fans doing nothing to disperse it. "I knew you'd be angry with me, Violetta. I thought maybe if you heard the danger from someone else, why you need to leave, you'd listen. You can leave with us, even. We'll take you where you need to go."

Okay, that was a new one. As much as I wanted to help her, we didn't have time to drive her around the country, not with Gus's life on the line.

She looked down at her slender hands. "Do you really think that I'm in danger?"

"Tell us about your friends in the Zetas," Javier said by way of answering. "Do they know about me?"

She shot him a wry smile. "Javi. You're not exactly big news down here. I'm sorry. You've got the Zetas, the Sinaloa, the Baja, the Gulf. The big boys. The big balls. Then you have a bunch of little ones that no one cares about. You're one of the little ones that no one cares about."

"Except for Travis," I said while Javier looked slighted at her description.

She nodded. "*Sí*. Except for him. Who is now with the Zetas. But even Travis isn't at the top of the food chain. Maybe in Veracruz he is. But it's Morales and his family in Nuevo Laredo who really run it. Not many people can take a gringo seriously, no matter how many men he tortured and killed to get to the top." She cocked her head at Javier. "I'm a bit surprised that you're not in Travis's position. I'm sure the cartel would rather have you there than a white man."

"I have had loyalty," Javier said simply. "To our family. As should you, you who is hanging out with these men like it's no big deal."

She shook her head. "Oh, relax. I'm just friends with two guys who do the deliveries, the transporting of the money." She shrugged. "It's a good job for them. And no, of course they don't know who you are or that I even have a brother. You make it easy to pretend you don't exist."

He looked grim. "And that may have helped you before, but you can't afford to take that chance now. I have no doubt that there's been word about me traveling down the Zeta chain. My cartel might be small, but when it comes to Travis, I'm as big as it gets."

She raised her hand in the air and snapped her fingers for the waiter, who until now had been ignoring our table. "I can't talk about this anymore without food."

The waiter came by, and we promptly ordered coffee, beer, and food. Though my stomach was growling, I had zero appetite, so just munched the tortilla chips and fresh salsa that came with our drinks. Javier spent the rest of the time trying to figure out a plan for Violetta. She was too busy stuffing her face to talk back but I could still see she was going to try and evade this idea for as long as she could. Like her brother, she was stubborn, even in the face of imminent danger.

And, unfortunately, we all knew the danger was getting closer with each passing minute on the clock.

CHAPTER FOUR

IT WASN'T UNTIL we were done with our meal—Javier taking care of the check, much to Violetta's delight—and were walking back to her apartment that he finally wore her down.

"Fine," she said, wiping the sweat from her brow and giving him an exasperated glance. "I'll go pack a bag. But I'm only going for a few days. I have a job here, a life, I have no intention of leaving it for good because of you, Javi."

I was going to ask her where she was planning on going, if she had friends she could stay with, but thought better of it. Though we were steps from going into her building, we were still in a public place, and I was starting to feel the slightest bit uneasy. As she fumbled in her purse for her keys, I paused on the curb and did a quick sweep of the area, shielding my eyes with my hand.

Jose was parked across the street, looking like a mangled wreck, but two cars down there was another mangled wreck, so at least the car didn't attract any

attention here. The sun was damn strong, the air even
thicker and browner than before, like hot soup. There
were a few squalid-looking apartment buildings across
the street, white stucco like Violetta's place but stained
with green sludge. Beside them were tiny, colorful
houses in bright greens and yellows. On the balcony of
the yellow house, an older woman sat in the sun, sorting
through her basket of laundry. In the yard of another
house, a skinny dog lapped up a bucket of water.

"Something wrong?" Camden asked quietly as
Javier berated Violetta for being disorganized.

I looked up at him and gave a small shake of my
head. "I don't think so. Just had a weird feeling."

He pursed his lips and looked around at all the
things I was just surveying. Finally he nodded at Violetta, who brought out her keys with a whoop of joy.
"Worried for her? Or about her?" he whispered.

Though I guess I had a right to be suspicious about
Violetta herself, I wasn't for some reason. She wasn't
like her brother. Maybe that's why I liked her. Or maybe
she *was* like her brother and that's why I liked her too.
There was that familiarity. Better the devil you know.

"I just want to get moving again," I said, and we
walked up to the door that Violetta was proudly holding open for us.

The weird feeling didn't leave, even as we went inside
the elevator and up to her apartment, Violetta protesting
it was always too hot to take the stairs. Outside her door,
I reached down and made sure my Ka-Bar knife and
gun were still secure in my boots. When I straightened
up, Javier was staring at me with an air of approval.

Violetta went to put the key in the lock, but Javier quickly grabbed her wrist, his eyes burning into hers with warning. He nodded to the door then pushed her out of the way, grabbing his gun from his waistband and holding it loosely at his side. Camden and I took a step back.

Swiftly, Javier kicked open the door and sprung into the room, his gun drawn. I grabbed my gun from my boot and followed after him, heart racing in my throat as we quickly searched the rooms.

When it was all clear, he waved at Violetta to come inside.

She crossed her arms and huffed her way into the middle of the apartment.

"My landlord is going to kill me." She scowled and waved her hand at the broken lock on the door.

Javier didn't smile. "That shouldn't have been so easy to break down. You need to be more careful."

"Well, I'm taking off for a few days, isn't that careful enough?"

He grunted and told her to go pack her bag. She sighed and disappeared into her room, muttering obscenities under her breath.

"Did you think you heard something?" Javier asked me.

"Why, because I was checking my gun and knife?"

He nodded.

"I was just being cautious, Javier," I told him, slipping my gun back into my boot. "I have learned *something* from my line of work, you know."

He raised his brows in disbelief, and I knew he was

close to bringing up the foolish mistakes I'd made that had allowed him to catch me in the first place. I didn't need the reminder that I wasn't as good a con artist as I thought I was.

I guess he could see the warning in my eyes, because a small smile tugged at the corner of his mouth and he turned around.

Camden cleared his throat, and I looked at him. He was leaning his good shoulder against the wall near the door, observing us. I couldn't read his eyes, though he was swallowing hard and his jaw looked tense. One hand was on his shot shoulder, pressing down lightly. I wondered if he was in pain or had been taking the pills when I wasn't looking.

I was about to ask him when a god-awful sound buzzed through the room, causing me to jump.

Javier whipped around. "What the hell was that?"

It sounded again, coming from the intercom. Violetta came out of her room, wiping her hands. She looked at our expressions and said, "Don't worry, it's probably just a friend," and went for the intercom. She pressed the button and asked, "*Hola?*"

There was no response.

That wicked feeling was sweeping through me again, causing all the hairs on my arms and neck to stand at attention. This was bad.

While Violetta tried the buzzer again, I ran to the window and looked out. The glare from the sun and the dirt on the glass made it hard to see through, so I quickly went into Violetta's room and out to her balcony.

There was a sea of roofs spreading out before us,

only one story below. I craned my neck to look up at the building. I didn't even know what I was looking for; someone who didn't belong, I guess.

"What is it?" Camden asked, standing in the doorway.

"That feeling I had?" I asked. "I think we have to get out of here. Now."

Suddenly the apartment erupted in gunfire and I heard Violetta scream. Instinctively, I ducked, pulling down Camden, and brought out my gun again. Violetta burst into the room as another round of gunfire went off and I quickly motioned for her to come onto the balcony.

"What happened?" I asked her frantically.

She was shaking her head and screamed again when more shots went off. The window in the living room exploded into a storm of shattered glass, and then seconds later a tall man went flying out of it. He landed on the roof below and then staggered to his feet. The minute he looked up at us on the balcony, he yelled something and pulled out his gun.

I was faster. I aimed, said a prayer, and squeezed the trigger. The gun roared in my hands and the bullet hit the man in his chest, causing him to fly backward. My first thought was *Thank god I was a better shot this time*.

Then Violetta let out a small sob and it hit me.

It was a good shot.

And I'd actually killed a man.

Me.

Suddenly I heard Javier's voice ring out from the apartment amid the gunshots.

"Run!" Javier yelled.

Right. I quickly shook my head, trying to focus. There was only one place for us to go.

Camden was already climbing over the railing and helping Violetta over.

It was only a twelve-foot drop or so. It wouldn't kill us, but it wouldn't feel good, either.

"Ellie," Camden yelled, "come on!"

I nodded absently, still dazed, and brought my legs over the side of the railing just as Camden and Violetta dropped to the roof. Camden's large frame landed with ease, sending the terracotta tiles of the roof flying, while Violetta quickly crumpled to her knees, her flip-flops providing no traction. Within seconds Camden was helping her up.

The roof was almost totally flat, just peaking a bit at the spine, but I still had to be careful how I landed.

"Jump!" Camden yelled up at me as a bullet whizzed past my shoulder.

I turned to look in time to see Javier bursting through Violetta's bedroom, simultaneously running toward me and shooting at someone who was in pursuit, the assailant's gun aimed at me. Javier shot him in the shoulder and in seconds he was beside me, yelling, "What the fuck are you waiting for, the circus?"

I stared at him for a moment, wondering why I felt relief coursing through me at the sight of him.

Then he put his hand on my back and pushed me off the balcony.

I screamed in surprise but managed to land in the right spot, my shins taking a beating, but I still remained on my feet. Gunshots followed, and Javier landed beside me seconds later.

"You ass!" I yelled at him.

"Keep running!" he yelled back and started sprinting past me.

Another bullet went screaming past my ear. Too many close calls and too soon. Too dangerous to even think about.

I started running, the tiles sliding under my boots, following behind him. Camden and Violetta were a few paces ahead, slowing down as they came to the edge of the roof. Luckily the next building was the same height and there was no gap in between them. In fact, the roofs on the block all seemed to be together, like one giant, distorted house.

Another gunshot rang out, and beyond the thudding of my heart in my ears I could hear the assailants landing on the tiles behind us. Motherfucking shit, they were persistent, whoever they were.

We kept running, and I willed my legs to move faster as we went from tile to shingles to gravel to stucco, roof to roof to roof. Somewhere in our retreat, Camden and Javier got ahead of us and Violetta started to stagger, her flip-flops causing her to stumble often. I grabbed her by the arm and kept her upright, running alongside her.

But I knew the men were gaining on us. And I knew we would run out of luck.

I squeezed her arm and told her to keep going, and then I stopped and spun around.

A few yards behind us was a lean, dark-complexioned man with an eye patch, ready to take a shot at us. I pulled my trigger before he could, getting him in the stomach by accident.

The man went down with a scream, his gun shooting at nothing. Fucking Mexican pirate.

Unfortunately there were three more men behind him, albeit farther back. I didn't have much time to try my luck. I tried to take in a deep breath, my lungs burning from the air pollution and the exertion, and aimed at them. I fired off three rounds and hit only one of them. The remaining two kept coming.

Time to move.

I turned around and started running again, surprised to see that not only were Camden and Javier farther away, but that Violetta had stopped and was looking down at something. I booked it over to her and saw what made her pause. There was a large gap between this roof and the next, though it fortunately was half a story shorter. We could make it if we had a running start, a running start we'd both just lost.

"Fuck!" I yelled, then whipped behind me to see how much time we had before our pursuers were at us. Not much. I grabbed Violetta's arm and started running with her back a few steps.

"Ready?" I asked her.

She nodded, her eyes welling with fear.

We both started running, as fast as we could, my hand holding hers until we both launched off of the roof and into the air.

I landed on the roof below, my ankles shuddering in pain from the impact. Thanks to my scarring, they didn't always hold up after a lot of wear and tear, and I immediately fell to my knees, my legs getting scratched up by the tar shingles.

Violetta's scream came through a second later.

She had hit the roof, scrambled to hold on, then disappeared, falling down the gap to the ground below.

I looked over the edge and saw her lying in a heap in the dirt alley, holding her arm in pain and crying out.

Another shot came dangerously close. The men were coming closer. There was no time to think.

I ran along the roof for a few steps, then jumped down onto a rickety iron balcony that swung with my weight, then launched off that to the ground below.

I ignored my throbbing ankles and hurried over to her just as one of the men appeared at the rooftop. I aimed and fired, all instinct, and got him right in the head. When he pitched off the roof and fell with a thud to the ground beside us, I dragged Violetta up to her feet. There was no time to be gentle. Her arm was probably broken and it was going to hurt like a bitch, but it was better to be hurt than dead.

"We have to run, okay?" I told her, and she cried in response. I had no idea if Camden or Javier even noticed we weren't behind them, but that couldn't be my concern. We had to get ourselves safe; then we'd get to them.

And then, then maybe I'd have a moment to think about the people I'd killed.

Together we scampered down the narrow alley, dirt flying from our feet, just as a bullet ricocheted from the wall. We yelped but kept going, zigzagging our way toward the street, knowing the last asshole standing was firing at us from the roof.

As soon as we hit the street that ran along the block of buildings, we were a tiny bit safer. At least I figured, since there was light traffic on the roads and people were going to and fro. However, despite the fact that I was running across the street and darting between the cars with Violetta in tow, both of us bruised, scratched, and bleeding, my gun visible in one of my hands, no one really seemed to bat an eye. I wondered how bad Mexico City was for crime, then decided it didn't matter.

We ran up the sidewalk until I saw another alley, then brought Violetta down it and around a corner. I stopped us beside a Dumpster that sat behind a café, a couple of stray cats sleeping in the shade.

"Violetta," I said to her, putting one hand on her good arm and trying to get her to look at me. Her cheeks were wet and dirty, a mess of mascara and tears. She was shaking and sobbing softly. "Violetta, listen to me. Do you know who those men were?"

She shook her head. "No," she cried. "I didn't recognize them. Javier told me to go to my room, but I wanted to see what was going on. It looked like he heard something out in the hallway. He hid near the door and suddenly a group of men came in the room and started shooting."

"And you didn't recognize them?"

She let out a loud sob, shaking her head even more, her forehead scrunched in pain. "No, I don't know. They looked like cartel men. Bad men."

Obviously.

"My arm, I think it's broken," she whimpered.

I nodded. "I know. We'll get it fixed, but we have to get Camden and your brother."

"Screw Javier!" she yelped. "He's what got us into this in the first place."

I smiled grimly. "I know. But you don't mean that. You can't leave him behind."

"He left me behind! He forgot I existed."

"And we're better than that." I gave her a steady look, my eyes imploring hers. "Okay? We're going to go back to your place—"

"No!" she cried out.

"We're going back to your place," I said, my voice harder, "and we're getting my car. Then we're going to find them. And then we're gone. You can do this."

I stared at her for a few moments until she relented with a nod. Then we moved down the alley that ran parallel to the main road until we were back on her street. Jose was still sitting on the side of the road.

Only now I realized that Javier had the car keys.

"Fuck," I muttered.

"What?"

"I have to hotwire it."

"So do it."

I gave her a wry look.

Suddenly the air was filled with a flurry of shouts and Spanish. I looked over at her apartment building and saw a few men on the balcony of one of the apartments, pointing at us and flipping out.

"Do it I shall," I said. I opened the door—no point in locking it, since half the windows were shot out—ushered Violetta into the backseat where she could lie down, and then jumped into the front. Even though I'd been driving Jose for most of the last six years, my car-stealing skills were still pretty sharp. After crossing wires for a few seconds, Jose roared to life, his engine loud and proud, and I gunned him out of the parking spot just as a group of men came running out of the apartment for us.

"Persistent," I grumbled and spun the car around the corner. Despite the circumstances, it felt fucking great to be driving my car again.

I took Jose zooming down the one-way street, swerving in and out of traffic while trying to keep an eye on the roofs that whipped past us. Dust flew up in our wake, coating us through the windows, and I narrowly missed smashing into a motorcycle. I was glad Violetta was in the back and whimpering softly; it made it easier to concentrate when the only screams you heard were in your head.

My stomach began to twist on itself when I realized I had no idea where Javier and Camden were, if they were still alive, still running. The houses in this barrio kept going on and on, family after family after family packed into these ramshackle dwellings like sweltering sardines.

I'd almost clipped a bus in front of me when I suddenly saw a dark figure running on the roof, his head disappearing behind the occasional awning and the back of the bus. It was one of the cartel men and he was chasing someone, which had to mean that Camden and Javier were up ahead.

I exhaled briefly with hope before pushing the pedal to the floor and going up the shoulder, trying to get ahead of the bus. There was a stack of bicycles up ahead, and I was either going to hit them, the bus, or the people on the dirt sidewalk.

I chose the bicycles. I gunned the car harder, the rear wheels spinning furiously, and braced for impact.

"Hold on!" I yelled to Violetta and then screamed as Jose plowed into them. The bicycles flew up onto the hood, cracking the windshield in the corner before clattering across the roof. "Sorry!"

Then I whipped the car in front of the bus to a round of angry honks from the driver and finally saw Camden and Javier on the roofs, still running for their lives. I grinned to myself, despite the severity of the situation, and let out a relieved laugh. Somewhere in the back of my masochistic head, I had been so certain that Camden would be done for. I hadn't wanted to think about it, but I was sure that Javier would have ditched him along the way. Or killed him.

"I see them," I told Violetta.

"Camden's still alive?" she asked weakly.

I wasn't the only one with that idea.

"So far," I told her.

"I can tell my brother wants to kill him," she said.

I rubbed my lips together, my hands gripping the wheel harder. "He hasn't yet." I shot her a look over my shoulder. "Just hang tight, okay? I'm going to try to get their attention and pull up ahead."

I drove a bit faster, trying to keep up in the traffic that was growing increasingly heavier, and was about to start honking my horn like crazy when I saw the unthinkable happen.

Javier and Camden both jumped from one roof

to another, the gap not too wide, but when Camden landed, it looked like his weight broke through part of the roofing and he went down, sinking in until I could only see him from the shoulders up.

I gasped, slowing the car so I could watch, the bus behind me honking again.

The man in pursuit started firing at them, closer now.

Camden was fucked.

A sitting duck.

And Javier...Javier stopped.

He stopped and raised his gun and tried to fire off a few rounds at the man, but I could see from the frustration in his face that he was out of ammo. He hastily tucked his gun back into his pants and then crouched down to help Camden up.

"What's going on?" Violetta asked, trying to sit up. "Why are we slowing?"

"Javier is helping Camden," I said absently. I wasn't sure what to make of it, other than the fact that I was grateful. Cautiously grateful.

"How noble of him," she said, her voice acidic.

It didn't matter. Soon Camden was on his feet again and they were back to sprinting. I took the car around a rickshaw and started honking the horn wildly. I didn't care if everyone in the barrio looked over at me. I just wanted them to see me.

But they didn't. And I could see we were coming up to an intersection where the roofs would end and they'd have to come down. The intersection that had the street on a red light so that cars were starting to slow in front of me.

I had to act fast. I brought the GTO onto the dirt sidewalk to get past the traffic and kept laying on the horn, now to get Camden and Javier's attention as much as the attention of the people I was about to run over. Fortunately, everyone got out of the way, and there wasn't another group of bikes to smash through. Unfortunately, because we were right up against the buildings, Camden and Javier wouldn't be able to see the car.

I stuck my head out of the window and started yelling for Camden, shouting his name over and over again. I hoped he could hear me above the noise of the city. There wasn't much time left. I was almost at the intersection, and if they got off the block of roofs and started running, there was a chance I could never find them again in this city.

The light was still red when we came to it, and I wasted no time.

I spun the car out, turning left into oncoming traffic, and kept another scream inside my burning lungs. Cars were honking as they came toward me. People were yelling and swearing, fists waving outside of windows.

I slammed Jose into park and climbed out of the window onto the roof of the car. I stood up unsteadily, mindful that I was precariously perched in the middle of a rush of cars in all directions, some of them slamming their brakes dangerously close to me, and looked to the roof.

In seconds, Javier and Camden appeared, looking over the edge, trying to figure out a way down, before the commotion I had created caught their eye. I waved my arms over my head until they both spotted me.

"Get the fuck down here!" I yelled.

Camden squinted then nodded, and I noticed he wasn't wearing his glasses anymore, while Javier pointed at an awning that unfurled above a convenience store. They ran over until they were above it, Javier glancing nervously over his shoulder, then with one fluid leap they jumped down onto the awning.

It crashed and collapsed under their weight and brought them down over crates of fruit, but they were quickly up and running across the road to the car. All while the store owner was emerging from the wreckage and swearing his head off.

I jumped down from the roof and quickly pushed the seat back to make room for Javier. He could sit with his sister and comfort her.

Camden was sitting beside me.

"Get in," I told them.

Javier's eyes locked with mine briefly and he said, "Thanks" before slipping inside.

I slammed the seat back and got in just as Camden got in the passenger side. Two bullets exploded nearby, one hitting the street, the other hitting the trunk of the car. The man was firing at us from the roof. I had half a mind to fish out my gun again and finish him off, but we had an opportunity to escape and I wasn't going to lose it.

I put Jose into drive and peeled out, avoiding the cars that were now making their way around me, meandering in and out until we were on the right side of the road and speeding through the city. The traffic was growing thicker by the moment, but still moving fast enough that I was able to keep up my speed as long as I paid close attention to the road.

"What happened?" I cried out at the same time that Camden did. He was missing his glasses—his big blue eyes looked startling—and covered in sweat, but other than that he looked okay.

"What happened to your arm?" Javier asked Violetta. She whimpered in response.

I eyed him in the rearview mirror. "We were running and came to that first gap. She fell. I think her arm is broken. I jumped down and we ran back to the car."

"Did you kill the rest of the men?" Javier asked, his eyes meeting mine. They danced, looking alive. If he was a lion, his tail would be twitching.

I swallowed hard and ignored the lump in my chest. "Yes. I had to."

His lips curled in delight. "I'm impressed."

I looked away and back at the road before I nearly took out a green and red taxi cab.

"Do you know those men, Javier?" I asked.

"No. But I bet my little sister here does."

Violetta moaned from the back, and at that Camden quickly pulled out a few of his pills from his pocket.

"Violetta doesn't know them," I told Javier while Camden twisted around in his seat and dispensed the pills to her.

"So Violetta says," Javier said.

"We've got to get her to a hospital," Camden said.

"Not yet," Javier said calmly.

My eyes flew back at him. "Not yet?"

He smiled, lips tight together. "We have to go straight

to Aguascalientes. It's about five hours from here, four if you hurry. My friend Dom will be able to help us."

"Is Dom a doctor?"

He shook his head. "He's part of my cartel and he's really into bullfighting. I have to talk to him first, tell him the situation. Then we can get Violetta sorted out."

"But she's in pain," I said.

He shrugged and sat back in his seat, looking away from me, away from her, out the window at the city's smog-filled sky. "She got into this mess when she started spreading her legs for the Zetas. She can afford to suffer for a bit."

Violetta groaned, writhing in discomfort.

"You're a sick fuck," Camden seethed at him.

"You're going to have to start coming up with more original insults. I believe you've already called me that before." Javier looked at him briefly, his face lighting up at the sight of Camden so angry and bothered. "Don't make me regret not leaving you on that roof to die."

Silence filled the car.

It was going to be a long drive to Aguascalientes.

CHAPTER FIVE

WE MADE IT to Aguascalientes in just under five hours. Traffic on the main highway was thick, and we had to stop to use the restroom and fill up on gas. Thankfully, Camden's pills worked well on Violetta, and she was out like a light for most of the drive, her head on Javier's shoulder—though I was sure it wouldn't remain that way when she woke up.

I only got to speak to Camden alone, briefly, when I went into the store to pay.

We were waiting in line for the cashier and he grabbed a bag of the ubiquitous pork rinds you find all over Mexico and tossed them to me. I caught them one-handed and found myself smiling shyly.

"What happened to your glasses?" I asked him.

He bit his lip, his eyes darting to the car. "They fell off somewhere. Probably when I fell. I can't remember. That whole thing was . . . a blur."

"Can you still see?"

He smiled, all beautiful white teeth, full lips, and

dimples. "I'm nearsighted. Which means I'll be a lousy shot until I get a new pair or some contacts. But at least I can see you clearly. The things up close. The things that matter."

Boom. There went my heart.

In the middle of a Mexican convenience store.

I had a sudden urge to step closer to him, press myself into his chest, find out how clearly he could see me then. But then the clerk was calling us forward and Camden gave me a little nudge. His fingers felt hot and rough on my arm, awakening my skin.

I smiled at the clerk and awkwardly asked in Spanish to pay for a full tank on our pump, but the clerk figured some of it out on his own. While I was handing over the pesos I had, Camden whispered in my ear.

"I know Javier helped me back there," he said deeply, shivers going down my neck, "but don't you dare start thinking he's on our side. He's not. He's not even on his sister's side."

"So who is on my side?" I whispered back while the clerk counted the money. Funny, back in the day I would have been busy trying to scam my way out of paying for the gas, but the idea wasn't even an option anymore.

His lips brushed against my ear, his presence behind me so large and commanding it seemed to fill the whole store. "I'm on your side. I'll be on your side. All the way, until we get home."

Then he turned and walked out of the store and back to the car.

Until we got home.

Home seemed like such a strange concept now.

And what would happen to us then?

When the clerk was satisfied, I went out to the car, Camden already pumping away. I met his eyes, wondering if I was a blur to him at that distance or if he could fill in the details. Giving him a grateful smile, I got in the car.

Javier was sitting stiffly in the back, Violetta now sleeping against the far window. The hot and dusty breeze from the highway swept in through the shattered back window, messing her hair. Javier was watching me observe her, thinking, always thinking.

"You like her, don't you?" Javier asked.

I raised a shoulder. "Why not? She seems like a good kid."

He grunted in disgust and started examining his fingernails. "Good kid. Right. You think associating with the Zetas is good now?"

I gave him a sharp look. "You don't know that those men had anything to do with her. They're after us in the end. Isn't that what matters?"

"They're after *me*, angel," he corrected.

"Then why take Gus?"

"They think Gus is of importance to you. They think you are of importance to me. That's how it goes."

They thought I was of importance to him—but was I? I shook my head, not seeing why I should care, and looked at Violetta. "Anyway, she didn't know you were coming, Javier. She didn't do anything. You're the one who is after Travis."

"*We* are."

"*I'm—*"

"After Gus, yes, you've said that," he filled in sharply.

Camden opened his door and climbed in. He eyed me, the tension in my jaw and shoulders, and then looked to Javier. "Everything all right in here?"

I had a feeling Camden wouldn't need much of an excuse to beat the shit out of Javier again. What I would have given to see that.

"Yes," Javier said. "Just getting our priorities straight." He tapped the back of my seat. "You better get this damn car moving again. I called Dom and let him know we'd be there soon."

"Is that safe?" I asked him as I started Jose and pulled him back onto the highway heading north. "I mean, calling people and letting them know where we are?"

Javier laughed. "Once again, angel, I am not Jason Bourne and the government isn't after me. No one is tapping my phones because no one has this phone number. Except for Dom now. And if I can't trust Dom, I can't trust anyone."

I definitely didn't trust Dom. And Camden would be happy to know, I didn't trust Javier either.

As soon as we got to the city limits of Aguascalientes, a pleasant-looking city at the base of ragged mountains, Javier instructed me to look out for the signs for the Aguascalientes Monumental Bullring.

"Are we seriously going to a bullring?" I asked. Violetta was awake now, not talking but obviously in pain. Camden had courteously shared with her the last of his pain medication, but apparently it wasn't enough. She was trying to keep it together, but little bursts of agony would occasionally squeak past her lips.

"Just do as I say" was Javier's answer. I half-expected him to tell me to trust him.

I grumbled, my hands sweaty on the wheel, my back aching from the drive, but did as he asked. It was all for Gus, all for Gus, all for Gus.

My mother's face came flashing into my head, the look of horror when she saw who I was, where I was.

Yes. This was all for her too, even though I knew she wouldn't do the same for me.

I sighed and focused on my new surroundings. The city was actually quite clean and civilized looking, well maintained, with lots of greenery and wide thorough-fares. It wasn't long until we came to a very high, very round building done up in pinks, oranges, and blues.

"It's like the coliseum on Gay Pride Day," Camden commented.

"You would know," Javier sniped.

I shot him a look. "Okay, we're here. Now what?"

Javier motioned to the giant parking lot across the street that was emptying itself of cars. "Pull in there."

"Looks like the fight is over," Camden mused, staring at the crowds spilling out of the bullring and into the surrounding plaza.

"We're not here to see the fight," Javier explained. Thank god. The idea of watching a bullfight made me feel sick to my stomach. I remembered being fifteen years old and actually donating money to some charity at school that was trying to make that event, and other animal sporting events, illegal. Obviously it did shit-all. Bullfighting looked to be as popular in Mexico as it ever was.

I parked the car in an empty spot and Javier tapped the back of my seat to be let out. I sighed and got out. It was cooler here in Aguascalientes, the sky blue even as the sun began to set.

He started to walk away, so I reached out and grabbed his hand.

"Where are you going?"

He paused and looked down at my fingers around his wrist, then looked back at me, brow raised.

I immediately dropped his hand like a hot potato and licked my lips nervously. I hated how I couldn't even touch him without him making a big deal about it.

"I'm going to see Dom," he said, trying to hide a smile.

I folded my arms. "I'm going too."

"Ellie, he doesn't know you."

"He'll get to know me. I'm not letting you walk in there, leaving me, Camden, and your poor sister in the car like easy prey."

He frowned and shoved his hands into his pant pockets. "You're so mistrustful, after everything I've done."

"*Because of* everything you've done."

"Such a short memory."

"My memory is just fine. I have a hard time thinking that any of the good you've done lately, for us, is because you've found your soul."

He chuckled. "Oh, angel, you forget. You're the only one who gave me a soul. If I don't have one anymore, it's not my fault."

I automatically dug my nails into my arms in

frustration. "I'm going with you," I said again, making each word sharp.

He sighed and brushed his hair behind his ears. "Very well. You may come. You better make sure your ape doesn't try anything with my sister." He walked off.

I turned and looked at Camden, who was leaning over my seat, hearing the whole thing. He gave me a grim nod, one I knew meant he'd stay and take care of Violetta, and then mouthed to me, "Be careful." I smiled uneasily and went after Javier. I hoped we'd be quick.

I also hoped Dom wasn't waiting for us with a loaded gun.

Javier didn't say much to me as we went into the building, and unlike the way he was in Mexico City, he was relaxed and confident. Considering the way his sister was, the way we all battled our way from death on those barrio rooftops, he was acting like none of that even happened. I don't know why I was so surprised—I guess from the way that Javier would describe his sisters before, they sounded like they meant a great deal to him. After this, I wasn't sure of that. I wasn't sure of anything involving him.

He looked over his shoulder at me as we walked down a cool, linoleum-tiled corridor. It felt like we were heading backstage at a concert or a hockey game.

"I can feel how nervous you are, angel," he said. "It's coming right off you, like sweat."

"Can you feel this?" I stuck up my middle finger at him.

He only looked amused at that. Great.

We went around the corner to a room that had a Spanish sign on the door, and Javier lightly knocked on it. A very distinctive knock. Code. Funny how cartels had the same knock as those "No Girls Allowed" clubs back when I was in middle school.

We waited for a few moments, Javier looking as cool and collected as he could ever be. Like he didn't fear a single thing. Like we were on his turf again.

That could be both a good thing and a bad thing. My gun tingled in my boot.

Finally the door opened, and I was somewhat shocked to see the face of a good-looking man staring back at us.

"Javi," he said with an easy smile. *"Entra, por favor."*

The man brought his dark eyes to me, and I could have sworn they were twinkling. His hair was black and cropped short to his head, a layer of thin stubble on his angular face. He was probably in his late thirties, and I could see a wedding ring glinting on his left hand. He looked like he'd be a family man, albeit one in Javier's cartel. He was built like a runner, tall and lean, but like Javier he had fluidity and grace to his movements. He opened the door wider to let Javier in, then extended his hand to me.

"And you must be his friend, Ellie," he said, his voice light but heavily accented. I gave him my hand and he shook it heartily. There was something impish in his expression as he watched me, and I had to figure that he knew I once was the infamous Eden, the heartbreaker.

"I'm not quite his friend," I said, my words coming out harder than I meant them to.

He smiled. "Of course not. Javi doesn't have friends." He dropped my hand and welcomed me into the room.

I went inside and stood against the wall, looking around the room. It looked like an ordinary office: filing cabinets, a messy desk, a fax machine. On the walls were a few colorful paintings of bullfighters.

"Take a seat," Dom said as he eased himself into his leather chair and gestured at the two chairs across from him.

Javier shook his head. "We have to make this fast. I need your help."

Dom smiled and brought out a cigar from his desk, pulling it out of the silver canister. He had no interest in making this fast.

"Care for a cigar?" he asked Javier. When Javier refused he looked to me.

I shrugged. "Sure."

Javier shot me a dirty look but I didn't care. A cigar would take some of the edge off the day. Hell, it would take some of the edge off the *right now*.

"I like you," Dom said. He lit his own with a thick match from an antique-looking matchbox. After a few satisfied puffs, he pulled out another cigar and offered it to me. I went over to him and took it. Both he and Javier watched me closely as I lit it, and once I showed that I wasn't an idiot and knew how to smoke a cigar, Dom murmured something in approval.

"Now that the formalities are over..." Javier said,

glaring at me for no real reason. I glared right back, my eyes cutting through the cigar smoke trailing up from my lips. "We have something urgent to discuss."

Dom nodded. "*Sí*. You've said so already. What is it?"

"I need a doctor, for my sister. Someone who won't talk."

"Which sister?"

"Does it matter?"

Dom shrugged. "No, I guess not. What else do you need?"

"I need you to get us to Travis Raines."

He frowned and looked at me. "Us? What does she have to do with Travis?"

"That's not important," Javier told him. "What's important is that you'll do it and do it fast. Dominique, I know you know where he is. This is part of your job."

Dom smiled wryly. He had this calm, bemused air about him, but underneath it all I could see there was that layer of fear. Whether it was for Travis or Javier, I didn't know.

"My job, Javi, is taking care of my men." He eyed the paintings on the wall.

"The matadors?" I asked.

He shook his head. "No. Well, yes. But only Americans call them that. We call them *toreros*. You see, after Javier decided to restructure the cartel, I was sent back to Mexico. There's money in bullfighting, yes? There's not much money in Javi's business. Not anymore."

I could feel Javier's posture snapping. It was like his mood could change the air pressure in a room, maybe even in a whole building.

Dom's eyes flew to Javier's face, which was struggling to stay calm. "*Disculpa*, Javi. You know it's true. Travis took a great deal from us. Well, anyway, no hard feelings from me. I much prefer dealing with bulls here than dealing with the bullshit in America."

Javier swallowed loudly. "You're still on the payroll, Dom. You owe me this."

Dom breathed out through his nose and put his cigar down on the silver ashtray. He folded his hands in front of him. "And I'll be on the payroll till my death, isn't that the case?"

"You have a lovely wife and two lovely little girls. What were their names again?"

Dom's eyes darkened momentarily, like a shadow passed over them. He and Javier stared at each other for a few moments, the clock on the wall ticking loud. Then Dom said, slowly, "Estella and Abril."

"Right. So lovely. They must be what, four years old now? Such a precious age. They live in Aguascalientes still? With your beautiful wife. Does she still work for the bank?"

Dom was starting to look nervous. I looked to Javier, who was as cold as stone except for that cunning look in his eyes. He was threatening him.

"Javier," I warned, hoping I wasn't jumping to conclusions, that they were still just having a simple business discussion.

"Ellie, shut up," he said, not even looking at me. "This is for you."

"This is extortion!" I cried out.

He shook his head. "No, this is loyalty. This is Dom

proving how loyal he is. He knows he'll help us get to Travis. I don't even have to take his children. He'll do it because he's loyal. I just like to remind him from time to time that what he has, what I gave him, can oh so easily be taken away."

Javier then leaned on the desk, coming closer to Dom's face, beads of sweat running down his temples. He started speaking in Spanish to him, fast and cutting, too quick for me to pick up on it. Javier's tone was so smooth that I couldn't even tell if he was further threatening him or what.

Dom nodded a few times and averted his eyes. "*Sí, comprendo.*"

This was ridiculous. I had to wonder what the hell Javier had said if Dom was agreeing to something that was nothing short of a death wish. I mean, that's all this could be, couldn't it? Me, Camden, and Javier heading off to find Travis Raines, now, when he knew we were out there, was a suicide mission. It wasn't until I saw how reluctant Dom was to get involved that it finally hit home for me, the futility of it all.

And just like that, my bravado was slowly slipping away like the wisps of cigar smoke that were trailing up to the ceiling. The thought that I may never get to see Gus again. The fact that Camden and I were heading into something that we most likely would never return from.

Javier turned his head to look at me, as if sensing my hesitation.

"Don't worry," he said. "Everything is good."

More lies. I couldn't smile. I licked my lips and put my cigar beside Dom's in the ashtray.

"Thank you for that," I told Dom earnestly. "I don't think it can help me anymore."

"He must really mean something to you," Dom said. I looked to Javier in confusion and Dom went on. "Not Javi. This man that Travis has."

I nodded. "He does. He came here for me. It's the least I can do for him."

"Very well," Dom said, getting out of his chair. "I will help you, Ellie. I will do this for you, because I like you. I am not doing it for him." He jerked his head at Javier.

Javier rolled his eyes. "You can think of any reasons you want to, Dom, as long as you get the job done."

Dom sighed and rubbed his chin. "*Sí.* Always getting things done. Okay, I will write down where to bring your sister. Then I want you to meet me here." He started scribbling on a piece of paper he tore out of a notebook. "We can talk there tonight. It's a bar. Busy but safe. There's a small hotel attached to it, also a safe place to stay."

Javier gently took the paper from his hands and narrowed his catlike eyes ever so slightly. "If you are trying to fuck with me..."

Dom gave him a small smile. "I'm not an idiot, Javi."

"That remains to be seen," Javier replied. Then he straightened up and grabbed my arm, wrapping his fingers around my biceps. "Come on, let's go."

Dom opened the door and Javier escorted me outside, his fingers digging into my skin.

"Don't you fucking touch me," I hissed at him as he brought me down the hall. People were passing us, giving us dubious glances.

"Oh, give it a rest, angel," he said, exasperated. "One minute I'm hurting you, the next minute you like it."

"I haven't liked it for a long time," I said through my teeth.

"Is that so?" He cocked his head at me. "I could have sworn it was just a few days ago that I last made you scream."

"Fuck you."

He grinned. "That you did, my angel. That you did."

I ripped myself out of his grasp before we exited the building. Outside the air was cooler, the sky layered with pink, blue, and orange, like the sand art I used to see in the gift shops along the Mississippi coast. As we walked toward Jose, looking more battered than ever in the fading light, I asked him, "Are you sure we can trust Dom?"

He shook his head. "Can I be sure? No. But he knows if something goes wrong, he will pay for it in the end. Or his family will pay, and he will have to watch."

"Does everything have to be a threat with you?" What I really wanted to do was call him a sick fuck, but he'd heard it too many times already.

"If there are no threats, then people die. I don't feel like dying anytime soon. Do you? Does Camden?"

I rubbed my lips together, wishing I had some lip balm on me. Actually, what I really wished for was a long, hot shower, then a drink or two, then a few hours by myself to think.

No. Not by myself. With Camden. I needed him to think with me.

When we got to the car, he was turned around in

his seat and speaking to Violetta. At a closer look, he was holding her hand as she lay in the back. My lungs pinched at the sight, as silly as it was. Poor thing was in agony and I was getting jealous.

"What are you doing?" Javier asked him as he got into the backseat, Violetta slowly sitting up.

"He's holding my hand, what does it look like?" Violetta asked snidely. She looked like utter shit. Her face was ashen, her forehead thick with sweat, her lips dry and cracking. A shiver occasionally rocked through her, despite my leather jacket, which Camden must have gotten out of the trunk, covering her shoulders.

Camden looked to me and said, "She's in a lot of pain."

I nodded. "We're taking her to the doctor now."

"Took you long enough," she said, then groaned. I noticed Camden squeezing her hand harder. I looked behind me at Javier, who was watching them with a look of utter disdain.

"Javier," I said carefully, slowly, until he looked at me. "Where are we taking her?"

He looked at the piece of paper that Dom had given him. "Outside of town. I know where this is. Take your first left until you see signs for the highway. Take it west."

I did as he said, hoping the cops wouldn't pull us over for driving with one headlight. It was Mexico, but Aguascalientes was a lot more civilized than Mexico City and Veracruz had been.

We drove for a few miles outside of the suburbs before we came to a ranch house that was surrounded by darkness, only a few lights on inside. It looked like a farm—not exactly the place I had been picturing in my head. You know, like a doctor's office or a hospital.

"This better not be another vet," Camden mumbled. "Though I could use a refill on the dog medication now that we've run out."

"Not a vet," Javier said with impatience. "Pull up beside the truck there. This is Alonso's house. He's part of my . . . family."

His cartel. I wondered if he was still on the "payroll" as Dom seemed to be, if he too was banished back to Mexico when Travis up and switched sides. More and more I was finding out that Javier didn't have the power I once thought he did.

We got out of the car, Camden easing Violetta to her feet and supporting her. Javier marched past them, apparently no longer caring that Camden was touching his sister—not like he was offering to help her himself—and went for the front door. The path lit up from motion-sensor lights.

He rang the doorbell and we waited a few moments.

A short man with thick gray hair and mustache eyed us over a pair of square glasses. "*Sí?*"

"Alonso," Javier said. "*Cómo está?*"

"Javier?"

"*Sí, que soy yo.*"

Alonso rattled off something in Spanish and eyed the rest of us.

Javier waved in our direction, said something about his sister needing surgery and something else. Probably that we were two gringos and inconsequential.

Alonso sighed dejectedly and opened the door wider, quickly motioning for us to come inside.

Camden helped Violetta through, Alonso staring at his tattoos with a mix of curiosity and revulsion. He then looked to Violetta's arm and nodded grimly.

"Okay," Alonso said.

Javier took her from Camden, much to her annoyance, and he gave us both a steady look. "He's going to fix her. You stay here. If you move, if you run, I will kill you. That is all."

Then he, Violetta, and Alonso disappeared down a darkened hallway until they entered a brightly lit room at the end of the hall. I could see Violetta's eyes glinting as she turned her head to look back at us. They disappeared behind a dark door, the latch echoing in the quiet house.

Camden watched the door for a few moments before he folded his arms and looked at me.

"What went on in there?"

"With Dom?"

"Yeah. Him. He a good guy or a bad guy?"

My lips twitched in a halfhearted smile. "I don't think there are good guys and bad guys anymore. I don't even know what I am."

"Ellie," he said, his voice becoming softer. "You had to kill those men."

I gave him a sharp nod. "I know."

"I had to do some things that I'm not proud of too." There was a rawness in his tone, like he was close to cracking open. "I don't think you and I can ever go back to being the people we were before."

His words hit me hard, splicing me open. It wasn't that I couldn't go back to being me—I was never very good to begin with—but if we'd both changed, could we find each other again as we had before? Did Camden lose himself in order to save me, and if he did, did that mean I'd lost the Camden that loved me?

Violetta's scream pierced through my thoughts, jolting me into the present. I was about to take off toward the room when Javier came out, strolling toward us casually, his face in shadow until the last minute.

"What happened?" I exclaimed.

"He set her arm," he said. He walked over to the bar and pulled out a crystal bottle of dark amber liquid, pulling the top off with a pop.

"Without any pain medication?" Camden asked incredulously.

He calmly poured the liquid into a textured high-ball glass and swirled it around. "We don't have a lot of time. She bit down on something, don't worry."

"Don't worry?" Camden sneered, stepping up to him.

Javier sipped his drink and winced, peering at the glass. "I'm fairly sure Alonso made this in his bathtub." He eyed Camden with amusement. "And yes. Don't worry. She's my sister. I know what's best for her. She'll be on some pain medication, the good kind, better than that monkey shit you were given."

Camden's fists clenched and Javier saw that too.

"Easy there, big boy," he said, grinning. He finished the rest of the drink and slammed the glass down. He wiped the back of his hand across his snaking lips.

"You're so overprotective of the ladies. They're a lot tougher than you give them credit for, you know."

Javier winked at me and went back down the hall. Camden went to the bar, snatched the booze off the table, and then stormed out the front door and into the emptiness of the night, perhaps hoping to drink the rage out of him.

I didn't know in which direction to go. Camden wanted to be alone and I didn't want to be with Javier.

I sighed and sat down on Alonso's couch.

And waited.

CHAPTER SIX

"ELLIE, DO YOU mind sleeping with me tonight?"

I looked behind me at Violetta. I was pulling Jose up to the motel that Dom had recommended. It was actually a clean-looking place, quite busy, with noise thumping from the bar at the end of the row. That was where Dom had wanted to meet us.

"I'd love to," I told her.

"If it's not one Bernal, it's another," Javier remarked.

I glared at him, though he didn't seem to notice. Instead, he merely tapped the front of the seat so I could let him out. Camden was still asleep from the alcohol he downed, his head resting against the window.

We had been at Alonso's for about an hour. Eventually Violetta was brought out to us, high as a kite on morphine and with a sling around her shoulder, protecting the makeshift cast covering her arm. Camden had successfully drunk half the bottle of mystery booze and had lapsed into an even more quiet and introverted state. Alonso didn't seem to mind, he just wanted us

out of his house and gone. I wondered if he really was
a doctor, and if so, if he was still practicing. The more
I learned about the cartels and the people tied to them,
the more their history interested me. I couldn't imagine someone like Javier being anything else before
becoming a drug lord, and I couldn't see him going on
to any other career if he had to. This was Javier's past
and future, this was his destiny, and nothing else would
ever compare to that.

I certainly never had.

Don't get me wrong, I wasn't feeling sorry for
myself. I know now what I didn't know then, that for
some people love is never enough. It's just sad that I had
to learn that twice, two lessons six years apart.

Okay, maybe I was feeling a little bit sorry for
myself. It was hard not to when I was reminded of what
I had with Camden and what my actions had cost me.

We stepped out of the car, Camden slowly stirring
awake, and surveyed the area. So far, so good. Nothing
suspicious, no one out to kill us. Not yet, anyway.

"I'll get us the rooms," I said, about to walk off, but
Javier pulled me back.

"With what money?" he asked.

I pulled out my wallet from my back jean pocket
and waved it at him. "There's more than a few lives in
that car, more than a few credit cards. One of them will
work."

He raised his brow. "Perhaps you should start taking inventory of your stuff before you begin making assumptions. You know what happens when you
assume, don't you?"

I rolled my eyes. "Yes, they make an 'ass' out of 'u' and 'me.'"

"They get you killed," he said quickly. He pushed me back slightly and took off for the motel office, tossing over his shoulder, "I'll get this. And yes, I'll make sure you and Violetta can share a room together."

Oh, of course, like he was letting us. The ass always had to be in control.

I turned to see Violetta and Camden standing beside each other and leaning against the car in matching poses: her dark skin glistening in the heat of the night, his body, strong yet tired. Both of them were a little fucked up in the head at the moment, their eyes glazed, their half smiles loopy. I had to admit, I was kind of envious. It would be nice to be oblivious to the shit going on around me at every given turn.

Javier did have a point though. Once he came back with the room keys—Violetta and I were sharing one, but Camden and Javier had separate rooms, thank god—I decided to take everything out of my trunk and start going through it. My aliases needed organizing. If we ever did return to America, I'd have to choose a new life to live, a new person to become.

I was exhausted thinking about it.

Maybe, just maybe, I could pick one life and stick with it for a long time.

I looked over at Camden, who was helping take stuff into my room: ziplock bags of license plates, boxes of falsified papers, IDs, checks. This new life felt entirely dependent on one thing.

Him.

The motel room was a lot nicer than the one we'd stayed at before. Sort of a Best Western, middle-ground quality of place. No roaches on the floors, no geckos on the wall. Shit mattresses, I discovered as I pounded my fist on the bed, but I didn't care.

Camden had just put the final box on my bed, Violetta sprawled out on hers in a state of drug-induced euphoria, when I noticed Javier lingering at the doorway.

"I'm going to be meeting Dom in about twenty minutes," Javier said to me. "Is that enough time for you to get ready?"

I frowned and he quickly added, "You know he'll want you there, if this is going to get anywhere. I figured you might want to shower and look nice."

He rapped his fingers along the doorframe, his mouth opening as if to say something else, then he turned and walked off.

Camden eyed me. "I'm going with you."

"You might be kind of drunk, Camden," I told him, though the determination in his voice warmed me like the finest cognac.

"I've never felt better," he said, enunciating each word. His eyes—my god, they were still such a clear fucking blue, even in the pallid light of the hotel room. They bore into me with such startling clarity, sending shivers down my back like trailing fingertips. He would be coming with me.

I wished he'd be coming in me. A vision of us in this hotel room, alone, him nailing me to the bed, the headboard banging, slammed into my head.

"Are you okay with that?" he asked.

I suppressed the thought, the flare of heat between my legs, and smiled quickly. "Yes, of course."

Meanwhile Violetta's head flopped to the side, her arm still bound to her stiffly in the sling, and started snoring lightly. I motioned to her. "Do you think it's safe to leave her here?"

He watched her for a few moments, blinking a few times, before saying, "I think she needs to sleep it off." He went and sat down on my bed. "I'll be here when you get out."

I grabbed the bag of clothes I had brought out of the car and brought it into the bathroom. I had a quick shower, trying to rub off all the grime—both real and imagined—with the flimsy hotel soap, then picked through my clothes. Everything that had been in my trunk was musty and wrinkled, some even dirty. I had a packet of unopened (and decidedly unsexy) Hanes underwear, a bra, another pair of jeans, a pair of gladiator sandals that I thought were dressy enough, a pair of Timberland hiking boots, a plain white T-shirt, a couple of wife-beaters, a coral-colored blouse, a plaid shirt, and a light blue tank dress that went to the ground. I wasn't exactly known for my fashion sense, and even with the cherry blossoms covering the scars on my leg, bringing me beauty that I didn't have before, I didn't see myself branching out anytime soon. Dressing up in my old clothes for Javier hadn't exactly helped either.

I slipped on the tank dress, opting to go commando for the evening, and put on the sandals. I looked at myself in the mirror. Once again, I felt like a different person was staring back at me. This me, this Ellie, was tired and hardened. I rubbed the residue mascara from under my eyes and applied a new coat. My skin was brown from the sun now and I didn't need much else.

When I came out of the bathroom, Camden straightened up on the bed. I felt strangely shy in front of him, especially as his eyes trailed up and down the length of me.

"Do I look okay?" I asked him, feeling the need to say something. "I mean, if you can see me, that is."

He bit his lip and stared, a multitude of emotions flashing through his eyes, too fast for me to pick up on each individual one. I thought I saw lust in there—maybe that's what I wanted to see.

When he still didn't say anything, I walked over to the dresser, where I had my clutch purse left over from the other night at Travis's, and rifled through it for my lip stuff. His silence at my back was a heavy weight, laden with too many uncertainties between us. It was eating at me, burning through me, rendering me with a lead heart. There were so many things I had to focus on, to worry about, fucking impossible things, and yet I needed him to tell me I looked beautiful. I needed him to tell me I was something to him.

I heard him get off the bed and walk toward me, that heaviness, that warmth that he brought with his body, teased at my back. He stopped, close enough to touch me, and I was about to turn around, perhaps to do something foolish, when he crouched down.

"How is my art?"

His hands found my leg, one of them lifting the hem of my dress, the other slowly moving over the cherry blossom tattoo. I sucked in my breath, holding completely still, trying to contain my nerves that were firing wildly as his fingers ran along the ridges of the ink. He touched me gently over every vine, leaf and petal, until I had to suppress a shaky moan that tried to escape from my lips.

"It feels fine," I said softly when I found my voice.

"It looks beautiful," he said.

"I had a beautiful artist," I told him. I turned at the waist and look down at him, my blue dress glowing in his tanned hand, his other one placed firmly around my calf, his strong fingers imparting heat that sunk deep. He was looking up at me, lips parted slightly.

I couldn't take a second more of this.

I turned and dropped to the ground, my knees rubbing against his.

I grabbed his face, his rough stubble pressing into my palms, and kissed him.

Hard.

There was surprise for a second, a hesitation, a pulse that refused to beat on. Then Camden kissed me back, his soft lips enveloping mine, his mouth opening to give me life. He put his hand behind my head, holding it there with power and control.

My heart was an elevator car, the cable suddenly snapped, and I was free-falling and falling and falling as his lips and tongue and hot, wet mouth took away every inch of my resolve. The more he kissed me, the deeper and longer we found each other, the thirstier I got for him. I felt like if we stopped, I would die, empty on the inside and forever longing.

"Ellie," he whispered into my lips. "I...can't."

And I was empty.

I pulled away and looked at him, fighting the tears of frustration that were tickling behind my lids. "You can't what?"

A jarring knock at the door prevented him from finishing his sentence.

The door swung open and Javier stepped in. He eyed the two of us, crouched together on the floor, our hands entwined in the other's hair, our chests heaving and unseen hearts hurting. Breaking.

He couldn't what?

Do this?

Love me?

I didn't even care that Javier was watching us, waiting for us to say something, to explain ourselves. I cared about what Camden was going to say next.

"Well, isn't this awkward," Javier said. Though his tone was light, there was no mistaking the fire that was burning in his eyes. He looked at me like he was ready to slit my throat and be done with it. He didn't even give Camden a second look—this was all about me.

He finally tore his eyes away from us and over to the bed where Violetta was sleeping soundly. He made a *tsk*-ing noise and shook his head. "And you were about to fuck each other in front of my sister, is that right?" He looked back at me, chin down, lips pouting ever so slightly. "I never pegged you to be such a whore." He smiled as if forgetting his manners, adding, "Angel."

It didn't sting. It didn't hurt me. I wouldn't let him hurt me anymore.

But Camden sprung up as if he had been waiting for this and launched himself at Javier, his fists flying. Javier was quick too, and managed to duck, though not without Camden clocking him on the side of the head with a powerful blow.

The two of them tumbled to the ground, crashing against one of the bedside tables. Violetta didn't stir, not even when I started yelling at them to stop it. I know I'd said I wanted to see this fight happen, but not now, not like this. This wouldn't bode well for Camden and me, especially if Camden won again. Javier would never ever let him live that down.

Perhaps not even let him live.

Javier was fighting back, dirty, of course. His physical strength was no match for Camden's, and he repeatedly went for Camden's injury on his shoulder with every jab and hit he had. He was cruel and ruthless and got the job done. That's how he'd been trained: quick and dirty. At one point Javier stuck his thumb hard into Camden's bullet wound until Camden released him, crying out in horror.

This was my chance.

I leaped onto Camden's back, wrapping my arms around his neck and good shoulder.

"Stop it!" I screamed in his ear. "This is what he wants."

Violetta mumbled something at that, then adjusted herself on the bed and fell asleep again.

I looked up at Javier, who was getting to his feet, his lip bloody again, his suit disheveled. He grinned, enjoying himself, and let out a wicked laugh. "You have no idea what I want." He wiped his fingers across his lips and raised his dark brows at the blood on it. "Huh. Not even sure how you managed to do that again. You know, if you're not careful, Camden, you're going to end up with nothing."

"And yet you still haven't killed me," Camden said with effort. I could feel his heart racing in his chest, the rage that wanted to keep flying out of him until Javier was lifeless pulp.

"I didn't say anything about killing you," Javier said. "I just said you'll end up with nothing. And you will. You want to help Ellie get the things she wants, you have to start playing a lot nicer than you have been. A lot nicer." He sighed and smoothed his hair behind his ears. "Ellie, if you want to see your Gus again, you come with me. Right now."

He went for the door and I climbed off of Camden and said, "Not without him. I'm not doing this without Camden."

Javier looked to the ceiling and mouthed something to the heavens, like he was arguing in Spanish with God. He exhaled long and slow through his nose. "Fine, bring the ape with you, as long as he can keep himself under control. Other people might not be as forgiving as I am."

Camden stiffened under my fingers and I willed him to calm down, even though I had to bite my own tongue to keep from saying something. The coppery taste of blood filled my mouth, but I only nodded and said, "Come on, Camden. We need to think about the big picture."

"The picture is bigger than you know," he muttered.

I was about to ask him what he meant when he brushed me aside and threw his shoulders back, walking up to Javier, looking large and in charge. Blood had soaked through his shirt from his re-opened wound and was trickling down his arm, but he just wiped it away with his hand.

"We're ready," he said loudly, standing right in front of him, his eyes bearing down. I watched their silent exchange for a moment, the complexity in their eyes as they matched against each other in a visual war. The snake against the bear, the man of stealth and lies against the man of soul and strength.

Both men who'd had a stake in my heart at some point in the game.

This ever-changing game.

Javier finally stepped back, flourishing with his arm. "After you," he said, his words dripping with venom. He looked to me. "Come on, angel."

I grabbed my purse and headed to the door. I was halfway out of it when Javier's hand slipped around my waist and he whispered, "You look beautiful."

I twisted away from his touch and quickened my steps so I was walking beside Camden. He didn't look at me, but his temples were twitching as he tried to keep his temper under control. I felt like we kept on taking one step forward together, two steps back, and Gus kept slipping away all the same.

The bar was dark but not dingy, small but not cramped. It looked like a good mix of locals and vacationing Mexicans who were staying at the hotel.

Camden and I were the only gringos in the whole place, but no one seemed to notice. They were all too busy laughing and drinking, having a good time.

In the corner of the bar, closest to an old pool table, was Dom. He was sitting with someone now and I could hear Javier mutter, "Fucking animal" under his breath. I turned to look at him, to gauge his reaction, but Javier pushed past me and went up the table with open arms.

"Esteban, you bastard!" Javier exclaimed, grinning from ear to ear.

The man, Esteban, got up and the two of them embraced. Once I got to the table, smiling politely at Dom, I got a better look at Esteban.

He was around six feet, medium build but muscular, light olive skin and bright hazel eyes, hair like a surfer, all shoulder-length straggles, dark brown with sun-bleached strands. He looked to be about our age, late twenties, and could have been Matthew McConaughey's evil doppelganger if it wasn't for the fact that he had a swath of lacerations on the left side of his face. It was weird to see someone so beautiful and ugly at the same time. He was scarred just like me, only his were visible for all the world to see.

And yet here he was, smiling and greeting Javier like old chums, not making any apologies for himself, for what had happened to him, for the scars he had to bear. He embraced it. Like, fuck it, this is me.

After the two embraced, Esteban sat back down and immediately looked to me. He didn't say anything, though, just pressed his pretty lips together into a small smile. His eyes did most of the talking. He knew who I was. He eyed Dom and a similar look was exchanged.

Javier looked to Dom. It was odd to see him so genuinely happy to see someone. "Why didn't you tell me he was coming?"

Dom smiled. "I wanted to show you that I too have a few surprises up my sleeve." He nodded at Camden and me. "Please sit down, Ellie. And you must be Camden."

Introductions were quickly made by me, since Javier wasn't stepping up to the plate.

"Got something on your lip there?" Esteban pointed at Javier.

Javier dabbed his bruised lip, a spot of blood coming away. He smiled quickly. "It's a tough business."

Camden quietly snorted beside me, but thankfully kept his mouth shut. Esteban eyed the fresh blood on his shirt and smiled smugly.

I leaned on the table, my hands clasped under my chin, and eyed Esteban and Dom. "Before we start getting into the real reason we're all sitting here, Esteban, why don't you tell me how you come into all of this."

Dom let out an amused gasp and sat back in his chair. He watched Javier for his reaction, knowing he was going to be slighted by me taking the reins of this whole thing, of his cartel. But fuck it. This was my mission more than anything. And if I was going to risk our lives to get Gus, I had to know exactly who everyone was and how they were playing into it.

Esteban raised his brows and said, in near-perfect English, "Well, Miss Watt. My brother used to work for Javi—"

"He still does," Javier interjected.

Esteban gave him a look. "Yes. But I haven't heard from him in a while, and I am sure you haven't either. Anyway, I joined in after Travis. I'm part of the new and improved cartel. The younger one. The stronger one." He grinned. "Of course, things don't always go as planned. I got into a, well, a scuffle down here with another cartel. I should say, the police that the cartel was paying off. Not the Zetas, the Gulf. But what does it matter what cartel it is, right? Alliances mean nothing these days. So in this scuffle, I took a load of shrapnel to my face and was presumed dead. I wasn't. Hey, but let them think that."

"You let me think that," Javier said. "You let Alex think that."

"It was for the best," Esteban said.

"Alex is your brother?" I asked him, remembering all too well the other henchman of Javier's.

He nodded. "I saw all the fine ladies he was pulling in with his new cars and suits and wanted in." He winked at me, then waved over the waitress.

We all shut up while she came by and took our orders—more beer, naturally—and then as soon as she was gone, I launched into more questions.

"So why are you here now?" I asked him.

He gave Javier a look, as if saying *ain't she the eager beaver.* Then Esteban gazed at me directly in the eye, unblinking, piercing, suddenly terribly serious. "Because Javier and Dom cannot do this on their own. You cannot do this on your own. Travis's compound is in the east part of Honduras. Right in the heart of the jungle. Not even accessible by road. They chopper in and out. We can't do that. We have to hike it and it takes several days. Then when you get whoever you've come to get, it won't be so easy to leave." He took a swig of his beer. My limbs felt leaden at the news. I had imagined him being in a house similar to the one in Veracruz, not a fortress in the middle of a jungle, not some place we'd have to hike to. "Speaking of, this man that you say Travis has, Gus? There's a woman too."

"My mother."

"Yes, so I hear."

"Will they be expecting Ellie?" Javier asked.

He nodded. "I think so. But maybe not you."

"How could they *not* be expecting Javier?" Camden asked suddenly. "They've been chasing us all over."

Esteban gave a half shrug. "It's just a hunch. Anyway, it doesn't matter who they expect, because we will go there all the same, and when we do we'll all be dead to them, equally."

I sighed and put my head into my hands. This was getting more and more impossible by the moment. I felt Camden's hand on my knee, giving it a squeeze, but even that didn't help.

"No one said this would be easy," Dom said gently.

Such concern from the cartel. How nice.

"When do we go?" I said, straightening up and running my hands down my face. "What do we need to do?"

Esteban eyed Javier, as if he was unsure of his place to speak now.

Javier took it and ran with it. He pushed his chair

back and leaned into it, his legs splayed, his beer dangling from his fingers.

"This is what we're going to do," he said smoothly. "The five of us will head to Honduras. I'm sending Violetta away in the morning. Dom, we'll need someone to take her to Puerto Vallarta. She can stay with her sisters or not, but I want her out of the picture. Este, you gather what information you can. You're the tech expert here. The logistics of the operation have to be sound. I mean asshole tight, you understand? If we need more than us five, then you bring a few more in. Just remember, I want this as small as possible. The more people who know, the more we're at risk."

"Can the five of us really get into Travis's place and get my mother and Gus out?" I asked.

Javier smiled patronizingly. "My dear, I think you're underestimating me. You don't need to match his team to win. Besides, I don't plan on killing everyone there. I only plan on killing him and whoever else gets in my way. The others, they will surrender to me once he is gone. We need a small team, maybe six of us if we have to. With the best weapons. The best tech. The best... depravity." He downed the rest of his beer and slammed it on the table. "Have a little faith."

His words rumbled through me like a heavy bass chord.

Faith.

Another thing I'd lost along the way.

CHAPTER SEVEN

WE DIDN'T STAY at the bar too much longer. After we said goodbye to Dom and Esteban—who started insisting I call him Este—we went back to our rooms. I desperately wanted to follow Camden into his, but I said goodbye to both men at once and Camden went into his room first. Javier was farther down, lingering at his door, watching me in silence. His face was in shadow, but I could still feel his eyes, his hesitation, as if he wanted to say something to me.

There was no hesitation on my end. I gave him a hard look and went to my room. Violetta was in the washroom, the tap running.

"Ellie?" she called out from behind the closed door.

"I'm here," I told her and climbed into my bed. A tank dress was no different than a nightgown, and I wasn't chummy enough with her to sleep naked.

The bathroom door opened and she staggered out. From the weak light that lit her up from behind, I could see she looked pretty wrecked. Or wrecked but still pretty, as seemed to be the case with her.

"How are you feeling?" I asked. "How's your arm?"

She gave me a sloppy smile and eased herself into bed. "I feel kind of sick and I can't feel my arm. But I don't feel any pain."

"Good."

"Ellie," she said softly. "What's going to happen to me?"

I turned my head on the pillow and looked across at her. "What do you mean?"

She sighed and stared up at the ceiling. I had an idea of what Javier's nose must have looked like before it was broken a million times. "I have a bad feeling. I've had it for a week. That I'm going to die."

"You're not going to die, Violetta. Javier wouldn't let that happen."

"You know that's not true. Javi always acted like he cared more than he did. Even when I was younger, he would be nice to me if it got him something, maybe a treat from Mom. Or he did it because it was expected. I don't know if he cares if I'm alive or dead."

I licked my lips, thinking back to the conversation in the bar. "I know he wants to keep you safe. He may have a funny way of showing things, but he does care about you. He wouldn't have come this way if he didn't have to. Tomorrow he's going to send you away from all of this."

She laughed. "Let me guess, to see my sisters?"

"You don't need to get mixed up in this."

"I already am."

"It's not too late to get out. And I, I will make sure you're taken care of."

She turned her head to look at me, her eyes glinting in the dark. "You're nothing like him, you know."

The back of my neck tingled. "I'm not?"

She shook her head slowly. "No. I thought you would be. But you're not."

I could barely find my voice. "I wasn't a good person. I was a con artist."

"I know. You left that out earlier when you told your little story, but I know. What difference is it what you were? You're not conning anyone now, are you? You're risking your life to save somebody. You risked your life to save me and you don't even know me. You could have let me fall and run on but you stopped and you helped me. I don't think there's anything more noble than that. You have more courage than any of those cartels do, those single-minded assholes with their money and their guns. They wouldn't even do that for each other. It's every man for himself. You're not like that." She paused. "And neither is Camden."

She was at least right about him. But when you're told over and over again about how immoral you are, how bad, how wicked, how unlikeable, how terrible you are, it's hard to hear anyone say any different. I felt like a fraud being good just as I felt like a fraud being bad.

"Camden is a good man," I whispered, a pit lodged in my throat. "Too good for me."

"And you say he's not your man?"

"No. He's no one's."

"If you say that, then you don't see what I see."

I smiled weakly. "What do you know? You're high on morphine."

She giggled. "This is true. But I know love when I see love. Take it from me, you never forget your first love."

Javier was my first love. That was always a hard pill to swallow. "No. I suppose you don't."

"First love or not, it's what you have now that matters. And you have Camden. You should be with him."

I thought so too. Camden understood me, he'd gone through the very things I'd gone through, the things that scar you, the pain that only your family and peers can inflict. Even when we were young teenagers, he knew my struggles first hand. There's nothing like finding that person who not only accepts you but...*knows* you. Knows the person you're too afraid to look at, your true self that hides deep beneath your armor. But I fucked it up in high school and I fucked it up now. I turned away from him because I was too weak to be the person I needed to be. To be the real me.

My chest squeezed. "It's not that simple."

"Things are only complicated if you make them. Believe me, I know. I wanted everything at one point. Then I lost my parents, a sister, and in a way I lost a brother. After Beatriz died, Javier changed. And then I realized I didn't need everything, I just needed people to love. That was it. Only people to love and to love me."

Tears welled up behind my eyes. I didn't really know Violetta. I didn't know exactly what she'd gone through. Yet still her words could have been my words.

"I'm glad I met you," I told her, my voice choking up. "Really."

"Same here. Just…" she trailed off.

"What?"

Her features softened in the dark. "Be careful. Javi may have loved you…and maybe he still does. But don't think he wouldn't throw you under a bus in order to get what he wants."

And what if what he wants is still me? I thought. *And what happens when he figures out he can't have it?*

"I'll remember that," I told her. We lapsed into silence, her breath becoming steady.

I fell asleep thinking about jungles and guns and death and blood. I dreamed about Camden, Gus, Violetta, and me buried under a landslide, and Javier on the mountaintop, one foot on my mother's severed head.

I woke up soon after that and never got to sleep again.

* * *

By the time the sun rose in the air, blanketing the surroundings in warmth, bare, distant mountains looking remarkably clear against a blazing blue sky, I was already dressed and packed. Violetta woke up in pain, so I left her to visit Javier's room for more medicine. I knocked on the door and held my breath, hoping he wasn't going to give me too much trouble over this.

He answered it, the chain across the door, one golden eye peeking through.

"Yes?"

I rolled my eyes at his formality. "Can I come in?"

"Oh, really?"

I stuck my boot in between the door and the frame. "Yes. Now."

He grunted and closed the door, forcing my boot out of the way. Then I heard the chain slide across and he opened it.

He was only wearing a towel again.

Fuck my luck.

Do you just walk around naked all the time? I wanted to say. But I knew the answer was yes and his ego would blow up at the fact that I'd noticed.

I didn't let my eyes stray south for a second longer and walked into the room, looking around.

"Where's the morphine?"

"A little early to be getting high, Ellie," he said, his fingers toying with the edge of his towel as it snaked across his waist. "Had I known you were into the poppies, I would have done away with all the cocaine."

I crossed my arms and looked at him dead-on. "It's for your sister and you know it is. She's in pain and she needs it. Now."

"You've really taken a shine to her, haven't you?"

"She's nothing like you, maybe that's why."

He nodded and walked slowly, very slowly, across the room to the desk. "She's weak and foolish, that's her problem. Though perhaps that's why you like her. You can relate."

I breathed in sharply through my nose and willed my heart to calm down. "Just give me the morphine."

He reached into a crumpled small paper bag and brought out the syringe and a vial. My eyes widened a bit at the sight.

"Got enough there?" I asked him snidely.

He pierced the bottle with the syringe and filled it a

quarter of the way up. "I told you that I'd only get the best for her. The rest, well, the rest *we* might need."

He walked over to me, each step with purpose, each step closer to shaking loose his towel. He smiled, all white teeth, canines showing, and proudly displayed the syringe and the medicine in his hands.

"I'll give you this if you do me a favor."

I did not like the sounds of that.

"Javier, there isn't time to play games."

"There is always time to play a game, angel. You've been playing them from the moment we met."

He took a step forward again and I backed up until the back of my knees hit the edge of the bed.

"Even your feelings for Camden are nothing more than a game to you," he went on. One step closer. "You want him because you can't have him. You can't have him because you *disgust* him. And once you do, if you get to him using those pretty eyes of yours and that tight as hell pussy, you won't even want him anymore. You'll toss him aside. Just like you did to me."

I'd had enough of this. I quickly reached for the syringe but he yanked it out of the way and grabbed my wrist, his fingers searing into me like hot knives into butter.

He jerked me closer to him until my chest was pressed against his, his erection hard against my thigh. "Now about that favor." He stared at my lips, his eyes full of lust and madness and victory. "Kiss me."

Was he seriously this sick, to make me kiss him in exchange for the medicine for his own sister?

"Forget it," I told him. I'd find another way to get it to her. I turned to walk away, but he held me in place and brought his face to mine. A wash of softness came over his brow, his mouth turning down, his lids heavy. "Am I that repulsive to you now?" When I didn't answer, he whispered, "You know I'm doing all of this for you, my angel. I wouldn't do this for anyone else, not ever." He cupped my face with his free hand. "You could still be the queen of everything."

A queen of everything, but still a queen with nothing.

"I have to go check on her," I said, closing my eyes, wanting to be free of him. I waited tensely, listening to my heart thumping in my ears, the shortness of his breath as he held me there.

Finally he released me and pressed the vial and syringe into my hand. "Take this to her, then. Make yourself feel better."

I turned around without looking at him, the medicine damp from the sweat of his hand, and got out of the room. The morning sun seemed glaring now after being with him.

I made it two steps out the door when the wall beside me exploded into a shower of cement and paint. I dropped flat to the hard ground on instinct, covering my head, looking around me wildly. Suddenly Javier's window exploded and I could feel bits of wayward glass raining down on me.

I reached into my boot and pulled out my gun, my eyes darting all over the parking lot. There was nothing unusual, just a few cars and Jose. But across the street was a long fence belonging to a house. If the shooters were hiding behind there, we were sitting ducks.

"Ellie?" Javier called out from his room. My ears

were ringing with the sound of the gunshots, my lungs seizing at the close call. The shots had stopped for now, but they were just waiting for an easy target.

"I'm okay!" I shouted back.

Camden's door swung open and he suddenly burst out, running fast as hell, gun in his hand, over to a high van that was parked near the entrance and closest to the fence on the other side of the road. He flattened himself against the back of the van and his eyes darted over to me. If I ran, the gunmen would try shooting and reveal their location. I looked over at the door Camden had left open. Could I make it there before their bullets got me?

Only one way to find out. I nodded at Camden.

Then I got to my feet and sprinted. Shots fired out in my wake, some of them far above my head, which showed that the shooters didn't have the best accuracy so far. I was just about to duck inside the door when Violetta came stumbling out of our door, looking panicked.

"Get down!" I screamed at her. I ditched Camden's room and ran for her instead. I tackled her to the ground just as the window to our room shattered with another blast of gunfire. Even though I smashed up my elbow in the fall and we partially landed on Violetta's arm, Camden took the opportunity to take out whoever was shooting at us. He popped off a few rounds, splintering the fence across the street, the noise punctuated by a few cries of agony and defeat.

Violetta moaned beneath my arms, her own pain taking over her. I rolled her over and peered at her face, the tears streaming down it. "I've got something for you, it will just take a few seconds, okay?"

"Who the fuck is shooting at us?" she cried out.

I looked up at Camden, who was peering around the van, being extra cautious. From behind us, I could hear another door open.

"Are you okay?" It was Javier. His footsteps stopped right behind us. I turned my head and glanced at his stern expression. He'd managed to put on his pants, thank god, though he was still shirtless.

I eased myself off of Violetta, and Camden came trotting over and helped me get her to her feet. "We're okay, thanks to Camden." I gave Camden a quick smile. "Can't see things from far away, right?"

"I got lucky," Camden said, but his tone and the darkness in his eyes said it was nothing as frivolous as luck.

"Well let's not start thinking he saved the world yet," Javier said. "We don't even know if they're dead." He took his gun out of his waistband and snapped back the clip. "But if they aren't, they will be."

He trotted across the parking lot, his shaggy hair blowing behind him, and crossed the street, gun held low. I looked over at the hotel lobby and saw a few people gathered, some on cell phones, perhaps to call the police.

I looked up at Camden. "We have to shoot her up and get her out of here." I held out her good arm and he grasped it around the forearm while I quickly found a vein near the crook of her elbow. "This will pinch. And then you'll be flying, okay, sweetie?" I tapped the vein and stuck the syringe in, injecting the morphine in one push. She immediately relaxed in my arms, but not too much. Javier had put enough in there to take away the pain, but not as much as she had the night before.

"Why don't you go wait in the car?" I told her, smoothing back her hair.

"Can I drive it?" she asked lazily.

I smiled. "Not yet. But you can listen to the radio if it will make you feel better." I put the car keys in her hands and sent her off.

I turned to Camden. "I think we have five minutes tops before the shit hits the fan."

He nodded at the broken windows and blasted walls. "I think it's already hit the fan."

"True, but—"

"No!" Javier's scream cut through us. We snapped our heads to look. He was running across the street toward us, screaming and waving his hands frantically. "No!"

I looked to Violetta, where he was headed. She had just gotten in the car.

She adjusted her seat.

She started the car.

Jose made a strange grinding sound.

My lungs, heart, soul collapsed.

And Jose exploded.

One minute I saw Violetta's dark hair through the back window, Javier running across the street for her, a look of absolute horror on his face, a look I'd never seen before and a look I'd never forget.

The next minute there was a fireball, hotter than hell, larger than life, and I was flying backward, blown into the wall by the fist of heat.

I slammed into the wall and fell to the ground, heat taking over my body, my brain humming with blood and echoes of the blast. I lay there for a few seconds, trying to figure out what had happened. Where was I? Why was the world on fire?

Violetta.

I lifted up my head and saw the flames that licked high into the sky, Jose a burning carcass of memories. Violetta. She'd been inside.

I had given her the keys.

She was dead.

Burning alive.

A messy, anguished sob came out of my mouth. Even though the heat was searing my eyeballs, I couldn't look away from the flaming wreckage, the cries around me muffled, like my ears were plugged with cotton balls.

I felt hands wrap around my shoulders and pull me up to my feet. A strong arm went around my waist and I was turned away from the inferno and brought into a room.

My hotel room. It seemed like a cave now with the fire raging outside. Violetta was dead. Jose was gone.

"Ellie?" Camden said softly, running his hands down my face. "Fuck, you're hurt."

I looked up at him, seeing him but not seeing him. He gently touched my temple and I saw blood on his fingers. "Come on, we'll get you cleaned up."

Cleaned up? Who cared about being cleaned up? What the fuck just happened?

"Violetta!" I cried out suddenly, tears rushing down my face. I tried to run back outside, but he held me in place.

"No," he said roughly. "There's nothing we can do for her."

I looked at him with wild eyes and he brought me closer to him. "I gave her the keys."

He shook his head. "You couldn't have known there was a bomb in the car."

"Javier!" I cried out. "Javier knew! He was running and yelling and... Oh my god, Camden, what happened to him?"

His dark brows came together and he bit his lip, his eyes searching me. "Ellie..."

I shook my head and pushed him out of the way. "No!" I ran out of the room and back to the scene of the crime.

People from the hotel were gathered around the blaze, some with fire extinguishers, trying to put it out with futile sprays of foam. I didn't see Javier anywhere.

I swallowed the bile that was coming up my throat. Had Javier been swallowed up by the same blast that was currently consuming his sister? Was he there now, a charred skeleton amid the flames?

I promptly leaned over and threw up on the ground.

Camden's hand was on my back in seconds. "Come on, come back inside."

I made a pitiful noise, wanting nothing more than to scream, cry, run.

"Please Ellie, you're hurt." I felt him reach for my head. I moved out of his grasp, getting hit with dizziness instead. I staggered a bit, then froze when I saw Dom coming out of the crowd of people, heading toward us, a gun noticeable in his waistband as the breeze lifted back his slick suit jacket.

We needed to run. But I couldn't even move.

Dom stopped right in front of us, a sympathetic smile on his lips. "You two need to come with me."

"Why?" Camden asked, his voice strong and steady.

Dom glanced at the burning wreckage, at the people who were now stealing glances at us.

"Because we have to go," he said simply. "You don't want to be here when the police get here. And the men who did this? They're still out there."

"Where's Javier?" I asked him, not quite certain that he wasn't one of the men who had tried to take our heads off and blown up my beloved car and Javier's beloved sister. And possibly Javier.

He looked over my shoulder into the room and said, "Just grab your stuff and let's go. I'm parked around the corner." Then he took off toward the bar. I watched until he disappeared around the building.

"What do you think?" Camden asked. "We don't have to go with him. We can go out on our own. It could be a death trap in that car."

I couldn't even think. I didn't even care.

Camden sighed and brought me to him, wrapping his arms around me and holding me tight. I could feel his heart beating against mine. I closed my eyes, feeling waves of darkness trying to swallow me whole. This was all too much, and my brain couldn't even take it in. It was spitting it all out, rejecting reality, leaving me with a numbness I welcomed too much.

"You tell me what to do," I whispered into his chest. "I can't."

I don't remember much after that. Maybe it's because

I had a concussion and pieces of Jose still in my hair, or maybe because my head was protecting me from the brutality of the truth. It was all like a dream. Camden brought me inside and we gathered up the rest of my stuff, everything that had been in Jose. Then we hurried along the row of rooms toward the bar. I could hear the cries of people behind us, as if we were the bad guys and we were getting away. But no one came after us as we rounded the corner and saw a shiny black Escalade at the curbside, its engine running.

It was all a dream until I got into the car.

Este was sitting by the door in the back to make room for me.

And Javier was sitting in the front seat.

Alive.

My heart churned like a cement mixer, a million competing emotions running through me. Relief he was alive. And fear because he wasn't dead.

I climbed into the middle seat, still dazed but feeling everything sparking back to life, like I went from black and white back to Technicolor.

Javier didn't turn around to acknowledge me. In fact, as Camden closed the door and Dom drove the Escalade down the street, no one said anything. The five of us were silent, though apologies were dancing on my tongue. I wanted to tell Javier I was sorry about Violetta. I wanted to tell him it was all my fault. I wanted to beg for forgiveness.

But I didn't. Because it wouldn't change anything. It wouldn't bring her back. It wouldn't make anyone feel better. Not even me.

Camden reached for my hand and held on to it tightly. His skin was warm, firm and soft all at once. I raised my eyes to his. He was here with me, a simple fact in a complicated world.

We stared at each other for a few beats, my thoughts lost in those baby blues, in the hardness that surrounded them, and the soulfulness deep inside. Violetta's words from last night swirled around in my head. Her wish for love, to love and to *be* loved.

I couldn't be sure I had the latter. I certainly didn't deserve it. But I had the former. I loved this man who was sitting next to me, who had been by my side, on my side, from the beginning. I had to hold on to that. I had something that Violetta died without—knowing that someone completely owns your heart. Camden owned my heart and the blood it pumped through me. He owned every atom and inch of my body, every crevice and dark shadow of my soul. From now on, he would possess it freely, easily. I was his. And if I blew up the next day, if I met my death trying to get back Gus and my mother, at least then I could die knowing my heart was put to good use. It wasn't wasted. And if it wasn't wasted, then perhaps I wasn't wasted either.

I squeezed his hand back, silent thanks for his comfort and devotion. Then I carefully leaned my head on his shoulder and tried to forget about the pain that the morning had brought me. The lives it had changed.

We sped south in a car full of love and death.

CHAPTER EIGHT

"HOLD STILL," CAMDEN instructed.

He had an alcohol-soaked cloth poised at the corner of my head, ready to sting the shit out of me. The pain that came with healing.

We were in a gas station bathroom, the floor sticky with unknown fluids, the walls crawling with winged creepy crawlies that would occasionally make a go for the bare light bulb before falling to the floor. I was sitting up on the sink and Camden was trying to treat my wounds while he had the chance.

We had driven pretty much nonstop all the way from Aguascalientes until just outside of the border to Guatemala, twelve hours in one stretch. During the drive, Javier hadn't said a single word, only stared out the window as the landscape of his country rushed past us. Dom and Este did all the talking, telling us the plan for the next few days as we went into the jungle. Apparently we were meeting another "friend" of theirs in Guatemala City who'd be joining us.

No one talked about what happened to Violetta or who was shooting at us. I assumed it was Travis, and I guessed from their silence the assumption was right. There was nothing to say, I suppose, except that his people wanted us dead and they were a lot more clever than I had given them credit for.

"Ow," I moaned as Camden gently pressed the cloth to my head.

"Sorry," he said, eyes soft as he gazed at me.

I watched him as he did this, wincing through the pain. He dabbed it on my cheekbone where I had another large gash that hurt if I smiled. Luckily, there wasn't much to smile about.

"How are your eyes?" I asked him, feeling like I needed to make conversation. The tension around us desperately needed to disperse.

He paused, cloth in hand, and peered at me inquisitively. "What do you mean?"

"Can you see me?"

He went back to stinging the wounds. "I told you I can see you clearly from up close."

I swallowed hard and swung my legs up and down, suddenly very aware that as I sat on the edge of the sink, I was pretty much straddling him. "Do you like what you see?" I asked quietly. My words sat in a fine haze over the room, my chest constricting from the silence.

His mouth dropped open, lower lip full and inviting, his pink tongue moving in his mouth, trying to make words that would not come.

"Am I still beautiful to you?" I whispered, feeling

my heart slowly leak open. I was raw and wounded and in his hands.

His face crumpled, such vulnerability in its strength. The cloth dropped out of his hands and into the sink and he sucked in his breath before saying, "Ellie Watt, you're more beautiful than you've ever been."

And then his lips, his soft, full, warm lips were on mine, sending sparks up my face to the back of my head, trailing down my back like brushes from angel wings. His mouth was greedy and mine wanted, needed, craved more. He made a fist in the back of my hair and I grabbed on to his, tugging it until he moaned, the intoxicating sound of his lust filling my mouth, my throat, my lungs. I couldn't get enough; I was afraid I'd never get it again.

It was wrong, it was wrong, it was wrong to be doing this with him, in here, when the whole world was dying out there, but I didn't care. I loved him and I needed him more than I ever needed anyone. I loved him and love had to be good in this life full of bad.

He put his lips to my collarbone, sucking and biting and making me forget everything, the worries coming off of me like the tank top I quickly pulled over my head and shed to the floor. He cupped my swollen breasts with his hands, his thumbs teasing my nipples until he pulled back the bra and exposed them to the humid air, pinching them with his teeth. I cried out from the pain, the beautiful pain that rocked through my body, making every centimeter of my skin feel absolutely alive. For the first time in a long time, I felt like I was living, breathing, present. Here.

"Please don't stop," I begged him between groans. "Please don't stop."

"Baby, I'm just getting started," he said, voice husky with unadulterated lust. He went for my neck, licking in long, smooth strokes that set off nerves all the way down to my clit, racing across my body like shooting stars. My legs spread wider for him, wrapping around his waist, tugging him close to me, desperate for friction.

He pulled away and pushed my legs together. With a hard tug he undid the zipper of my jeans and I quickly kicked off my hiking boots. He pulled down my jeans and underwear, the sink cold against my ass as I reached for his belt, fumbling to let him loose, like if I didn't free his cock fast enough I'd lose the opportunity forever.

When my legs were bare and wide for him, I brought him in closer with my calves, which were hooked securely around his back. The belt finally came free and his pants dropped to his ankles with a single snap of a button.

And here we were, naked from the waist down, his cock hard as concrete and silky against my opening, his hands gripping my shoulders as if I would try to escape. But there was no escape for me: I was in this deeply and I needed him to be in me just as deep. If he couldn't feel something for me in his heart the way that I did, then he could feel something in his balls. I would take what I could get, even here, in this dirty gas station bathroom, because I never wanted Camden more, never needed him more, than I did right there.

"Ellie," he whispered, pressing his hard ridge against

me, rubbing ever so slightly. The pressure on my clit made me wetter than water. I felt myself spreading open, eager for him, feeling so fucking empty and hollow until I had him inside of me.

I grabbed his face and kissed him, my mouth wanting more than he could give me, my tongue coaxing his until they melted into each other, that insatiable thirst that was plaguing me once again driving me to devour him, consume him.

He took my lip between his teeth and pulled back on it, biting down in sweet sinful pleasure.

"Ellie," he whispered again, and I reached down for his cock, stroking it smoothly, every hard, long inch of him. The illicit grunt that came out of his mouth, the way his eyes rolled back in his head, those gorgeous eyes of his, caused my hormones to flare up into overdrive.

"Just fuck me," I told him, my mouth sucking on his soft earlobe. "Just fucking love me."

He hesitated and pulled back, looking like I slapped him in the face.

"What did you say?" he whispered hoarsely.

"Please," I said, one hand a fist around his cock, my other hand digging my nails into his back. I was wrapped up in layers and layers and he was at my core, at my middle. This was me and I was in his hands and he had me exposed to the bone. "Please."

His eyes raged with lust, and then he kissed me so hard, my head slammed back against the mirror on the wall. He took his cock out of my grip and pressed the wet, smooth tip against me. With a single thrust, he entered me, sharp and fast. His size, his wonderful fullness, had me gasping for air as pain rocketed through my limbs, my insides tensing until he pounded me again and again, until he became a part of me and I couldn't have imagined life without this, life without anyone else. This was the puzzle piece, the part that made my heart stop hurting, my soul stop bleeding. With each thrust of him, up to the hilt, he filled me with hope. He erased the death. He gave me life, if only for that moment, when we were joined as one, and I was a better version than the girl I was before.

It didn't take me long to come, my fingers pressing hard into his ass as I almost slipped off the cold sink, my head still rocking against the mirror until I was afraid it would break. But it was only me breaking open from the inside, raw and vulnerable and ugly and beautiful all at once. He started moaning, his thrusts slowing down while my body spasmed me to new heights. And as I came, as the world was colors and I saw stars and felt unbreakable, unstoppable, the rush of emotions took over and buried me under them.

I cried out in pleasure and then I cried out in sorrow. I just plain fucking cried, grabbing him hard and sobbing into his neck, even as the last traces of him were milked into me.

He tried to regain control of his breath, our bodies sweating, rising and falling against each other, trying to make sense of the world and what had happened. "Hey," he said softly, voice aching with concern. He reached for my face and made me look at him through the tears. "It's okay."

I closed my eyes and the tears spilled over, leaving hot tracks in their wake. I shook my head back and forth, fighting for air, my chest expanding but unable to take in a breath. I could only sob, my face scrunching up as every rotten part of me came out.

"What's wrong?" he asked gently. "Ellie, please tell me."

I sniffed hard, my mouth wet with my sadness, the words so afraid to come out.

But they did.

"I love you, Camden. I love you so damn fucking much and it's so right and it's so wrong because people are dying, and we're almost dying and Gus is out there and my mother and we can't trust anybody and all I can think about is you. All I can think about is how much I love you and how badly I fucked everything up and I don't deserve you but I need you." I made a fist with my hands and pounded it against his chest, hard, my tears flowing. "I fucking need you and I need you to forgive me. I need that more than anything in the world! I need you to make me good."

He swallowed hard, letting me hit him, his fingers strong on my jaw. "Ellie, Ellie, Ellie. You *are* good—deep down you always have been. You don't need me for that."

"I am so sorry."

"I'm sorry too," he said. "I never wanted it to be this way."

To be this way.

To be this way.

My heart clenched painfully and I hunched over, fighting for breath.

"What way?" I choked out. "What way?"

"The way it is," he said, brows pinched together. "The way it will be."

There was a knock on the door, causing both of us to snap to attention.

"What is going on in there?" Dom's voice came through. "Camden, Ellie, we have to go. Now." He pounded on the door again until Camden yelled, "All right, we'll be out in a minute!"

He stepped away from me, quickly pulling up his pants and fixing his belt before handing me my hiking boots and slipping my jeans back up my legs. His hands lingered momentarily on the cherry blossom tattoo before sliding back up.

I pulled up the jeans and slipped my boots on before jumping down to the floor, my shoulder leaning against the weight of his body for balance. He hadn't really done the most thorough job of tending to my wounds, but at least all the action got the car parts and glass out of my hair, the particles now littering the bowl of the sink. I clung on to that bit of humor because that's all I had. I had hoped, wanted, needed us to be closer, for the sex to bring us together, to let him feel that he had me, all of me, and whatever happened between Javier and me was gone. It was his seed inside me right now. He had me body and soul.

But then he was looking at me like he was being torn in half.

And I felt like I was left with nothing.

"You ready?" he asked.

I wiped underneath my eyes and asked, "Do I look like a mess?"

He smiled, his eyes sad. "You're allowed to look like a mess, Ellie."

I guess he was right about that. I brushed my hair behind my ears and shrugged.

"Then a mess I shall be."

We left the dingy washroom and walked across to the car. It was night now, hot and dark with a sky filled with cicadas and stars. Dom and Este already appeared to be inside the Escalade and Javier was leaning against his passenger's-side door, puffing on a cigar, his eyes following our every move.

I stiffened for a moment, wondering what Javier would say or think. Then I realized it didn't really matter anymore. My heart broke for him, for the loss of his sister, but I refused to let it break because of Camden.

He watched us in the silence, still not having said a word to us since the explosion. Camden didn't even look at him—perhaps he couldn't. I thought maybe he would have looked smug about what had happened, about what we so obviously had done in that bathroom, but he didn't. He only kept his eyes forward and got in the car.

I paused by the door, watching Javier exhale a cloud of smoke.

He looked at me once, just briefly, and though I couldn't see clearly through the haze, I picked up on the pain in his eyes. Camden was right. I was a mess.

"I'm sorry," I said, wiping my hands anxiously on my jeans. "About Violetta."

He stared at me and it was almost as if I could see whatever sick ties he once had to me snapping one by one. The freedom was exhilarating. The uncertainty was terrifying.

"Get in," he said, his voice rough as sandpaper.

I nodded, taking what I could get, and got in the car after Camden.

*   *   *

We drove through the night, and after we passed through the border into Guatemala, our passports all checked and cleared, I fell asleep. I didn't wake up until dawn was breaking and the Escalade was pulling into the city.

We came to a stop outside of a small white house with a terracotta-tiled roof and waited for a few moments.

"Any way we can stretch our legs, maybe get a coffee?" Camden asked.

Este was in the driver's seat now and Dom was snoring beside me, completely out. He eyed Camden in the mirror. "In a bit. We don't want to stay a second longer in this city than we have to."

Camden nodded with a sigh and sat back in his seat. Javier unbuckled his seat belt and stepped out of the car, walking up to the front door of the house. Before he had a chance to knock, he was met by an extremely buff man in a wife-beater with a shaved head and ripped camo pants. He was white, with piercing blue eyes I could see all the way from the car.

"Who is that?" I asked.

"His name is Derek," Este said. "He's American."

"I can see that."

"He was in the Afghanistan war. Married a Mexican

woman. She died on the streets, caught in the gunfire
of two cartels. He decided to stay behind and clean
shit up."

"I see," I said slowly.

"He's good at getting in and getting out," Este went
on. "He's fearless and ruthless. Soulless."

"Like Javier," I found myself saying. My eyes darted
to Este, catching my mistake, but he only smiled.

"He's got training that none of us have. And as long
as you pay him well, he's loyal to the bone. If anyone
can get your people back, it's Derek."

Derek and Javier came over to the back of the Escalade, Derek with only a small backpack. Javier opened
the trunk and Derek quickly slid inside.

I smiled at him, but he didn't smile back. Instead, he
nodded curtly and then lay down, still as death, staring
up at the ceiling.

I exchanged a nervous look with Camden. Our little team was growing bigger, each new person adding
an uncertainty that wasn't there before. But worrying
wouldn't do me any good. This was out of my hands.
If I wanted to get Gus and my mother back, we had to
go through with it. I laid myself bare last night—no use
being guarded now.

We drove for a bit until the city was far behind us,
along with its overgrown trees and layer of smog. Este
finally stopped at a small diner where we all got cof-
fees and churros to go. It was stinking hot out, waves
of heat rising from the road, the sun bearing down
relentlessly.

"We're closer to the equator now," Este had said,

watching as I wiped the sweat off my brow as we stood around the car, waiting for Dom to get out of the restroom. "It will be cooler in the jungle."

"So how is this going to work exactly?" Camden asked, shoving the last remaining bit of the churro in his mouth.

Este looked to Javier, who was on his cell phone, talking to someone in Spanish. Javier ignored him and turned around, slowly walking to the other side of the car. Este shrugged at Camden. "Well, I have the coordinates on my iPad, picking up from a satellite feed. It will take us straight there."

"iPad?" Camden asked, almost laughing.

Este gave him a look. "Why mess with a good thing? You'd be amazed at the apps that the cartels have floating among them. You can't buy them on iTunes, but they can save your life. And your money. I've made a few myself. The one we'll be using, we can almost watch our own selves going through the forest in real time."

Este went on about the mission, how the six of us would go in until a certain point and then split up. There were the people who would need to go in silently, and the ones who would go in blazing. They weren't quite decided yet on who would go where. I guess that remained to be seen.

While he chatted with Camden some more, Derek listening and staying silent, I decided to go and look for Javier.

He had just hung up the phone and put it in his pocket, facing away from me. I walked over to him, carefully, like he could attack at any minute. He seemed wounded, and like any animal, ready to defend himself against predators. In this case, the predator was me.

"Javier," I said softly.

He turned slowly and I stopped where I was, dust flying up from my boots and settling in the air around us like spilled flour. His mouth was set in a hard line and his eyes were even harder than that, glinting like golden stones. He appraised me, taking me in, not sure what to do or say or feel. I could tell half of him wanted to hate me, hit me, make me bleed. And the other half—well, that was the sadness I could see masked far beneath. I knew him well enough to know when he was burying shit deep inside.

I reached out for him, slowly putting my hand on his shoulder. He didn't flinch, but he eyed my hand like I carried some disease. I left it there for a second, hoping the weight of it would translate the weight in my heart before I took it away.

I stuck both my hands in my back pockets and looked at the ground. "I'm so sorry."

He breathed in sharply through his nose, his eyes cutting into me with curiosity. "About?"

"Violetta." Even saying her name hurt.

He looked away for a moment and tilted his head to the side. "It has happened. It is done."

"I gave her the car keys," I said, fighting the stiffness in my throat. The terrible guilt that festered inside me, the guilt that wouldn't go away.

He nodded once and quick. "It wasn't your fault. I didn't realize soon enough what was going on. I played it too safe." He exhaled and checked the time on his phone. "No point dwelling on it though. If she had left right away back in Mexico City, none of this would have happened. She chose to get involved. She made her choices when she befriended the Zetas."

He was making it sound so simple. But, like Violetta said, maybe there was no point in making things complicated if they didn't need to be.

"She's dead," he said with finality. "That's the cost of doing business sometimes."

And just like that, whatever vulnerability, whatever hurt and pain I thought I had seen beneath the surface, was all gone. Wiped clean. All that was left was Javier Bernal, a drug lord with only one thing on his mind—his own rise to the top. He was steel and hard lines and ice in the middle of the tropics. He was the only thing that would never melt, no matter what pressure was applied to him. He was a human, a machine, a man who I knew had lost his soul forever. He lost it somewhere far away, and it was no longer my job to get it back for him. Maybe it never was my job.

I swallowed hard and said, "Well, just so you know. I liked her."

"And that was your problem," he said, giving me a dry smile. "If you hadn't gotten close to her, you wouldn't care so much. Let that be a lesson to you, Ellie. Don't get close to the people you know will die. Don't get close to anyone. We'll all die at some point."

Dom appeared at the front of the car, slamming back a coffee and climbing into the driver's seat. He eyed us over his aviators. "Time to go."

Javier left me standing there, slightly dumbfounded, going around to the passenger's side of the car. I shook my head when Dom slammed his door shut and I got in the back.

It turns out we were close to the Honduran border, which proved to be an easy checkpoint. I don't know what the guards would have done if they had searched the car and found stacks of weapons in the back with Derek, but from the giant wad of cash I saw Dom hand them, I had a feeling it wouldn't have mattered. Money went further than honor here, and we'd certainly paid our way.

Once in the country, it was another five hours of driving through piss-poor towns, crumbling roads, and rampant wildlife like monkeys who liked to dart from the overhanging canopies until we finally reached Catacamas for our last dinner in civilization. Of course knowing how wanted we all were, we sent Derek out to get questionable food from a street vendor and we all ate in the car without the air conditioning on, sweat pouring down our faces.

I hadn't had a chance to talk to Camden yet, and every time we were alone for a few moments he would suddenly busy himself with questions for Este. I don't know if he just wanted to be on top of everything and be a man with a plan, or if he was avoiding me. Part of me was feeling ashamed for opening myself to him last night, but the other part was glad I did it. It was out on the table. He knew how I felt and that's all I could do. I was a woman born of lies, but here I was being honest even when it hurt me the most.

When we were all done, Dom took us out of the city and toward a tiny village that consisted of a post office, a gas station, and a feed store. It was sleepy, quaint, and the place we were to ditch the Escalade. He pulled the car into an empty and abandoned barn and turned off the engine.

"You're ready for this, yes?" Este asked me as we climbed out of the car.

I shook my head. "No way in hell will I ever be ready for this."

We all gathered around the open trunk as Derek and Dom started distributing stuff. They handed me a backpack that I had already crammed with some of my belongings, another gun, and a change of clothes. Then they handed out minuscule walkie-talkies that resembled Bluetooth earpieces to each of us and made sure that I was carrying the first aid kit.

Dom slapped the car affectionately and I felt a funny little pang in my gut for the loss of Jose. I knew it was just a car and it was Violetta who died, but Jose had been with me for the last six years. He'd almost become a friend when I didn't have any.

"If we see this car again," Dom said, "you'll know we've done good."

"That said," Javier added, "if you do get back here without anyone else, my advice is to take the car and go. It's every man for himself out there, I hope you know that. You don't win wars by saving each other. You only get killed that way."

Well, that wasn't exactly the encouragement we needed before we started hiking off into the jungle on a rescue mission. I looked across at Camden, dust motes dancing in the barn light that shone between us. He looked right back. We were the only people here who would risk life and limb for each other.

I was forever on his team.

"Javier has never been one for speeches," Este said, shaking his head in amusement. "But all I'll say is, we can get in and get out. We can make this happen. Travis Raines is ours. What he has is ours."

"You mean Gus," I spoke up quickly.

Javier grinned. "Gus, sure. And the cartel."

I frowned, feeling a rush of nerves down my back. "You said you were doing this for me."

He let out a laugh to which only Este joined in.

"Dom is doing this for you," Javier said, gesturing to him with his gun. "And, if you're lucky, Camden is doing this for you. Derek just wants his paycheck. The gringo doesn't care who does what, fucks what, gets what. But me, Ellie, angel dearest, I'm going in and I'm taking over."

"This wasn't supposed to be a coup," I said.

Suddenly Javier was in my face, the veins pulsing in his head, spittle flying out of his mouth as he screamed at me, "And they weren't supposed to kill my sister!"

Camden was at my side in a second, ready to push Javier back, but the barn filled with the sound of three guns being drawn and I didn't have to look around to know that Dom, Este, and Derek all had guns trained on Camden.

The madness in Javier's eyes was quickly reined in and he stepped back. He wiped his mouth and smiled.

"As you can see, Travis has hit yet another nerve. You'll get your Gus back, your mother back, whatever you want, and whatever is left is mine. And if you step in my way, I won't hesitate to kill you. Both of you." He turned around and clapped his hands together, the sound giving me a jolt. "Now, let's head off into the jungle, shall we?"

Camden and I stayed behind for a moment while they all walked out of the barn and into the last remaining sunlight. He grabbed my hand and squeezed it and I was warmed where my insides had turned cold.

"Just focus on Gus," Camden said.

I nodded. Squeezed his hand back. And followed the drug lords out into the light.

CHAPTER NINE

THE JOURNEY STARTED off easy enough. The six of us, backpacks in tow, walked down lonely, dusty streets that wound their way through fallow fields and past shanty houses. Eventually the last signs of humanity gave way to the jungles of the Sierra de Agalta National Park, an imposing wall of vegetation and darkness.

We paused right before the foliage swallowed us, hesitating before the belly of the beast.

I looked up at the sky, now bruised purple from the twilight. "Are you sure we shouldn't camp out here for now?" I asked, my arm sweeping out over the valley below us. "You know, while there's still light and shit."

"I never thought you'd be afraid of a little jungle," Javier said, though his tone was flat. "We're moving through the night." He brought out a flashlight from his pocket and flicked it on. He looked at Este, who had his iPad raised up to his eyes. "How's your battery on that thing?"

Este smiled. "It'll last throughout the night until I

can get the sun to charge it tomorrow. I have my compass just in case anything goes wrong. We're good."

Javier slid a formidable machete out of his backpack and toyed with his grip on the handle. "Very well. I'll clear our path when needed. You just tell me where to go."

Este nodded. "Shouldn't be a problem at this level. Just head straight for a few kilometers. I'll correct us along the way."

Oh, just for a few kilometers. I looked up at Camden. He was looking uneasy, his jaw tense, his lips rubbing against each other, calculating something. Possibly our demise.

Javier disappeared into the trees until I could only see his flashlight and the glow from Este's iPad. Dom followed behind them. I expected Derek to go next, but he only nudged Camden with the butt of his rifle that he always had out, nodding ahead.

"I'm covering you," he said, his voice raspy like he'd blown out his vocal cords at some point in his life. His eyes were dead, emotionless, and even though I thought I'd feel some sort of camaraderie for the man since he was American and young, there was nothing. This man felt nothing for anyone, especially not Camden and me. We weren't the ones paying him. If anything, he was here to watch us, to keep us in line.

Camden hesitated, wrestling with the silence, before he grunted and walked ahead of me, following Dom. I guess he didn't like the idea of having Derek behind us. It made us feel more like we were prisoners, not cohorts.

Even with flashlights in our hands, the jungle was a terrifying place. We were lucky that the trees weren't too close together and the ground underneath was dry, but the occasional root would still try to fuck you up, or a branch sometimes came down too low and got you in the forehead. Not to mention the countless spider webs I could feel trailing past my arms. I wasn't a wuss over many things, but it had me walking right up behind Camden, cowering behind his tall and wide frame to shield me from the insects that I could only imagine were in a jungle like this.

We walked and walked and walked until I started feeling delirious from the dizzying darkness, that claustrophobia of never knowing what was out there. You could hear the occasional slice of Javier's machete as he cut through something, and Dom and Este were talking in Spanish. We were all getting farther and farther apart, especially Camden and I as we grew tired, our legs slowing.

"Want me to carry you?" Camden asked me. Though the idea of me getting a piggyback ride made me smile, I told him I was okay. I was just getting sleepy, that was the problem. An energy drink would have gone a long way.

I decided to pester Derek with questions instead, to keep my mind engaged.

I looked behind me, seeing only his flashlight and asked, "So, Derek. Where did you grow up?"

You know, like we were chatting at a café or something.

He didn't say anything at first. I could only hear the crunch of dirt and leaves below our feet. Then he cleared his throat, and in that raw voice of his said, "Minnesota. Small town."

"You must have been a hockey fan."

"Yeah," he said with surprise. "Though who isn't?"

"You're built like you play hockey," I commented, hoping my compliments would get him to relax a little.

"Built to fuck people up," he answered.

"Well, that's pretty much the same thing, isn't it?" I made sure he could hear the smile in my voice. It didn't work.

"Hockey is child's play," he said sternly.

I made a small noise of agreement, not sure what else to say.

We trudged along in the dark, in the silence punctuated by wild animal calls. Shivers stroked along the ridges of my spine.

Then Derek said, "Tell me about Gus. The man you mentioned."

I wasn't sure why he needed the information. Maybe it would help him pick better tactics going in. Maybe he felt bad and was trying to make conversation. But I needed to talk about Gus. To talk about him was to keep him alive, keep him as my goal. The further we got into the depths of the night, the more the goal seemed to be pointless. I couldn't let that happen.

"Gus is like...a father to me." The realization that my own father had died slammed into my gut, making my words that much more meaningful. With my own father dead, Gus really was the only family I had left. "He was friends with my parents for a long time, he'd always been around. He was like...one of the few constants in my life."

"What did he do?"

"He worked for the LAPD as an officer. Retired early. Maybe he was discharged—he doesn't really talk about it. He started providing false identities to people who needed it."

"People like you. Con artists."

"Yes. How did you know?"

"I've read all your files."

I nearly stopped in my tracks and Derek's arm swung into my back. I stumbled but kept walking, flabbergasted and horrified.

"You've read our files?"

"Even mine?" Camden asked from in front of me.

"Everyone's," Derek repeated. "Cartels are thorough."

"Then why do you want to know about Gus if you already know this stuff?"

"Because it's good to hear it from you. I need to know how involved you are and what you are willing to do when things get bad."

My throat tickled.

He went on. "Will you risk your life for Gus?"

I hadn't seen Gus for years. But he'd been there for me when no one else was. And he'd come all the way with Camden to save me, to bring me home. He gave his life for mine by doing that. There's no way I wouldn't do the same for him.

"There are very few people in this world who will go out of their way to save someone else," I told him. "Gus was one of those people. Camden is the other. I'd do anything for both of them."

I felt Camden hesitate as he walked, his head turning to look at me. I was grateful for the darkness, that he couldn't see my face or the heat in my cheeks. Still, after what I'd said yesterday, this was nothing.

"I see," Derek said. "And your mother? Who may or may not be considered a hostage at this point."

"What about her?"

"Would you do anything for her? Would you risk your life to save hers?"

I wish the first thought that entered my head was yes. I wish I didn't have to think about it, to weigh it, to wrestle with it. Because I honestly didn't know. Would I give up my mother to save Camden and Gus? Yes. I would. I was a horrible daughter, I know that, just to even think it, but it was the truth. Would I save my mother if it meant I'd die in the process? That...I didn't know. I just didn't.

I hated how that made me feel.

Like I had no humanity left. That I wasn't as selfless as I tried to be.

When it came to me or her, I had no idea how that would play out.

I swallowed the lump in my throat. "I guess I'll have to find out." I licked my lips and felt the need to explain. "My mother and I weren't very close. She—"

"I read her files," Derek said. "I know the story."

"Right," I said, wrapping my hands around the straps on my backpack, trying to ease the pressure off my shoulders.

"Why do you need to know all of this again?" Camden asked, a thread of tension in his voice.

"Because I never enter anything until I know everything about the people involved."

"So you must know everything about Travis," I said as I nearly stumbled over a rock.

Camden's arm shot out and steadied me.

"I do," said Derek.

"Enough to help Javier take over his cartel?" I asked.

"I guess we'll have to find out" was his answer. "Javier is all about expansion."

"I heard my name back there." Javier's voice rang through the darkness, rattling me to the bone. "How about you three pick up the pace a little. Derek, I'm not paying your gringo ass to have conversations and plod along like a bunch of burros. This is Mexico, not Afghanistan, you should know that."

Derek sucked in his breath sharply but said nothing. I could feel the tension rolling off him like waves of heat at my back. Apparently Javier got under his skin as well.

Derek stuck the butt of his gun into my lower back, this time on purpose. "Better get a move on."

We marched on.

* * *

Much as you'd imagine, the Honduran jungle is a brutal place to try to get a good night's rest. We stopped on a plateau of sorts where the trees opened up a bit and the ground was more level. None of us had packed for a camping session and Javier and his men were treating the outing like sleep was a luxury for the benefit of Camden and me. All we had were a few tarps that the men had laid out on the uneven ground and that was it.

"Shouldn't we be worried about things coming to

kill us in the night?" I asked them as we stood around the makeshift sleeping area that was nestled between three trees. Their bark glistened eerily under the glow of my flashlight.

"Are you talking about Travis or something else?" Este asked as he settled onto the ground, his scarred face lit up by his ever-present iPad.

"Well, *now* I'm talking about both," I said.

He laughed. "I've been watching him through satellite from time to time. His men don't come out this far. In fact they rarely patrol the area outside of the compound, but now, well, if he thinks you're coming, that might be a different case. Still, we're good. As long as we stay low, don't light any fires and refrain from shooting anything"—he gave a pointed glance at Derek—"we should be *bueno*, hey."

"And aside from Travis?"

Este exchanged a look with Dom, who tugged at his shirt collar. "There are a few poisonous snakes, spiders ... frogs," he said slowly. "The worst of all are the bullet ants—most powerful sting in the world. Rumor has it that Travis has been using them now as a means of torture. Seems acid no longer cuts it for him."

"Figures," Javier muttered under his breath as he sat up against a tree. He gave Camden and me a funny look. "Well, are you two going to try to get some sleep or stand there like a pair of monkeys?"

Fuck you, I thought. But if I said it, I knew what he would say in response, and I did not want to go there, not after what had happened between Camden and me.

God, what I would do to get him alone again. The

things I wanted to say. Maybe without crying like a fool this time.

"Come on," Camden said, gently grabbing my wrist for a moment before walking over to the other tree, the one farthest from Javier. He sat down, his back to it, and motioned for me to come sit between his legs.

I could feel Javier's eyes on me as I walked across the tarp and sat down, Camden's knees on either side of me. He wrapped his arm around my chest and pulled me close to him, the small of my back pressed against his crotch, the back of my head against his chest, hot, sweaty, breathing steadily. All man, all this very protective man. The warmth and strength of his arms encasing me made me feel like I was being wrapped in a cocoon, a security blanket for the night.

"Good night," he whispered softly into my ear, his lips brushing against my lobe.

I squeezed his forearm in response, so grateful for him, so damn grateful.

"Sleep well, lovebirds," Javier said, his cynical voice echoing into the night.

*   *   *

I woke up to my arm being tickled.

I opened my eyes, and in the gray dimness of the morning light saw a giant black spider crawling slowly up my arm. I immediately cried out and jumped back, brushing the spider off me, feeling waves of revulsion and a million little spider legs covering me from head to toe, my body turning it into something more than it was. Like a panic attack, the feeling was impossible to stop, and I shook my body vigorously, swatting at nothing.

It was only then that I realized I was completely alone.

The tarps were all gone. Everyone was gone.

Even Camden.

Holy fuck.

The jungle started spinning around me and I saw nothing but madness in the never-ending trees, faces made out of foliage, darkness in the limbs.

What the hell happened?

"Camden?" I cried out. "Camden!"

No, no, no. He couldn't have left me alone.

I started running around where we had slept until I found my backpack, the contents strewn across the leaf-covered forest floor. Sweat poured down my face, stinging my eyes, as I knelt down and frantically sorted through everything. My other gun was still there, my fake IDs, my passports, everything I didn't want to leave behind in the Escalade. Whoever raided my stuff had left me everything. Why?

I needed to think. I screamed for Camden again and again, then tried everyone else's names. I screamed until my throat was sore and I realized that I needed to shut up. If something had happened to everyone, if I was let go or missed for some reason, I was only making things worse, only calling attention to myself.

I branched out in a small radius from our sleeping area, going around the trees and then around the next ring of trees, always keeping my backpack, which I had placed in the middle of the trees, in my sight.

Eventually, a yard or two out, I found the tarp. Shredded into bits. Blood on it.

Shit, oh fucking *shit*.

I dropped to my knees, feeling absolutely powerless. I was alone in the middle of the Honduran jungle, halfway between nowhere and Travis's compound. I had nobody. Something had happened to them, and more than that, Camden, my beautiful Camden, was gone. The last thing I remembered was his arms around me as I fell asleep. How could I have gone from that to this?

I wanted to cry. I wanted to crawl up against the hollow of a tree and close my eyes and let the animals take me away into the night. After so much, after so long, I wanted to give up.

But Gus was still out there. My mother too. There were people facing a much worse fate than this. I was able. I was willing. I would save them.

I took in a deep breath and dropped the bloody tarp from my hands and walked over to my backpack. I took a swig of water from the Camelback that was inside, shoved a tasteless portion of an energy bar in my mouth, then put the pack on my shoulders. I brought out one of the compasses that Este had given everyone and started walking in the direction that we were originally headed. I wasn't the best at reading trails, but I would do the best I could to find out where they went and if they were going to the place I both hoped and feared they were.

I made it about three minutes before I heard a bunch of macaw parrots squawk above me and fly across the canopy. Then the jungle went eerily silent.

Soon I was running before I even knew what was happening.

I kept going, leaping over tree roots, maneuvering around rocks, keeping my legs and arms pumping as fast as I could. Breathe in, breathe out, keep going.

I ran until I collided into what I thought was a tree.

It wasn't.

Hands dug into my upper arms.

I screamed.

"Ellie!" Camden exclaimed.

I stopped trying to fight him, to get away, and looked up at the man who held me there in the middle of the forest floor. It was Camden. His head was bleeding from a gash in the middle of his forehead, running red into his eyes, but it was him.

"Oh thank god!" I cried out and immediately wrapped my arms around his middle, holding him to me. "Camden, Camden, what happened?"

"I don't know," he said. I could feel him shake his head against me. He held me for a minute, our breath slowing down together until we were breathing as one. Then he pulled away, holding me at arm's length and peered at me. "Are you okay?"

"I'm fine!" I cried out. "Except for waking up alone and thinking you were dead! I found the tarp—it's all ripped and there's blood. Camden, oh what the fuck happened? Why was I left behind?"

"I don't know," he said, his forehead scrunching, which then brought out a wince of pain from him. "I don't know what... They came in the morning. Maybe an hour ago? It wasn't light out yet, but birds, birds were singing. I heard someone yell something. You were sleeping…I got up and I could see these men walking around, but without my glasses and in the dark I couldn't make them out. Next thing I know I was hit over the head with something and dragged into the jungle. I wasn't unconscious but I couldn't do anything. I couldn't move. I don't know if I was drugged or what. Then they started yelling at each other."

"Did you recognize the voices?"

"I think so. I thought I heard Derek. He was pleading something, arguing. In Spanish. Like he was begging for his life. Or my life. I don't know. Then they dropped me and I guess I passed out until I heard your voice." He put his hand to my cheek and rubbed his thumb along my cheekbone.

"What do we do now?"

"What else can we do?"

"We don't even know where Gus is."

He stepped back and lightly touched his fingers to the gash on his forehead, grimacing at the touch. He pulled his hand away and frowned at the shiny smear of blood. "We have the compasses that Este gave us. Last night, as we were falling asleep, as I pretended to be asleep, I heard Esteban tell Javier that it was less than a day's walk from where we camped. That it was roughly northeast where we needed to go and that we would know it once we started seeing signs warning about poachers. Apparently Travis's compound is in the middle of a reserve. 'Course you wouldn't know it because I assume he bribes the hell out of the government. Fucking fingers in every fucking pie."

"So we just go for it then?" I asked.

He nodded sharply. "I think we have to. I don't know which way we came in, but I know which way we're going."

"And if Javier..."

"Is dead?"

I shook my head. "Worse. If he's out there. If this is a setup."

"You wouldn't put it past him, would you?"

"No," I said, though it hurt to say it. "I wouldn't."

His lips twitched up into a smile. "Good." He brought his compass out. "I don't have any guns. They took them."

I took mine out of my boot and then brought the extra one out of the backpack and handed it to him, placing its solid and deadly weight in his palm. "Now we both have one."

His fingers curled over it and he slid back the clip to check it like an old pro. I had to admit, as wrong as it was, there was something so goddamn sexy about seeing Camden handle a gun, the shiny metal against his big arms and wide chest, muscle against muscle. With the blood smeared on his face, dripping down onto the tats that teased at his neck, he was 100 percent man. I just wished he was 100 percent mine.

"Ready?" he asked.

I adjusted my pack, brought out my compass, and said, "Let's go."

CHAPTER TEN

"ROUGHLY NORTHEAST" wasn't exactly the most detailed direction to go by. Our compasses worked fine, but as Camden and I traversed the depths of the jungle, sticking to a straight line wasn't as easy as we had hoped. The elevation was proving to be more difficult the farther along we went, mother nature putting rocky outcrops, fallen trees, and ravines in our path. We were both tired, sweaty, and irritable, and I was letting my fear get the better of me. The fear of who might be lying out there in the dense foliage, watching me, springing a trap. The fear that Gus and my mother were already dead and that this was all for nothing. The fear that the man who was walking in front of me might keep walking one day and never look back.

"Seen anything yet?" he asked, glancing at me over his broad shoulders.

"No, nothing," I told him. The whole time I'd been looking for some sort of sign that the men had come through here, but my tracking skills weren't up to snuff in a place like this. It was too wild and unpredictable, much like the men we were looking for.

At that, thunder rumbled ominously. We both paused and looked up. Through the tall tops of the overgrown trees dark clouds had moved in, blocking the sun. It felt like we were being closed in. The air around us shifted and changed and when we started walking again it wasn't long until I was completely coated in a new layer of sweat.

"Do you think this whole thing was a setup?" Camden asked me after a few moments. He was breathing heavier now, the rising elevation and intense humidity breaking him down as well.

"I don't know how it could be," I said honestly. My lungs were burning, my feet aching in my boots. I had stopped wiping the sweat off my face a long time ago. "What would be the point of bringing us out here?"

"Maybe we're supposed to be a diversion. Maybe Javier is setting you up to distract them while he swoops in and takes over. Maybe that's why you were left behind."

I shook my head, droplets of sweat flying. "I don't think so. Why were you left?"

"I'm a diversion too."

"But if we're a diversion, then it means we are being set up to fail. They'd want Travis to take us...worse, kill us. Javier wouldn't do that."

He stopped and turned to look at me. "You just said that you wouldn't put it past him to set you up." His voice was ragged, and unmistakable anger burned deep in his eyes.

I threw up my hands and sighed. "I don't know. I

don't know what to think. I…." I remembered what Violetta had said about Javier throwing me under a bus if he had to. I swallowed hard. "I think he'd use me, use us, to get what he wants. But I don't think he'd ever put my life in danger." Or, at least he wouldn't try to flat out have me killed. I knew there was nothing between Javier and us now and I knew he'd use me for his own benefit but I still believed, foolishly perhaps, that my life was at least worth something to him.

He raised his brows, then laughed wickedly, looking up at the sky. "Wow. You have got to be kidding me."

"What?" I asked, my heart began to thud loudly in my ears.

"What? Ellie, from the start he has been pulling all the puppet strings and you've been pulled willingly. You say he wouldn't put you in any danger, but he sent you to Travis's house to kill him. He made you cozy up to the sick bastard. If that's not putting you at risk, I don't know what is. I would *never* do that to you."

"And then he saved us. He also saved you again. On the roof. He didn't have to do that."

"Didn't have to save a human being's life? Who wouldn't?" he scoffed.

"Why are we even arguing about this?" I said. My pack was feeling too heavy, so I put it on the ground. I hated fighting with him, though I knew where it was all coming from. There was a lot of truth in Camden's words and still a lot of resentment. Toward me.

"Because…" He sighed and turned away. "Because I can't help it. I can't stop thinking about… what we did."

My lungs were definitely working overtime now, my

heart feeling as if it were being squeezed by icy fingers. I didn't like where this was going. Why couldn't we get over this? Why couldn't my heart stay intact for a fucking minute?

"What we did?" I asked carefully. "You mean when I fucked you in the bathroom? Or was it what I said?"

He gave me a dirty look. "Was that what it was to you? Just a fuck?"

"Oh my god," I exclaimed. "What is wrong with you?"

"What's wrong with me?" he repeated. He smiled coldly. "Excuse me if I have problems taking your words at face value."

That fucking hurt. No, that fucking killed me, knife to the heart.

Another hit of thunder slammed through the sky and in seconds the clouds broke open. Heavy rain pounded down on us, soaking us in seconds. The forest roared with the sound of raindrops hitting the leaves. Just perfect.

I didn't even know what to say to that. My mouth fumbled for words, the rain streaming down my face. If I started crying he wouldn't be able to tell the difference.

"Why can't you just forgive me?" I pleaded. "I'm not lying, Camden. I'm being more honest than I've ever been."

"How could you sleep with him so easily and then do the same to me?"

I put my face in my hands, trying to contain myself. I took in a shaky breath and looked at him. He was barely visible through the sheets of rain.

"I can't take back what I did," I told him, my voice raw, threatening to crack. "I have my reasons and you know what they are. I can only control what I do from now on in. I slept with you because I love you. I told you the truth in that bathroom. You can decide to forgive me or not, but it's not my problem anymore if you don't. I gave you my heart. You have it. You should know you have it. If you can't find it in yourself to give me another chance, then that's your problem. Stop punishing me for the past when the only thing we have is right now!"

"I'm not punishing you."

Oh, that did it. I stormed over to him, nearly slipping in the mud, and shoved my hands against his wet chest, pushing him back a step. I was unable to contain the stream of words that had been dying to come out. "Now you're the fucking liar here. You've wanted me to suffer the minute you found out about Javier and me. And you've been doing a bang-up fucking job about it. You think I don't hate myself already for what I've done? Now I just hate myself even more because every time I look at you I see a man who once loved me, a man whose love I should have believed in, should have had faith in, and I didn't. So I lost that love and I lost you all for nothing! All because I'm a stupid, scared little girl with scars on her leg who never deserved anything good in her life and who believed it. A girl who took her pain out on the world, who followed the footsteps of her parents because it was the easy way out. Now for the first time I think I might be better than I thought, better than I ever gave myself credit for, and you're the one who won't let me believe it." I blinked hard, trying to control the tears. They stayed put, but the pain in my chest was unbearable. "You told me I was good, Camden. I know you want to believe in me, but you're stopping yourself. Why can't you just love me again?" I grabbed his face with my hands, his skin slick from the rain that continued to fall steadily. "You own my heart. Please let me have yours."

He closed his eyes, his lashes dark and wet. He breathed hard, his mouth open. I kept my hands on his face, trying to hold on to him even though I felt him slipping away.

"I don't want to love you, Ellie."

All my air left me. I was nothing inside but bones and blood. I was hollow, scooped out, unlovable. Undeserving. I was dying in the jungle, holding on to the one with the knife.

A small sob escaped me. His eyes flew open, a blue ocean of pain. He swallowed hard and put his hand behind my head, staring at me with stark determination. "I don't want to love you, Ellie, but I *do* love you. I can't stop myself. I've been trying to since the moment I saw you with him. You broke me, you broke my fucking heart." He closed his eyes again and rested his forehead against mine, our noses pressed against each other. "You broke me into so many pieces that I didn't think I could find myself again. And I'm so damn scared, I'm scared just like you. You've always been my love, Ellie Watt, since the very beginning. Since the moment I saw your face, your beautiful, young face on that hot, dry day in Palm Valley. You were water for my soul, even in high school. You made me feel like I had another half, someone else who understood what it was like to be unwanted."

Oh Jesus. I was melting in his hands.

He gazed at me, so close, raindrops hanging from his lashes. "But the pain... Oh please, I can't go through that again. I look at you and I see him and I just want to see you again. I want to know that this can work. I want you and me to go home. Make a home. I just want my heart to be safe in your hands, because yours is safe in mine."

"You're safe with me," I told him, my voice choking up. "Camden, you're safe with me."

I kissed him, wet and slick, and his fingers pressed harder into my face. I pulled back and whispered, "Please believe that you're safe with me." I stroked his lower lip with my finger. "I gave you pain and I can take it away, if you let me. If you let yourself love me."

His eyes went soft and dreamy for a few moments before they flared with a wild hit of lust. The look made my blood hot. He placed his lips on mine, drawing out a deep, hard kiss, pressing himself into me, his tongue warm and feverish against mine. He moaned, the vibrations sinking into my core, heat radiating between my legs. Inappropriate. Once again, so fucking inappropriate.

But fuck it.

And fuck him. Literally.

"Camden," I murmured into him, wanting him right there in the rain, his body and soul and heart.

He went for my neck, his tongue swooping up just

behind my ear, licking the rim, then sliding back down
my jawline. He grabbed my hair hard with both hands,
tugging sharply, and looked me dead in the eyes. He
was all fire and hard angles.

"I love you," he said, his voice gruff. "And I'll have
you. Keep you. Own you. You belong to me, only to
me, from now on."

Feather-soft butterflies swarmed my heart, filling
me with beauty and light and all that was good.

"Until the waves crash at our feet," I said softly as
his full lips pressed at my cheek.

"Beyond that," he whispered. "Beyond the ocean
and the world and the stars. You're mine beyond that,
baby, and I'm yours." His hands suddenly dropped to
my jeans and he swiftly unzipped them, slipping one
of his long, skilled fingers down past my underwear
until it found my clit, swollen and ready. Steady hands,
indeed.

"And now I'm going to make you mine. I'm going to
make you forget you've ever been with anyone else. I will
own you from the inside out, with every hard inch of me."

With his dirty mouth and his deft fingers, I nearly
came right there. Camden wasn't messing around. And
now I would have his body and his heart. I would have
him, all of him, every corner of his beautiful soul,
every part of his hard, strong frame.

He began swirling his fingers around, dipping down
into me.

"Christ, you want this," he murmured as he pushed
in, my wetness soaking him to his knuckles. I gasped at
the intrusion, then ground myself into him.

"I always want this," I said, kissing him, the frenzy building up inside of me. "I always want you."

"You're getting me," he said. "My beautiful girl."

With his hand still down my pants, he took my arm in the other and led me backward until I was up against a tree. He carefully pulled down my jeans until they were at my ankles, then slid his whole hand between my legs, rubbing me back and forth. I quickly pulled my soaking wet tank top and bra off and his mouth went for my breasts, licking, pinching, making my nipples throb, an exquisite pain. I cried out, rainwater pouring into my open mouth.

"Tell me you love me again," he commanded, pressing me harder against the tree, the bark digging into my back.

"I love you," I whimpered as he pressed his fingers to my wall, massaging in tight circles while his thumb did the same to my clit. I couldn't hold on anymore. "I love you."

I came fast and hard, every part of me throbbing, clenching, pulsing as his hand continued to push me over the edge. I surrendered to him, to the rain that continued to pound down on us. My cries carried out into the jungle. "Oh god, oh god. Fucking god."

He removed his hand, grinning at me while I tried to get my bearings. The world was still spinning and I was lost in my own delirious state, just pulses of pleasure that fired through me. I barely felt it when he grabbed me by the waist and turned me around so that my hands were clamped on the tree. He put his arm around my stomach and pulled me back, making my back arch.

Next thing I heard was his pants coming off. His T-shirt went flying to the muddy earth beside me.

"You're so fucking beautiful," he groaned, and I knew he was stroking himself. I tried to turn around and only got a quick look at his hard, tatted body, all firm lines and rigid angles, his magnificent cock in his hands, the rain streaming all over him. He was a wet god, and I was about to get pounded.

He pushed me back around. "Grab the tree. This could get messy."

I did as he asked while I heard him moan again. He pressed the tip of his dick to the small of my back, then slid it down my ass crack, my skin extra slick from the rain. I couldn't hide the shivers that rolled through me and I arched myself more, pressing my ass into him.

"Slowly," Camden grunted. He put a hand at my waist, holding me in place, and continued to draw himself up and down until my clit calmed down and I needed friction all over again. I wanted him inside me, filling me to the brim, buried to the root. I tried again to get him inside me but his hand was firm. "Slowly," he repeated. "I don't know if we'll get a chance to do this again."

I knew what he meant by that. Where we were. What we were about to do. It made our coupling that much more urgent, much more sweet, much more poignant. I couldn't die without having him inside me one more time, feeling him as part of me, knowing he did love me, lust for me, need me.

I heard him suck in his breath and exhaled shakily, trying to contain himself.

"Now," he said with a grunt. He slammed his cock

into me and I shuddered from the impact, crying out, my hands slipping as I tried to hold on to the tree. He started hammering into me fast and smooth, groaning, his breath rapid, his hands tight around my waist. He thrust out and in, all the way to the hilt, till I felt like he'd taken over half my body. The pleasure-pain was all encompassing, radiating from my core to my fingertips and toes, and he kept pounding and pounding and pounding, his balls smacking against my ass, my breasts swaying from each hit.

Then I started slipping, my boots giving away beneath me, my hands too slippery to grip the tree.

"Camden!" I cried out.

He quickly grabbed me around my chest, keeping me upright. Then he pulled out for a moment and turned me around. While I leaned on him, he bent down and took my boots, jeans, and underwear off until we were both stark naked, standing in the rain and looking at each other. He was so fucking gorgeous, inside and out, it almost brought tears to my eyes. I needed him back inside me. Immediately. In any way I could get him.

I dropped to my knees, sinking into the warm mud, not giving a shit if I got dirty, and took his cock into my mouth. I ran my teeth lightly over the hardened ridge until he gasped, then soothed it with my tongue. He moaned. "Fuck." And moaned again.

I tightened my fist, taking him in as far as he could go, sliding him in and out until the grip he had on my hair became vise-like. "Not yet, not yet," he gasped. I looked up at him standing tall over me, the rivulets of water running over his beautiful ink and sculpted muscles. His eyes were lid-heavy with lust.

"Get on top of me," he said, and before I could respond he was lying down on his back, right on the muddy earth, and pulling me down on top of him. "Ride me. Fuck me. Fuck me as if it were the last time."

I straddled him eagerly and he grabbed me by the waist, lifting me up before impaling me on his cock. I moaned from the tension, then started to grind myself into him. His muddy hands gripped my waist, and when I leaned forward they squeezed my swollen breasts, thumbing my nipples. I didn't give a fuck if I was covered in mud from head to toe, if we were drowned, dirty rats. I was going to ride the hell out of him, right here on the forest floor.

He pumped me up and down on him until I leaned back, letting the rain cascade down my chest, and he worked on my clit again. I felt utterly primal, alive, loved. We were animals fucking, humans making love, two wounded, tortured people bringing each other to ecstasy beneath tropical skies. I rode him hard until we were both going over the edge. I came first, screaming gibberish, my body letting loose, my walls gripping and milking his cock as the spasms went through me, each one more powerful than the next. When it was time for him to come, I looked down, making sure I watched the pleasure on his face, the pleasure he was getting from me and only me. His eyes rolled back, his head pressed harder into the earth, mud smeared all over his beautiful body. He moaned, grunting, "Fuck, fuck, fuck" over and over again, gasping for breath, his mouth open in surprise like he couldn't believe what was happening.

I knew how he felt. I couldn't really believe it either.

I was so lucky to have this man. My heart couldn't have been more full. I couldn't have been more high.

God, I don't think I could have loved him more.

When we both calmed down, I went to get off of him, but he quickly grabbed me and brought me down to his chest. "No," he grunted into my ear. "Stay where I can see you. Where I can feel you."

I nodded and nuzzled my face into the crook of his neck. He smelled like musk and damp earth, fresh and manly. "I love you," he whispered hoarsely. "I was never meant to love anyone else. No matter what, Ellie Watt, you own me. And I'll keep you safe."

My throat felt thick and I blinked back tears. Above us, the rain was tapering off a little. I ran my hands over his face, my finger over his perfectly straight nose, over his dark, arched eyebrows, over his square jaw, the spots on his cheeks where I knew his dimples appeared when he smiled. I owned him. And he would keep me safe.

I kissed him softly, sweetly, then lay my head back on his chest. We lay like that for a while, until the rain stopped and we finally realized we were lying naked in the middle of the Honduras jungle. As much as I wanted to keep lying there, keep feeling his heart beat against mine, his strong arms around me, protecting me, loving me, there was reality to face. A job to be done. A mission we were both committed to. It was heart-wrenching when I finally got off of him and slipped my clothes back on. The moment would be forever committed to my memory, keeping me going when everything else got scary, dangerous, hopeless. I would return to that moment when it was just him and me for a brief time, and nothing in the world mattered. No one could hurt us. It was just love and it was all we needed.

When we were both dressed—and still partly splattered with mud—we resumed our duty. We brought out the compasses and started walking again, heading northeast. I felt like I left something behind on that forest floor: the us I hoped we could return to.

CHAPTER ELEVEN

IT WAS DUSK when we saw the first lights in the jungle. At first I was certain that it was a pair of animal eyes, maybe a panther, watching our every move. But the eyes turned into several eyes and the forest began to open up and suddenly the lights belonged to a walled fence and a pathway and the roof of a sprawling mansion.

We had found it.

This was Travis's compound.

"Now what?" I asked Camden as we stopped a football field's length away, sticking close to the trees for cover. We couldn't really see anything because of the high stone wall that went on forever, hiding the mansion and who knows what else behind it.

"You don't happen to have a pair of binoculars in there?" he asked, gently taking the backpack off my shoulders and opening it. "Maybe night-vision goggles?"

"No. Javier had them."

"Of course he did," he said. He sighed and rubbed his hand on his face. He looked up at the trees. "Well, we won't have any idea of what we're dealing with if we can't see it. You good at climbing trees?"

I smiled. "World's best date palm climber right here."

A weird flash came across his face, as if something dawned on him. "I had a dream about you and me last week. We were in high school and climbed to the top of one of your uncle's date palms. There was a fire coming across the valley."

"Did we get burned?" I asked, reaching for his hand and pulling him toward me.

He smiled sadly. "We did. But at least we were together." He cupped my face in his hands and my eyes closed at his touch. "My Ellie. My beautiful girl. I will burn for you. I will die for you."

My heart skipped and burst, overflowing until my chest was radiating with heat, love, peace. I turned my face and kissed his palm. "You give me life, Camden. Death doesn't seem so scary after that."

He pulled me close and kissed my forehead. "How about we climb this tree, see if we can get a good look before it gets dark?"

I squeezed his hand and looked up at the tree closest to us. Sure, on the date farm I had a ladder to help me, but the way this tree's branches were spaced out it was like a ladder anyway.

Camden gave me a boost up to the lowest branches, but after that it was easy to climb. The only problem was the ants I saw crawling on the trunk. I hoped they weren't the really poisonous ones that Dom had warned us about.

We paused about halfway up, at a part where the branches separated a bit and we could see out.

Jesus.

Travis's compound was a lot bigger than I had thought—it was like a palace. On the other side of the wall there was the main building, the mansion that seemed to go on forever, wings and levels and sections. There was a courtyard in the front with fountains, a huge pool among landscaped gardens, as well as a few other houses that were scattered about. Golf carts littered the manicured lawns, lit pathways snaked their way through outdoor sculptures and statues. There was also a helicopter pad with a helicopter resting on it.

"I can't really see that far," Camden said, squinting at the distance. "What does it look like?"

"It looks like he's trying to re-create Versailles," I said honestly. *Off with her head.*

"What about people? Are there guards?"

There had to be. I tried to take it all in, paying attention to the details. There was a man driving a golf cart down a path, heavily armed of course. It looked like two guards were stationed by the front door, talking to someone I didn't recognize.

"There are some," I told him, relaying what I saw.

"Could be more, too. How about getting over the fence?"

My eyes followed it, searching for an opening. "It's too tall to scale, I think. And I don't have my grappling hook. There are a bunch of trees in the left corner though...If we kept walking straight we'd hit them. I think we could maybe climb over the fence that way, so long as the branches can hold us up."

"You'd at least be able to go over," he said.

I eyed him fearfully. "I can't do this alone."

"You won't," he said. "I promise. We'll do it together. We'll find a way."

"So when we get in, then what?"

He shrugged. "Get Gus and your mother. They are there. We will find them. You can break in. I have faith in your B and E skills." He smiled for a second. How far away that seemed now, how insane I was to break into Camden's house and rob him. That seemed like a lifetime ago.

My cheeks flushed with embarrassment. "I can get us in. Then I guess we case the joint and see who we can find."

"I wish it was going to be that simple. The odds are against us, you know."

"I think the odds have always been against us, Camden. Don't you?"

He grinned. "You're right about that. Okay. If that's the plan, then that's the plan. Let's go get Gus and your mother."

I nodded and was about to head back down the tree when I remembered something.

"You said something about a big picture the other day," I noted. "What did you mean?"

"When did I say that?"

"In the hotel room. You said the bigger picture is bigger than we know."

"You don't know?"

I worried about the look in Camden's eyes. His brow was pinched together, eyes sullen, almost sad. I shook my head.

"Ben," he said gently. "I need my son."

A heavy brick was placed on my heart. Of course, Ben. His son. He'd barely mentioned what happened to him with Sophia. It must have been killing him to not have him. I'd been so wrapped up in Gus and my mother, in Javier and in Travis, that I'd forgotten all about his little boy. Camden had been suffering in silence all this time, knowing we were being pulled one way when his son was the other.

"We'll get him back," I told him.

He nodded grimly. "I hope so. I can't... I can't let him stay with her. Not after what happened. You don't know how hard it was for me to leave him."

I smiled sadly, feeling pinched with guilt. "I can imagine. I'm sorry you had to come for me."

His face fell. "Oh, Ellie. No." He reached over and kissed me. "I don't regret coming to get you. I had to. I didn't have a choice. I was wanted... I couldn't have gone to get Ben without being caught. I would have been put away. And then what would have happened? I never would have seen him again. Never would have seen you again. I had to come for you. And then I promised myself that when I had you safe, we'd come back for him." He swallowed hard, his blue eyes watering. "We are getting out of this alive. We are getting my son back. I don't care what it takes."

His pain was breaking my heart. "I will help you do everything and anything. You'll get Ben. You'll be the father you weren't allowed to be before."

He nodded. I hope he believed me. Camden McQueen deserved to have all his wrongs righted.

He exhaled loudly, blinking hard, then said, "Come on. We better hurry while we have some light left. We better stay quiet too. We don't know if they've got people listening at the wall."

We went back down the tree and I could hear him sniffing. More of my heart fell to pieces. But I had to be strong for him. To do this job. And get him home.

Once on the ground, we walked along as silently as we could, mindful of every single leaf we were treading on. I was actually glad that we still had the mud from our sexual romp all over us still; it darkened my white tank top and arms and made us blend in a bit more with the vegetation. We were a few coats shy of looking like we'd rolled out of *Apocalypse Now*.

It wasn't long before we came to the group of trees that went dipping over the top of the wall. On closer inspection it looked like the branches were firm enough to support Camden's weight. I guess we had no choice but to find out.

I stopped and pointed up, motioning for us to climb. I quickly checked the gun in my boot and my knife in the other, making sure they were secure. I was nervous as hell. Like, heart-racing, lungs-seizing, pins-and-needles-shooting-up-and-down-my-spine-and-massaging-my-head kind of nervous. Panic-attack nervous.

Camden placed his hand on my shoulder and held it there until I felt like I could push through it and go on. There was no choice. We committed to being heroes— we couldn't back out because I felt like a coward at the last minute.

Heroes. I liked the sound of that.

I gave him a smile that probably looked depressing as hell. Then, with another boost from him, I climbed up the tree until we were at the right set of branches. I lay down on it, straddling it with my arms and legs, and shimmied my way across the branch. It dipped a bit with my weight, but not by much. I moved as slowly as possible, not wanting anyone to notice a tree with leaves shaking for no reason, and hoped it would be passed off as an animal or something.

I looked down. I had cleared the wall, but it was a fifteen-foot drop to the ground, thankfully in an area behind a set of flowering bushes. I hoped my ankles would forgive me.

I glanced over my shoulder at Camden, who was waiting at the end of the branch, barely visible against the tree. I nodded at him, then quickly swung under the branch and let go. I landed on the ground with a soft thud and then rolled, once I realized my legs weren't reliable. I lay on my back and looked up at the tree, staying low and waiting until Camden had joined me.

I could barely see him go across the branch, but I did see the branch start to sag dramatically under his weight. Fuck, him being 6'2" and all muscle, he had to be at least sixty pounds heavier than me. He paused, probably unsure of whether he should continue or not.

Suddenly a light lit up the wall in front of me and I could hear the whir of a golf cart's engine in the distance. I froze and prayed they wouldn't come any closer, that they wouldn't shine up in the tree. Camden stayed completely still. So did my heart.

After a few nerve-bursting moments, the light finally moved along the wall and the golf cart continued on its way. I slowly turned over and poked my head around the bushes. It looked like this was part of their nightly patrol.

"Camden, hurry," I whispered as softly as I could. He heard me. The branch started moving again, the leaves shaking. I winced.

Then the branch broke with the loudest snap.

I gasped as Camden and the branch came crashing down to the ground. I quickly scampered over to him and looked around in a panic, hoping no one heard anything. Camden got up, staying low, and put out his hand to let me know he was okay. We stayed huddled next to each other, frozen in fear, waiting for time to pass, for our passage to go unnoticed.

When no lights came back on us and we didn't hear anyone approaching, we exhaled in unison. I patted him on the back to let him know we were okay so far. He nodded to the row of hedges that lined the lit path nearby. If we stayed behind them, there was a chance we wouldn't be seen and it would lead us all the way to the back of the mansion.

We got down on our stomachs and started crawling on the stiff grass, sticking as close to the hedge as possible. I almost found it amusing that we were doing moves that belonged in a *Mission Impossible* movie, but considering this was an actual life-and-death situation and Tom Cruise wasn't going to start sprinting out of the bushes to save us, it wasn't very funny. Maybe one day I'd look back on the impossibility of this all, what we had to go through, the things we had to do. One day, if I was lucky.

We crawled until my limbs were thoroughly scratched up and I had added grass stains to the things I was currently covered with, but we eventually came to the house. Camden stopped and I crawled up around the side of him. He brought his mouth to my ear and whispered, "There are lights on at the farthest end of the house and upstairs. There are no lights here and there's a door. Do you think you can tell if it's alarmed?"

I nodded. I knew when security systems were up and running, and with luck I could defeat them. That is, if Travis had your regular home alarm system. If this place was wired like Fort Knox, I had no chance in hell. Only problem was, it would be noisy.

I whispered back, "Smash and crash. I can use my gun. But if there's anyone around where the alarm panel is, they'll hear it."

"Let's hope it's not alarmed then."

"Let's hope there's no one on the other side of that door, period."

He quickly kissed me. "If anything goes wrong, you get out. You run like hell. Don't worry about me."

Like hell I would run away. But I nodded to placate him and took in a deep breath. We looked around to make sure the coast was clear and ran across the path for the door, flattening ourselves against the wall. We waited a few moments, and then I quickly reached into my pocket where I had stuck the lock-picking tools from earlier. Same ones I had used to break into Camden's house.

It didn't take me long to pick the lock. That was the easy part. The hard part was having the courage to open the door. Though Travis's house wouldn't have a system connected to the police in any way, it would be connected to some monitoring station in the house or even outside of it. If the door was alarmed, I had thirty to sixty seconds to find the alarm panel and smash it with the butt of my gun. If we were lucky, the beeps wouldn't be too loud and no one would hear me destroy the panel before it had a chance to signal that someone had broken in.

If we were unlucky…well…

I readied myself, getting my head into game mode, finding the confidence I had somewhere inside me, and opened the door.

I didn't realize I'd been holding my breath until we were both inside. It was dark where we were, with tile floors. Maybe a laundry room. I heard the beeps being set off, sounding like sirens in the night even though in reality they weren't too loud. I followed the sounds, walking as quietly as possible with Camden right behind me, then found the alarm in a closet. I took out my gun and with a quick jab smashed the panel, Camden's hands catching the falling plastic and glass before it clattered to the floor.

The alarm was disabled. Now we had to stand there and wait for our fate, for the guns that would be inevitably drawn on us if we'd been heard. We listened, hearing only the crickets outside the door that was still open and the sound of each other breathing. It must have been the longest couple of minutes of my life, and yet I was terrified to move, to open the door and explore the rest of the house. I felt safe in the darkness of that room with Camden at my side.

Finally his hand grasped mine. It was wet with sweat, and somehow knowing he felt as scared as I did made me feel better, that I wasn't alone.

He brought out his cell phone from his pocket and shone it around us briefly. We were in fact in a large laundry room: two washers, two dryers, and a linen closet where the alarm had been. He aimed the light at the closed door that led into the rest of the house and then put his phone away. I heard him reach into my backpack and withdraw his gun. I gripped mine tightly in my hands, and he went for the door, opening it as slowly as possible.

We poked our heads out into a long hallway, the only illumination coming from a green glass lamp on a table at the end of it. The walls were done up with stoic portraits of Mexican men, posing gallantly like royalty. I had to wonder if Travis actually built this place or if he just took it over from someone else in the cartel. The thought of him, his cold inhuman eyes, made me shiver, but I had to let the feeling go. This was far from over.

I wondered where we could go next. Though there were a few doors and rooms coming off of the hallway, it wasn't exactly smart to start opening each one and asking if Gus was there. We'd have to spy, observe, hunker down somewhere until we knew what was what and who was where.

I placed my hand on Camden's arm as a way of telling him to stay put, then quickly crept back into the laundry room. I gently closed the door to the outside, closed the door to the linen closet, hiding the pieces of the broken panel underneath some towels, and then closed the laundry room door. If we were going to be spending a few hours in the house, then everything had to look exactly like it had before. We had to go undetected.

If Camden was confused by my actions, he didn't show it. Now we just had one thing to do and we had to do it right. We had to find a place to hide. Because the laundry room had access to the back, it would be a high-traffic area. We had to find something that was more off the beaten path.

I took Camden's free hand in mine and started leading him down the hall, away from the light at the end. He had said this end looked completely dark from the outside, and we needed to be heading away from the people who lived here.

The second room down the hall was dark, but there were large windows that had the outside lights streaming from in between the curtains, casting some illumination into the room. It was a library. Lots of leather couches, chairs, tables, and bookcase after bookcase. In the beam of light I could see layers of dust on the tables and motes floating in the air—a room that was rarely used. It's not like Travis started a reading habit in his spare time. This place would have to do.

I brought Camden into the room and did a quick sweep of the area. Where to hide? We had to be close enough to the hall to hear people, but we couldn't be visible. Taking a chance, he brought out his phone and flashed its weak glow around the room. Then he aimed it upward. There was a whole other level up there, a small balcony that wrapped around the room. A sturdy-looking ladder led up to the loft. We both eyed each other. If we lay low up top, just above the door, we wouldn't be seen and we could hear everything.

We quickly climbed up the ladder, wincing when it scuffed a bit against the hardwood floor from our movement, and crept along the balcony until we were above the door. Like below, it was lined with more books.

I lay down on my stomach as flush against the bookcase as I could muster and Camden did the same, our heads facing each other. We both brought our guns out and laid them on the floor beside us. Another advantage we had: if someone did come into the room and discover us, we could pick them off easily.

I rested my chin on the floor and Camden did the same. I leaned forward and kissed him, then took his hand in mine. We stared at each other, his eyes shining in the darkness, and waited. Waited for signs of life. We waited until we fell asleep, Travis's house lulling us into dreamland.

CHAPTER TWELVE

SCATTERED SPANISH entered my dreams until my brain somehow figured out that this was reality and I needed to wake up. Camden's hand on my face helped too.

My eyes flew open and I immediately froze as I remembered where I was. I was lying down on my stomach in the loft of Travis's library. Camden was across from me, his head inches from mine, one hand stroking my face, the other on his gun. He implored me with eyes not to make a sound or panic. I swallowed hard, trying to still my heart, and listened.

A bunch of men were yelling in Spanish to one another. It was coming from outside the room, most likely from outside the house. My suspicions were cleared up when I heard the front door slam and someone stomp inside.

"Idiots," a man yelled angrily.

Travis.

I knew that voice too well. I had to fight against the urge to pick up my gun, leap off the balcony, and hunt him down. It would be so simple. I'd probably die in the process, but for a split second I didn't care. I only wanted him dead. Then I realized how badly the revenge still ran through me, the pain his presence still brought me.

Knowing this, knowing everything about me, Camden brushed the hair off my face. And my thoughts went to him. How silly we both looked in the daylight, dried mud caked on in splotches all over ourselves.

There was someone else walking out in the hall, the footsteps going past the library and stopping not too far away. Perhaps by the laundry room. I prayed they wouldn't need any towels.

"Is everything all right, sir?" the person asked in a near-perfect American accent.

"No, it's not all right," Travis answered rather snidely. "I don't understand how they haven't been found yet. When was the last time they were spotted?"

"Aguascalientes," the man answered. "Still nothing different. We are trying—"

"They should have died. They should have been in that car. I don't understand how something so goddamn simple could go wrong."

"At least they were heading north. Not coming here."

"I couldn't give a shit if they were coming here or not. I want them fucking dead so I don't have to worry about them fucking things up again. They made me look like a damn idiot. The whole cartel, we looked like damn idiots. All of us."

"If you don't think they're coming here, then why don't you just…"

A pause. "Just what? Kill her? What kind of barbarian do you think I am? She's my wife."

The word *wife* stabbed me. My eyes flew to Camden. He couldn't have been talking about my mother. Could he?

"I don't mean any disrespect," the man said quickly. "I just figured from the way you were...talking...the other night. From what she's gone through...that it was on the agenda."

Travis chuckled maliciously. "Agenda? There is no agenda. I will deal with Amelie when I am ready to deal with her. Until then, keep her down there." He grunted, his footsteps echoing down the hall. "Fix me an omelet, would you? It would be nice if someone here wasn't completely incompetent."

Amelie. My mother. A bunch of thoughts flew into my head. My mother was Travis's wife, even though that made no sense at all. I never saw a wedding ring on her finger, and my father had died. But he had mentioned she was "down there," which I had to assume meant someplace in the house like a basement. That at least gave us a direction to go in, and I could try and make sense about all the other shit later.

Then there was the fact that he didn't once mention Gus.

At least Este's hunch about Javier not being expected here was true. Then again, if he said the last place that we'd been spotted was Aguascalientes, then whatever happened to Javier and the crew out there in the jungle wasn't orchestrated by Travis.

Which meant...Oh, fuck.

My eyes widened, and judging from the way that Camden narrowed his eyes into a steely gaze, he was realizing the same thing. Nothing had happened to Javier.

We were set up.

They had planned for us to come here.

And here is exactly where we were.

Motherfucker.

I was pretty sure my blood was boiling over. I could feel my veins pulsing at my temples, my face growing hot and red. I was ready to go fucking apeshit. I was ready to lose my fucking mind.

Camden let go of his gun and put his other hand to my face and held me firmly.

"Hey," he whispered softly. "It's going to be okay."

I tried to shake my head, but his grip increased.

"Ellie. It's going to be okay. We know your mother is here. We can get her out."

"We were set up," I hissed harshly. "And Gus?"

"We'll get him too."

"Where is he?"

"If he's here, we'll find him. But we find her first. She can help us."

"They probably know we're in here."

He smiled, briefly, softly. "They probably do. But we don't know how this will play out. You want your mother and Gus. They want Travis dead. We might be able to have both those things and walk out of here alive. We at least have to try."

I understood what he was saying, but it didn't stop the burning pain in my gut, that feeling of utter foolishness.

I hated myself for not seeing what Javier had been doing. He was spiteful more than anything, spurned by my devotion to Camden, angered by the death of his sister, the death that I inadvertently caused. He was a loose cannon, mad for power, and I had told myself that when I least suspected it, that's when he'd pull the rug out from under me. And even though I told Camden I wouldn't put it past Javier for setting me up, I still hadn't believed it. I thought he loved me enough to want what's best for me. To see me well. I believed in his love without remembering what kind of love it was.

Gus, my dear sweet Gus, had once told me to never mistake obsession for love. He was so right, time and time again.

Javier had set Camden and me up. To come here. Perhaps to walk free or perhaps to fail. He left me in that forest, using me as a pawn, walking blindly forward for Gus and my mother. He was both doing me a favor, leading me to what I wanted, and cementing my doom. Because whatever Javier was after, it wasn't my happiness. It was his. And at this point in our lives, what made us both happy was very far apart. I wanted family. I wanted love. I wanted Camden.

He wanted power. Just power and only that.

I closed my eyes, trying to escape the humiliation of how wrong I was about everything. I didn't handle being made a fool of very well. We listened a while longer to the sounds of the mansion. It sounded like someone was at the other end of the house, perhaps the man in the kitchen, making the omelet. When those sounds quieted down, I could only assume that the breakfast was being delivered to Travis in some other room in the house.

As long as we didn't stumble across that room, this was our chance.

I nodded at Camden and we got up.

It wasn't until we had carefully climbed down the ladder and onto the main floor of the library that I realized how badly I needed to pee. That was the thing about this that they don't show you in the movies—everyone has to pee at some point, no matter how inconvenient the circumstances.

I grabbed Camden's arm and whispered, "What are the chances of me finding a bathroom nearby?"

"Are you serious?"

I nodded, eyes wide. "I don't joke about peeing."

"Go behind the couch," he said. "Maybe do it on a stack of first editions while you're at it."

I nearly smiled. Pissing on Travis's floor was a small bit of sweet revenge.

I went behind the couch, which was right by the windows, and did my business. When I was done I peeled back just the tiniest bit of curtain and peeked out. I could see the wide front steps leading out to the elaborate courtyard in the front, a row of golf carts across it. There were two men with rifles stationed at the foot of the stairs, looking alert, two men we'd probably end up having to take out when it came time to get out of here.

I pulled up my pants and Camden suppressed a smile as I stepped out from behind the couch.

"See anything?" he whispered.

"Just the two men with rifles that I saw last night. I

don't think this place is as heavily armed as I thought. Or I'm terribly wrong."

He rubbed his lips together and breathed out sharply through his nose. "I hate it when you're wrong."

"Me too." I shook out my arms and legs, took my gun out of my boot, and said, "Let's go down and get my mother."

Of course we didn't know where "down" was. We slinked out into the hallway, making sure the coast was clear, and sidled our way down the walls, careful not to brush off any of the ugly paintings. We checked every room down at this end of the house and, with great trepidation, every door. There were bedrooms, studies, game rooms, all untouched and unused, but nothing that would lead to a basement.

We stopped at the end of the hall and I rubbed my palms against my jeans. There was only one way for us to go, in the direction of the kitchen and Travis. I looked to Camden, who closed his eyes and took a calming breath before giving me a short nod.

We crept back down the hall, my pulse quickening once we passed the safety zone of the library and the laundry room. Everything beyond this was unknown and occupied. It was going to take either a lot of luck or a lot of bullets to get us through this.

And first, we had to cross through the foyer.

We stopped at the edge of the wall and I peered quickly around it. The foyer was all marble and gaudy accents, tile floors and hanging chandeliers with a giant winding staircase leading up to the second floor. I could see through the front stained-glass windows the shadows of two guards outside, seemingly closer to the door than the pair I had just seen.

I held up four fingers to Camden, letting him know there were four of them in total now. Four of them, two of us, and who knew how many others there were in different parts of the compound. The odds were continually stacked against us.

Lightly, silently, as if we were running on air, Camden and I scampered across the foyer before we were spotted by anyone and didn't even relax once we were safely behind the wall of the adjacent hallway. I could hear noises, clattering of pots and pans, coming from the room closest to us—the kitchen.

I motioned for Camden to stay still. I didn't know what I was doing now. The fear inside was struggling to take over, to become free. But I wouldn't let it. I would control my fear. I would use it in my favor, to work for me.

My fear was about to help me make some very hard decisions.

I crept silently over to the kitchen doorway, crouched low, and poked my head around it. There was a man—his back to me, thank god—putting away stuff in the fridge. I didn't know if he was the same man I heard speaking to Travis earlier, but it didn't matter. He had to be taken out if we were going to get out of here. The risk of him seeing us was far too great.

Unfortunately, I didn't have a silencer on my gun, so I couldn't shoot him even though I currently had a clear shot. I also didn't have any means of knocking the guy out without causing any racket. He wasn't as big as Camden, but he was still bigger than me and would put up a fight. At the first sound of struggle, I knew Travis or the guards would come running.

So it had to be me.

I had to do this.

Very slowly, very carefully, I pulled the knife out from my boot. It felt cold and slippery in my sweating hands and I held on to it as tight as I could, channeling my fear through my hand.

I stayed crouched, stayed low, and eased my way toward the man.

I got close.

Really close.

Hoped he couldn't hear how loud my heart was beating.

I straightened up.

Knife out.

Hand shaking.

The man reached further into the fridge, grabbing something.

I was right behind him.

I raised my arms, one ready to put over his mouth, the other to draw the blade across his throat.

A tear leaked out of my eye.

He suddenly stepped backward, into me, and turned around in surprise. Wide, dark eyes met mine.

He probably expected to see Travis.

Not me.

And before either of us could even react, Camden was sprinting across the kitchen.

Grabbing the knife out of my hand and shouldering me out of the way.

He put his hand over the man's mouth and pushed the man's head back into one of the shelves in the fridge.

Camden took the knife with one swift motion, slit the man's throat.

The man's eyes widened even more then froze, blood spilling out of him and down his white shirt. Camden held the man there until he was certain he was dead. Then he took the man in his arms and nodded to the pantry, trying to get me to open the door.

I couldn't move. My body rocked with terrors while everything inside of me froze. Blood pooled around my boots.

Camden managed to open the pantry and put the body inside, closing the door quietly behind him. Then he came over to the sink, took paper towels from the dispenser, and quickly wiped up the blood at my feet. He shoved the reddened towels under the sink, closed the fridge door, and grabbed my shoulders. I looked down at his hands, covered in blood, leaving bloody prints on me.

"Ellie," he whispered, shaking me. "Ellie. Look at me. Look at me."

I raised my head and looked at his eyes. They were wild, pupils completely dilated, but they were familiar. He was still my Camden.

Oh god, what had he done?

What had I been about to do?

I opened my mouth to speak but nothing came out.

"Ellie," he said again, his voice hoarser now. "I couldn't let you do it, you'd never forgive yourself. I'd rather this be on my conscience than yours. I'm getting my son back and I'm going to do whatever I can to make that happen." He reached into his back pocket and pulled out another gun. "I found this on him. Do you want it or should I?"

I licked my lips and managed to say, "You have it."

"I'm keeping you safe," he said and quickly kissed my forehead. "Come on."

He grabbed my hand and led me out of the kitchen back to the hallway.

As sick as I was with shock and horror at what we had just done, I felt a twinge of relief deep inside. The man, who would have no doubt killed us, was dead. We didn't have to worry about him. And I now knew, I *saw*, that Camden was prepared to do absolutely anything to keep me alive and get back to his son. I could only hope that he'd make peace with it one day, if we managed to get out of this on our own two feet. The human heart had the capacity to take on only so much, and I knew Camden's heart was overburdened as it was.

We continued down the hall, pausing every few steps to listen. There was some shuffling from one of the rooms at the very end. The door was open and the room faced to the back, where the morning sun was spilling into it. It seemed like a place that Travis would sit and have breakfast, perhaps a sunroom where he could sit and think about all the money he was making, drugs he was distributing, people he was killing.

I wondered if Camden was going to take me straight there. Take himself straight to Travis, kill him and have it all over with.

But someone else's voice came from that room, speaking in Spanish. Travis answered him, also in

Spanish, albeit rusty. I couldn't really figure out what they were talking about—the news, perhaps, some event in Honduras. Unfortunately, that made two of them in there. It wouldn't be so easy now. I doubted we could go in the room the way we were and take them out.

Camden paused, then instead of continuing toward the voices, he carefully tried the handle on the first door to our left.

Locked.

And locked for a reason.

He looked to me questioningly. Could I do this?

I nodded and brought out the lock picker with fumbling fingers. I kept hearing Travis down the hall, knowing how close we were to him, how close we were to getting my mother out. Though it took longer than normal, I managed to pick the lock. We carefully pushed the door open and I held my breath waiting for it to creak loudly. It didn't.

And there were a set of stairs leading down into the dark.

We had found it.

Camden motioned for me to go first. The stairs were lit by a bare bulb, and he ever so carefully closed the door behind us. We went down slowly, step by step, my legs feeling weak, my jaw clenched hard.

We had found it, but I was afraid to see what it was.

I stepped off the last step, my boots on hard concrete. There was darkness all around us, the light from the stairs not reaching very far.

Suddenly a flashback came into my vision. Me, eleven years old, walking down the stairs to Travis's basement by accident, looking for money that wasn't there and only finding the chemicals that would change the course of my entire life.

It wasn't quite ironic, but it was definitely something.

A moan came from the corner of the room, and I realized that though we couldn't see what or who was down here, they could see us.

I squeezed my gun for assurance and then took a step forward.

"Hello?" I whispered softly. "Mom?"

The moan got louder. I walked toward it, and then Camden quickly brought out his phone, shining the weak light straight ahead of us.

My chest was shredded by what I saw.

There was a cage in the corner of the room, a large cage, like one you'd see when transporting animals to a zoo.

My mother was in the cage.

She was sitting half up, leaning against the bars, wearing what looked like the same dress I had seen her wear at Travis's party. Her hands were gathered behind her back. Duct tape around her mouth. Her eyes were crazed, filled with tears, pleading for us.

"We need light," Camden's voice came through, calm and steady. He shone his phone around, and found another bare bulb hanging from the ceiling and pulled the string.

Everything lit up. I glanced around quickly, taking in a very familiar sight. It was like the same basement he scarred me in, but worse—much, much worse. It looked like a meth lab crossed with a mad scientist's lab. And very close to where my mother lay in her dirty cage was glass jar after glass jar of crawling black insects. Ants. Bullet ants. Este's assumption about Travis using them for torture wasn't just a silly hunch after all.

I looked back to my mom and immediately crouched down beside her, trying to ignore the welts she had all over her bare arms and legs. Insect bites.

"Mom," I said, my voice breaking. "It's me, Ellie. Your daughter. We're going to get out of here, okay?"

She shook her head back and forth, tears spilling down her cheeks, and I reached into the cage and pulled the duct tape off of her mouth in one go.

She winced from the pain and I whispered, "Sorry."

"Ellie," she cried softly, and her voice reached down into my very soul. If I didn't hold it together I was going to lose it.

"Mom, it's okay."

"You won't get out of here," she cried.

"Yes, we will," I told her, my throat closing up. "Together. This is Camden. He's going to help us." I motioned behind me to Camden who was crouched down at my back. "Where is Gus?"

"Gus?" she asked. "What are you talking about?"

My veins had more ice than blood in them.

"Gus," I said again, fighting to keep my voice steady. "He was taken by Travis. You know Gus, Mom, you *know* Gus. He came all the way to Mexico with Camden to get me. We have to save him, I owe him this."

"I'm sorry, sweetie," my mom said softly, shaking her head. "Gus isn't here."

CHAPTER THIRTEEN

HER WORDS SETTLED over me like fine, cold dust.

Gus. Wasn't. Here.

"But Javier said…" I started. I didn't even bother finishing the sentence.

"Javier lies," my mom said. "How do you think I ended up here with Travis?"

I narrowed my eyes at her, the rage building up inside, threatening to spill out. "Because you're weak. And you're a fool. And so am I."

"Ellie," Camden warned me.

"No," I hissed at him. I was about to lose it. About to lose everything. I squeezed my gun so hard I could feel the ridges cutting into my palm. Javier had lied to me. He told me Gus was here. All along I was chasing after something that wasn't real. Where was Gus?

"Why?" I cried out. "Why did he lie?"

"Because," she said, her eyes avoiding mine, "he knew you'd never come for me. But you'd come for your father."

"My father?" I asked while I heard Camden suck in his breath behind me. "He's dead. I know he's dead. Don't tell me Javier lied about that too?"

"Ellie, I think we should get her out of here first," Camden said quickly. "I hear something upstairs."

I ignored him and my mom went on. "The father you know *is* dead, Ellie. I'm sorry, sweetie. He was... Travis killed him. To take possession of me. We never knew what we were getting into when we came here. We only wanted... revenge. For you."

"The father I know?" I asked, suddenly recalling Javier wording things very similarly.

She gave me a sad smile. "Ellie, I'm sorry. Gus is your real father."

"What?"

What?

This was too much. My brain started to shut down on itself.

Gus. All this time. Gus. The man I was looking for, the man who was like a father to me more than my real father was in fact my real father. This shit couldn't even be digested. My mother had an affair with Gus. Who the fuck didn't she have an affair with?

"Fuck," Camden swore under his breath. "I had a feeling."

I whipped my head to look at him. "You had a feeling and you didn't tell me?"

"I didn't know for sure and I didn't know how," he said quickly. "I knew you wanted to get him back badly enough as it was."

"And Javier knew that too," my mother went on, trying

to adjust herself. I was both so angry at her and her lies and hurting because she was hurt. "He knew you'd come here for Gus if he told you that Travis had him."

"But why?"

"To kill Travis."

I shook my head, trying to get some sense into it. "Still? Again? Why doesn't he just do it?"

"Because if you do it, he cannot be blamed. It won't be a coup. And he'll just take right over. Everyone's allegiance will be to him. Cartels, my girl, are archaic."

"Don't call me that," I hissed at her. "I am not your girl. I cannot put up with any more of your lies. Everything you've ever told me is a lie. You're just like *him*." Whether I meant Travis or Javier by that, it didn't matter.

"We have to go, now," Camden said louder.

As if on cue, the building rumbled and shook slightly, the light bulb swaying.

"What the hell was that?" I asked, automatically looking to my mom.

She looked bewildered. "I don't know."

"Javier," Camden said.

My mother's mouth dropped open. "Javier is here?"

"He brought us here," I told her. "How else would we have found you? How else would he have insured that I would keep going after Gus?" My voice cracked over his name.

"He ditched us in the jungle on the way here," Camden filled in. "Obviously knowing we would keep coming. I guess he was waiting for us to make the first move. Either he's gotten impatient or they somehow know we're down here with you."

"Well, fuck this," I said and quickly took my lock-picking tools to the cage. Once I had gotten that open, I crawled in beside her and got her handcuffs off.

She rubbed her raw wrists and looked at me proudly. "I taught you well. You always were the best at picking locks."

My lip automatically curled. "You shouldn't be proud at me for being a con artist, for being like *you*. You should be proud that I'm bothering to get you out of here after everything you've done to me." I grabbed her by her arm and pulled her up and out of the cage, ignoring the look on her face, like I'd slapped her. "Can you walk?"

She swallowed hard but nodded. "Yes. I've only been in there for a few days. I...I talked back to him the other night and..."

I raised my hand, not wanting to know about her torture. "I don't want to hear it." I looked at Camden. "You'll take care of her, okay?" Before he could answer, I snatched the other gun from his pocket and ran toward the stairs just as I heard gunfire breaking out upstairs.

"Ellie!" Camden screamed at me, full-on horror.

But I kept running, gun in each hand, taking the stairs two by two to the top.

I was getting Gus back.

And I was going to make everyone pay.

I kicked the door open into the hall and was surprised to already see a guard running toward me. I quickly raised my gun and shot him in the head before he had a chance to aim at me. Then I slammed the door shut, my gun already pointed straight forward, and saw Dom at the opposite end of the hallway. I figured the guard was running toward someone.

Dom froze where he was, his gun also drawn.

"Don't you fucking move!" I screamed at him. "Don't you fucking move."

To his credit, Dom stayed put. I had a feeling it's because he wasn't allowed to kill me. I was going to have to make that work in my favor.

I ran down the hall toward him, but when I crossed the foyer I was met with glass breaking and bullets riddling the walls. I kept running, noticing there was fire coming up from behind where Dom was, filling the end of the hallway.

I stopped in front of him and immediately pistol-whipped him across his nose. He cried out, grabbing his face and dropping his gun. I scooped it up, sticking it in my boot. Now I had three guns. I had a feeling I could never have enough.

More bullets and shots came from the foyer. I quickly grabbed Dom and swung him around the corner into the laundry room, shutting the door behind us. I slammed his head against the door, stuck the end of my gun against his temple, and yelled, "Talk! Tell me every fucking thing you know or I will kill you."

He looked at me in utter fear, at my eyes which must have shown the rage that was flowing through me. What had Javier said earlier about depravity? Well, he must have known I had that in spades, just waiting for the right moment for me to snap.

And I had *snapped*.

"Talk!" I screamed again, my spit flying into his bloody face.

"You were set up," he said, panicking. "From the start."

"You fuck! And you said you liked me."

He blinked several times. "I do like you. But I love my family."

I pushed the gun harder into his head. "What was the plan? Where is Gus?"

"You were supposed to be a diversion. You'd kill Travis and we'd swoop in, secure the compound. I don't know where Gus is, I don't. Javier said he was being kept somewhere for future use. I don't know what that means. He's alive, though."

"Take me to Javier," I told him, pulling him off the door and jamming the gun into his lower back.

He looked over his shoulder. "He's in a firefight."

"No," I said, "Derek and Este are in a firefight. Javier is somewhere else, biding his time. Waiting for me. Take me to him. Now."

"Please, I have a wife and child," he pleaded.

"I won't kill you if you do as I say," I told him, meaning it, too. I didn't want to kill Dom, but I was realizing I was prepared to if absolutely necessary.

"You won't, but Javier will," he said.

"That's your problem."

Another explosion rocked the house, this time from the opposite wing. We stumbled a bit and Dom went for his gun, but I had my gun back on him in no time.

"I don't think so," I said. I nodded at the door I had broken into last night, the one leading to the backyard. "Let's go."

I kicked open the door and hoped that Camden and my mother were somewhere safe. "Who is setting off the explosions?"

"Derek," he said. "Improvised explosive devices."

"If he accidentally kills Camden or my mother, everyone here dies, including you. Tell him to rein it in."

"I can't—"

"I know you're communicating with each other, do it now!"

Dom sighed and pressed the Bluetooth device in his ear while I did a quick scan of the area. I could see the pool glistening in the distance, a single body floating in it. Several statues on the grounds were cracked or knocked over.

"Derek," Dom said. "Stop the explosions and hold. Take out only Travis's men. If you see McQueen or any of the Watts, do not shoot, do not engage. We need them alive. Copy?"

Dom nodded at whatever Derek said in his ear. "Okay," he said to me. "He's been called off."

"Lucky you," I said. "Where's Javier?"

His eyes darted to the pool house, a small cottage with a single darkened window that was open a crack. Just enough space for a gun to fit through. Of course.

"He's not going to kill me, right?" I asked Dom as I readied myself to run across the lawn.

"Javier? No. We were ordered not to kill you or Camden."

Or Camden? "How nice. The bombs don't really help."

"We didn't know where you were."

"Well, here I am." I looked around then nodded at the cottage. "I'll try to cover us."

We started running for it, both Dom and I running as fast as we could, knowing there was a lot of ground between the main house and the pool house. We were only a few yards away when bullets started whizzing past us.

I turned and looked up at the roof of the house to see a sniper there, taking shots at us as we ran. I aimed both guns at the roof and fired.

My aim was terrible.

I didn't hit the sniper.

Instead, the sniper hit me.

My leg exploded in pain, and I stumbled to the ground as the bullet seared through my calf. The cherry blossoms offered no defense.

I cried out, my gun falling away from my hands, and tried to crawl toward it. I barely managed to get it and quickly rolled onto my back, aiming the gun at the roof, when the sniper was hit before I could even pull the trigger. He stumbled backward and then slid off the roof to his death on the hard patio below.

I turned around to look at Dom, who had been brought down to the ground with me.

He wasn't moving.

A shadow appeared overhead. I looked up.

Javier was standing over me, blocking out the sun, a rifle in his hand.

"Is Camden still alive?" he asked me in a strangely hopeful voice, as if Camden mattered to him more at the moment than me.

I pointed my gun straight up at him, my hand shaking from the bursts of pain that rocked my body in pure agony.

"Yes. But you won't be."

"You going to pull the trigger, angel?" he asked. "After I just saved your life?"

I ground my teeth together in nauseating anger. "You lied to me. You lied to me." I tried in vain to keep my hand steady. "You lied about Gus."

He smiled, eyes glowing with madness. "I did lie. You wouldn't have come here otherwise. You would have never fulfilled your destiny. To kill the man who ruined so many of our lives."

I was done. So fucking done.

"Tell me where Gus is or I'll blow your fucking brains out."

"You don't have it in you, angel. You're too good for that now."

This was no longer a matter of good or bad.

This was all gray.

Hazy, fuzzy gray.

I squeezed the trigger.

The chamber clicked.

Loudly.

Empty.

And though Javier's face was shadowed from the sun, I saw something in his eyes that I had never seen before. Absolute disbelief. Absolute shock. Absolute...fear.

And I felt relief that he was still standing there, alive. I did have it in me to kill him, that dark part of me that wanted him dead. But now I had nothing to regret.

I whimpered and rolled over, grasping my leg as another wave of pain rolled through while he stood there above me, in the middle of a firefight, absolutely dumbfounded by what had just happened.

Suddenly the ground around us erupted in another spray of bullets. I screamed and quickly rolled over, trying to get out of the way.

And Javier turned and ran back toward the pool house, toward safety, leaving me there on the grass, bleeding, while the bullets came closer.

Leaving me alone.

Leaving me to die.

I guess I had pulled the trigger first. The honeymoon really was over.

I rolled over onto my stomach, avoiding getting too close to Dom, who lay dead beside me, and watched as Javier ran, wondering if there was a point in me crawling after him. I wondered how long I had before I died. I wondered if I'd ever see Camden again. I wondered if my life made a difference to anyone out there.

I just wanted another chance at it.

Another chance to be me.

Scars and all.

And while I was lying on the grass, my leg bleeding out, soaking my jeans, I heard a few more pops of bullets go out.

Javier was running into the pool house when he was struck in the back.

I screamed bloody murder.

He fell down flat, legs sticking out of the door, motionless.

Javier.

Shot.

Dead.

No.

No.

Not yet.

His legs twitched and he managed to pull himself into the pool house until I couldn't see him anymore.

"Ellie Watt!" a cold voice bellowed from across the lawn. I could barely tear my eyes away from where Javier had disappeared, fighting back a range of emotions I couldn't even pin down, but I managed to turn my head. The voice had reached into me, holding me tight with an icy fist.

Travis was standing on the lawn where it met the edge of his patio, gun in hand.

In front of him were my mother and Camden on their knees with their hands behind their heads.

No.

Not this.

Not now.

My heart couldn't take any more of this. Every part of me was shattered, from leg to soul.

"What do you want from me?!" I screamed at him. I grabbed my gun out of my boot and staggered to my feet, crying softly from the pain as I touched my right leg to the ground.

"Come closer and we'll talk," Travis yelled back. "You might want to keep your gun down, though. You know you can't save both of them."

I sobbed in pain and anger and started limping

toward him, practically dragging my bloodied leg behind me, gun at my side. Each step I took riddled with more pain, more sorrow, more hate toward this man who had taken everything away from me.

I wouldn't let him take Camden.

I wondered if he knew that would be my decision. He figured I came all this way for my mother, when that wasn't the case at all. He was betting on me picking her, saving her.

I remembered when Derek had asked me what I would do if I had to save my mother, how I said I'd have to let the situation dictate my choice.

I knew my choice back then, and I knew it now.

I stopped a few yards away and looked at Camden, at his beautiful soul in those blue eyes. We stared at each other locked in our gaze, locked in love. He wouldn't want me to make this choice either. I could only hope he wouldn't make it for me.

"You don't look as lovely as you did when you were Eleanor Willis," Travis said, smiling like the devil, his gun in the middle of the two of them but leaning more toward my mother.

"You don't look so hot either," I retorted. His normally neat, dark gray hair was messed up with pieces of plaster in it, his slick Italian suit covered in blood, his terrible eyes red. "Your age is showing."

He kept smiling and nodded at me. "Sorry about your leg. Hope it doesn't leave a scar."

I swallowed hard, overtaken by the anger and the pain and the determination to walk out of there with the love of my life. I chose love over everything.

Love over gold.

I raised my gun in the air and pointed it at him. "I hope this doesn't either."

"You kill me, Ellie," he said quickly, a rare tremor coming through, "your mother dies." He trained the gun to the back of her head.

"You wouldn't kill her," I said, and though I wished it weren't true, I had to wish it was true. "You love her, don't you?"

His eyes narrowed. "No. But she loved me enough to make up for it. You can't love in this business, Ellie. Sooner or later everyone dies."

Javier had said that to me. Now I didn't even know if he was alive or not.

"Then why are we standing here like this," I said, hiding the weakness in my voice. "Do you want me to come join you, is that it? Do you want me to be like my mother? The only reason she was with you is because she wanted to get revenge for what you did to me." I didn't even know if that was true, despite what my mom had told me, but maybe it could knock his ego down a few.

He pressed his thin lips together and smiled. "You're here because I'm humoring you. I've got a sniper trained on your head right now. None of you are walking out of this alive. I just wanted you to see what love gets you in this world, in the real world. Death. You can escape love, but you can't escape death. Not here. Not anywhere. And not right now."

This wouldn't be our fate.

"And neither can you," I said, pulling the trigger.

It all happened so fast and so terrible.

The bullet went straight into Travis's forehead, but not before he had the chance to pull the trigger on his own gun. My mother leaned to the side in anticipation and the bullet ended up striking her neck instead of her head. I immediately dropped to the ground as the sniper's bullets came out, Camden doing the same. I rolled over, getting as close to him as possible, not even feeling my leg anymore, and aimed in the direction of the bullets.

There were two men on the roof now. One with the gun. The other going behind him and snapping the man's neck with a quick twist of his hands.

The man fell down dead. The other man waved at us, just once, then started running down the roof until he was able to slip inside an open window on the second floor.

Derek.

"Ellie," Camden said, crawling to me, taking me into his arms. "Are you okay?"

I shook my head, words not coming, and immediately tried to get to my feet. I fell back down and then crawled over to my mother, who was lying on the ground, making gurgling sounds from her throat.

"Mommy," I whimpered, trying to turn her over. Blood poured freely from the hole in the crook of her neck, soaking my hands. She was still breathing, weak and shallow. Her brown eyes blinked at the sun, then slowly looked over at me, softening when she saw my face.

I couldn't stop the tears. I bawled, chest burning for

air, and she reached for my hand and held it as strongly as she could. "I'm sorry," I gasped. "I'm so sorry."

"Ellie, sweetheart," she tried to say, but could only cough.

"I am so sorry," I cried again, shaking uncontrollably. "I love you, Mommy, and I'm sorry, I'm so sorry I did this."

She shook her head slightly. "You did nothing wrong," she croaked, her lips turning white. "I'm sorry. For everything I did to *you*."

Her lungs wheezed and she coughed again and I could feel Camden crouched beside me, a hand on my arm. He was going to tell me to go, that we had to leave, but I couldn't leave her here, not dying like this.

She swallowed, a stream of blood coming out of the side of her mouth. "I love you, Ellie. Remember that."

In that moment I forgave her for everything. I only hoped she could forgive me. And that I could forgive myself.

And then, as I kissed her forehead, I heard her take in her last breath of air. My tears spilled onto her head and I slowly pulled away. She was lifeless, frozen, hopefully taken away somewhere where she could finally find happiness.

"Ellie," Camden said softly, sticking his shoulder under my arm and pulling me up to my feet. "The game is still in play, and you're shot. We have to get out of here."

My heart was a stone, a brick, a mountain, weighing me to the ground. I looked at my mom, then over at the pool house, and I wondered how things went so wrong, so fast. She and Javier weren't the constants in my life and they weren't the good, but at least they weren't *always* the bad. Like me, they were gray and they shaded every step I'd taken.

I moved like I was in a dream, the pain in my leg overshadowed by my sorrow. Camden helped me limp a few steps before he bent down and scooped me up into his arms, instructing me to put my hands around his neck. He ran forward, but I stared backward until the bodies were farther away.

"You two okay?" Derek's voice broke through.

Camden stopped and I raised my head to look. Derek was standing at the corner of the house, a large gash across his face but otherwise all right. I wasn't sure if we could trust him, but he did just take out the sniper for us. Then again, he was wearing a bulletproof vest.

"She's been shot," Camden said, his voice on the verge of panicking. "In her leg."

Derek gave it a quick glance and then looked at us gravely. In his vest, ammo, and weapons, piercing blue eyes and shaved head, he looked like he was in his element. Nothing fazed him. This was routine.

"I can help you," he said. "If you pay me."

"What?" Camden exclaimed and his grip around me tightened.

Derek was motionless. "I know where Gus is. I needed to know how much he meant to you, what you are willing to give, Ellie. I can take you to him. I can fix you. But you have to name your price."

"Fifty thousand," I said, knowing how much Javier

had given Camden for me. I was sure, even in death, Javier wouldn't mind if it went to save my life. "Give or take."

"I'll give you a break and let's call it thirty," Derek said. "It's still more than what Javier paid me to stick around and help take over this place."

The words were stuck in my throat but they managed to come out. "He's shot, you know. He's in the pool house."

He nodded. "I saw. I took out the original sniper as well. But whether he's alive or dead, he owns the Zetas now and they're coming. I did my job for him, now I want out."

"And how are we getting out of here?" Camden asked.

The tiniest hint of a smile appeared on Derek's lips. "I learned to fly a few choppers in Afghany."

He jerked his head toward the landing pad.

"Shouldn't we...shouldn't we make sure Javier is okay?" I asked, knowing it wasn't the popular opinion.

Derek shook his head. "We don't have time. You have no idea what that man is capable of, do you?"

"She knows," Camden said quickly. "She just has a big heart."

"A big heart will get you killed. If Javier's alive, he's at the top of the food chain now. And we're all just chum."

I let that sink in and tried to forget the guilt. He had left me behind to die. I would have to try and do the same to him. And hope that if he did pull through, that he wouldn't come after me again.

Soon we were in the helicopter, Derek at the controls, Camden beside me in the back, ripping open a first aid kit for pain medicine. I stared out the window as we rose from the ground and took off toward the horizon. We left my past—my broken and sometimes beautiful past—behind us.

CHAPTER FOURTEEN

"ELLIE, WE'RE HERE."

I moaned and opened my eyes and saw a repeating shadow crossing above my head. Chopper blades. I had that one sweet moment between sleep and waking when you think everything is fine.

Then I was slammed with unbearable pain. In my leg, where the bullet went in. And in my heart, where my mom and possibly Javier had died. Grief for people who perhaps didn't deserve grief but I was drowning in it all the same.

Camden was at my side, gently pressing his lips to my cheekbone.

I reached out and grabbed his strong face, needing to feel him, that he was here, alive. I had him. He had me.

"Where are we?" I whispered, my voice dry.

He put his arm under my shoulder and gently lifted me up. He quickly unscrewed a bottle of water and poured some of it in my parched mouth. I was sitting in a field right beside the chopper. In the distance was the barn we had parked at and the black Escalade was coming out of it.

"It's just Derek," Camden explained. "We're getting you to a doctor and then we're getting Gus."

"We have to get Gus first," I said, grabbing his collar.

He gave me a steady gaze. "No, Ellie. Derek says Gus is safe. You can't save him if you're dead, and I don't want you losing that pretty leg of yours either. It would be a shame to lose such art."

"But who knows how much longer he'll be safe?"

"Ellie," he said sadly. "I couldn't save your mom, even though I tried. Travis found us before I could even get a few rounds off. But I can save you. I will save you. I promised I'd keep you safe, even at the expense of Gus. You've been shot. You're lucky to be alive and I'll do everything in me to keep you alive. No ifs, ands, or buts."

Derek pulled up to us and leaped out of the driver's seat, quickly ushering us into the back of the car.

"Why can't we take the helicopter?" I asked as Camden lay me down in the back. My jeans had been torn off at the knees and mounds of bandages had been wrapped around my calf.

"Out of gas," Derek said as he got back in the driver's seat. "And the Zetas would be coming by copter anyway. This is safer."

He drove that Escalade like a rally driver, bounding us from rough road to rough road, and after a few precarious turns on mountainsides I wondered how much safer it could be.

The pain was slowly growing worse too, to the point where I had a death grip on Camden's hand, body covered in sweat. It felt like my leg was on fire and stabbed with a million knives at the same time. It was all encompassing and all consuming.

"How much longer?" Camden asked Derek.

"An hour," Derek said. "Tops. I know a doctor right before the border into Guatemala."

"Hold on, baby," Camden said, squeezing my hand. "I've got you."

Even Camden couldn't save me from my agony. My eyes rolled back into my head and I tried to divert my attention from my leg. Questions. Painful questions. I had a lot of them. I had time to ask them.

"Derek," I choked out. "If we're paying you for all this, questions are included, right?"

Silence. Then, "Yes. What do you want to know?"

"My mother. The truth. What happened to her? How did she end up married to Travis?"

"She wasn't married. That's not how Javier put it."

Of course *he* had known.

He went on. "Javier recruited your parents to work for him right after Travis went and switched sides. I heard from different sources that it was so Javier could have closer ties to you. But I heard from Javier it's because they wanted revenge on Travis. They'd stopped conning at this point and had their hands in a whole bunch of work from the cartels already, so it was not a big career change for them. Then one day they left and Javier tracked them down to Veracruz. To Travis. He was angry. That's where you came in."

"His angel of death, six years in the making," I muttered, then groaned as another wave of pain went through me. "Why not kill them all with one blow?"

"To his credit, Javier seemed shocked when he learned you were going to Travis's house back in Veracruz," Camden spoke up, surprising me. "I don't think he meant for you to kill them all."

"What does it matter?" I snapped. "I was being used, just like I was used here. Javier got his way, he got his wish. Even if he's dead, he's still won. My mother is dead. And so is Travis. And *I* killed them both." The tears teased me again, moisture swelling in my throat, but I refused to give in. I ground my teeth until my jaw was sore. "I was the fool who did as he asked."

"Don't say that," Camden said. "You didn't have a choice and you know it. You can grieve for your mother, but I will not let you punish yourself for this. You don't deserve this burden. None of us deserve what went on in there."

The memory of the man dying by Camden's hand filled my head, and I remembered I wasn't the only one who lost a piece of myself back in the jungle.

"Then why would my parents go to work for Travis? What happened then?" I asked, wanting the distraction.

I saw Derek shrug. "I don't know."

My mother had told me it was revenge. For me. I wanted to believe that now, though it didn't make things hurt any less.

"And she never married Travis. Travis took her in because he was obsessed with her. Killed your father, kept her as his own. *Kept her* is the key term that was thrown around a lot. I can't say what went on. I don't know all the facts, I only know what I read and what I've been told. I'm guessing it was something like Stockholm syndrome. If they were ever officially married, I never heard about it. I just know it was a fucked-up, messy situation."

I had my fair share of that. I held Camden's hand tighter again and hoped that the Watt cycle of being sucked into codependent, obsessive, and unhealthy relationships was finally over. As long as I had Camden, I had broken free of that. I wouldn't end up like her.

"Did you know that Gus was my real father?"

"I did," he answered simply. "Javier was supposed to tell you, it was part of the plan. But he held off at the last minute. Maybe he was afraid that when the time came and you found out that he'd tricked you after finding out the truth about Gus, you'd come after him. I guess he was right about that, wasn't he?"

Was he fucking ever.

"So what happens next?" Camden asked. "After we get Ellie fixed up and get Gus. What happens to us? And to you? How do we know you won't kill us or come after us?"

Derek eyed him in the rearview mirror. "Because so far, that's not my job. And, believe it or not, it wouldn't become my job. I like you two. I fucking hate dealing with the cartels, and yes, I do it for a living, but some jobs are better than others. I take what interests me and that's it. I want you to get to Gus and I want you to get home to California. Then I want to take a nice long week of drinking and fucking tourists on a beautiful beach." He paused and scrunched up his brows. "I will say this to you, man, Camden. When we took off in the jungle that morning, I was certain we were only leaving Ellie behind. Javier wanted to take you with him. I told him not to, that it would slow down our operation. So he left you behind. He didn't want to."

"Of course," Camden scoffed. "He wanted to off me somewhere."

"No," Derek told us. "That wasn't it. We all had specific instructions to keep both you and Ellie safe. But the emphasis was placed on you, Camden. You were the priority."

I coughed at the tickle in my throat and threw a bewildered look to Camden. "What the hell does that mean?"

"I have no idea, honestly," Derek said. "But that's what we were told. There were too many other things to question than to focus on that."

Camden looked at me, lips pursed, and I could tell he had no clue either.

*   *   *

The next couple of hours were a blur. Instead of some farmhouse like the one where Javier had taken Violetta, Derek drove me to an honest-to-god medical clinic. It was after hours, of course, since gunshot wounds attracted at least some attention, but the woman who ran the clinic was quick, silent, and efficient. And by efficient, I mean she pumped me full of drugs until I couldn't tell what was up and what was down. Not quite morphine, but something that made me stop wanting to chop off my leg.

She had no problems pulling out the bullet; at least it didn't seem that way in my drugged-up head, and she said I was lucky it didn't strike an artery. She gave Camden the medication, painkillers, and antibiotics to fight infection, wrapped me up, and I was somewhat good to go. Derek handed her a handsome wad of American bills for her effort.

"So," Camden said as they put me back in the Escalade. "Now we've all been shot. You, me, Gus. Quite the team, right?"

I jerked my head. "We'll be a team once we see him again. Derek, that's our next stop."

"Yes, ma'am," he said, seeming to lighten up a bit. "Back to Mexico you go."

We drove through the night, passing through the Guatemalan and Mexican borders with ease. Now that my leg was fixed, we weren't attracting any suspicion. Just three gringos with Mexican plates. And even if they did search the car and found the guns and ammo we still had in here, Derek was ready to bribe them. Or take them out. Whichever came first.

Derek had told us that Javier kept Gus in the city of Oaxaca, a place we had already driven through on our way to Guatemala and Honduras. That fact made me rage inside, pushing away the euphoria that the drugs had laced my brain with. All this time I was wrong. All this time I was being led like a puppet on a barbed wire by Javier, and Gus was alone somewhere, hurt, wondering if we'd ever come for him. We had been so close, so damn close, and I had believed Javier. I fell for his lies time and time again.

At least I wouldn't fall for them anymore. My chest choked up with feelings of sorrow and fear. I didn't know if I could ever find peace knowing he was alive. I didn't know if I could ever be relieved knowing he was dead. There I was, still caught on the drifting cobwebs of the past.

It was the middle of the night when Derek pulled the Escalade into the suburbs of the city. Despite taking another dose of painkillers, I was wide awake, anxious to see Gus.

"I don't understand why they even have Gus, though," I mused darkly. "Like, not that I wanted this to happen, obviously, but why didn't Javier just kill him? He must have told you why?"

"I don't know," Derek said. "Perhaps he had some affection for him. Or maybe if you thought Gus was dead, you wouldn't go with Javier."

"Oh, please," I said in disgust. "Like I would have anyway."

"Javier is used to getting what he wants," he explained. "I think in the end, he still wanted you."

Camden stiffened, and I put my hand on his knee to comfort him. We road in silence for a few moments, and I did my best not to dwell on Javier, how he could both still want me and be someone who would leave me behind to die.

How the hell did his love for me get so fucked up?

"Are you sure they'll let Gus go willingly?" I asked Derek, shaking memories out of my head. "I mean, you're not the one running this show."

He eyed me over his shoulder and gave me a

handsome smirk. "Who said anything about willingly? We're taking him whether they let us or not."

Oh great. Another one of these.

"Obviously you're staying in the car," Camden filled in beside me, stifling a yawn. "You're not going anywhere on that leg."

I cocked my head at him. "Oh really?"

His eyes were serious in the darkness of the car. "Really. Ellie. You need to stay safe. I'll get your father back."

Father.

My heart warmed.

And filled me with determination. I wasn't letting the men do this without me. Gus had come for me, now I was going for him. After everything I'd been through, I wasn't leaving without him, the only family I truly had left.

We stopped on a quiet, wide road in the suburbs and Derek turned off the lights and the engine. He nodded at a house in the distance that had a few garbage cans knocked over in the front yard and a real estate sign. "That's the one. It's usually a stash house. Guess they're stashing people there now too."

He turned around in his seat and looked at Camden. "What guns do you have?"

"None. I had to drop mine back at the compound."

Derek jerked his head to the back of the car. "Come around back."

Camden put his hand on my shoulder and applied light pressure. "Stay here, Ellie. Please."

I couldn't promise him anything. I just watched as

he got out of the car and went to the back. The trunk
opened and Derek started going through the guns
that the team had left behind before we went traipsing
through the jungle. I watched them with curiosity as
Derek handed Camden a shiny new 9mm and picked
up a sawed-off shotgun for himself, his eyes glinting
feverishly at the weapon in his hands. Derek was in his
element once again. I only hoped it was enough to get
Gus out of there in one piece.

Derek and Camden both shot me one last look
before they closed the trunk.

"Be right back," Derek said. Then they ran off
toward the house, their feet quiet on the street.

I waited a few moments, watching them as they split
up and disappeared around the back of the house. In
my emotional, drug-infused state there was something
supremely romantic about the sight of Camden running
off with a gun to save my father.

I still couldn't believe it. Gus was my father. I had
to say it to myself again and again. It's not that it didn't
feel true; it's just that I had a hard time wrapping my
head around what family meant.

Which, of course, is why I reached into the back and
searched for a pistol until my hand closed around a .40
Glock. Gus and Camden were my family now, and I
had to protect them.

I opened the car door and climbed out, careful not to
put any pressure on my bad leg, and limped as swiftly
and silently toward the house as I could.

I turned at the neighbor's yard and hid behind one
of the lemon trees, peering around the trunk at the

stash house. The lights in the house were all off, and I couldn't hear anything, not Camden or Derek, not Spanish. Just the sound of the breeze as it ruffled the leaves around me.

I took in a deep but shaky breath. The pain in my leg was starting to flare up again, and I needed to push past it. I looked up at the second story of the house. Climbing was out of the question. Almost everything was out of the question with my injury.

That was until a light upstairs went on, streaming out the window between the cracks of a blackout curtain—in a stash house, its purpose wasn't to keep out the sun, but to keep eyes from looking in. That's where Gus had to be.

Before I could even formulate a plan or try and figure out how far Camden and Derek had gotten, voices rang out into the humid night air.

Yelling.

Spanish and English.

Camden.

The curtain at the window moved.

Shots were fired, echoing down the street.

It was all happening so fast.

I jumped away from the tree, wincing at my leg, just as there was a terrific crash and a man fell from the window in a shower of glass onto the lawn below, landing with a thud.

Gus.

It was Gus.

I gasped, heart lodged at the back of my throat, and scampered over to him as quick as I could. Just before I reached him, I looked up at the window and saw a man with a gun pointed at him.

Not Camden. Not Derek.

And therefore he had to die.

I aimed just as the man spotted me and fired three times.

One of the bullets struck him in the chest, causing him to pitch back into the room.

I dropped to my good knee and rolled Gus over, holding my breath, holding on to every second that passed for fear of the next one.

He rolled onto his back. His eyes opened. I hadn't seen those eyes in years.

He blinked once. Twice. Looked at me, face scrunched up, all beard and gray hair and friendly eyes.

"Ellie?"

"Gus!" I exclaimed.

He tried to sit up and then looked past me, his expression of terror. "Ellie!"

I twisted at the waist, gun out, and was about to shoot without even lining up.

I was lucky I didn't.

I would have shot Camden, who was running up the side of the house toward me, weaponless.

He at least saw me and my gun clearly enough to drop to the ground and duck.

Leaving the man chasing him an easy target.

With Camden on the ground, I pulled the trigger and hit the man at the knees, bringing him down. He struggled, reaching for the gun that he'd dropped, but I shot him in the head before he could even move.

I hated how easy this had become for me.

But then Camden lifted his head and gave me an incredulous look that said it all. That took my soul from black to gray.

"I promised to keep you safe, too," I told him earnestly.

I turned back to Gus as Camden pulled me up to my feet. "Are you hurt?"

"Oh, I'm hurt," Gus said, grunting as Camden pulled him up next. "But I'll live."

"Where's Derek?" I asked.

Camden shook his head. "I don't know. We have to go back to the car, now."

I looked back at the house and still heard yelling inside, the breaking of glass. There was still chaos. Still a fight and someone was losing.

"We can't leave him behind."

"Ellie," Camden said, sharp enough to make my head snap to him. "We have Gus. We have each other. We can't lose that. We have to go."

He was right. He was always right.

We took off running toward the Escalade, Camden supporting both me and Gus the best he could. Gus was bent over, the fall probably reopening the bullet wound in his stomach, wheezing for breath. It was so weird being with him now, knowing what he was to me. Did he know himself? I thought back to all our interactions over the years, the way he talked to me, kept in contact with me, watched over me. He must have known. All this time.

We got Gus in the back and I climbed in the front,

just as Camden got behind the wheel and started to peel away. We drove past the house, an explosion now blasting open the front door in a mess of flames, and it wasn't until we were zooming halfway down the street that Camden's eyes went to the rearview mirror.

"Shit," he said.

As I turned to look, he popped the SUV in reverse and we started speeding backward toward a man running toward us, hell-bent, Tom Cruise–style.

Derek.

Camden screeched to a stop just before he collided into him, and I leaned back to open the back door for him.

"Thanks," he said as he jumped in beside Gus. His face was covered in a layer of soot, the gash on his face reopened, and he smiled, widely, for the first time. "That was a rush."

Camden shook his head and pressed his foot to the pedal. We roared away from the fire and destruction, and though Gus was hurt and I'd been shot and Camden was missing his son, it felt good to have all three of them. They were my family. They were my home. And we were going to California.

CHAPTER FIFTEEN

WE ENDED UP saying goodbye to Derek in Acapulco. Even though we felt a camaraderie with him after everything we went through, he still wanted his money. All the money we had was still in checks that we hadn't cashed yet, so we had to promise him an IOU through monthly PayPal installments. The funny part was that he trusted us to do so, and I knew I would make good on my promise. Maybe I'd picked a lot of locks in the last few days, but the scamming days were truly gone for me. I had the second chance I'd asked for.

After we dropped him off—and after he bought us all clean clothes from a local Walmart—we continued on with the Escalade to Zihuatanejo, a beach town that Gus had always wanted to go to because Morgan Freeman ended up there at the end of *The Shawshank Redemption*. I'd put fake plates on the Escalade back in Acapulco, knowing now that I could never ever be too careful again, though we planned to steal a new car once we were heading up to California. For now, we needed to catch our breaths and take stock of the fact that we were still alive.

The three of us were sitting on the patio of a restaurant that lined the silky sand beach, enjoying gigantic margaritas, when Camden got up to go to the washroom.

"So, Ellie," Gus said, sitting back in his chair with controlled movement. In the end, his gunshot wound was healing nicely. For whatever reason, Javier hadn't mistreated Gus. After he'd been shot by Raul and after Camden came running for me, Javier took Gus immediately to a doctor who removed the bullet and stitched him up. Then Gus was knocked up full of roofies—Javier's drug of choice, it seemed—and the next thing he remembered was waking up in the stash house where he was guarded by three formidable men and two idiots, according to him. He wasn't allowed to leave the bedroom upstairs and was tethered to the first half of the room by a chain around his leg, thus not allowing him to reach the windows. He was permitted bathroom breaks, though, and he could watch TV and eat whatever food the rest of his captors ate. He was more comfortable than I thought he would have been, certainly more than my mother had been. If that was the way Javier treated the people he captured, he had shown he wasn't as much of an animal as Travis was.

Of course, he'd shown he was an animal in so many other ways.

"So, Gus," I said, pulling my shades up so I could look him in the eye, even though the sun was setting, causing the ocean to refract in beams of light.

He gave me a smile that could only be described as shy. And Gus was not a shy man. Suddenly I realized why Camden had excused himself with a knowing look on his face. Gus and I had not discussed what I'd learned yet. But I had a feeling it was about to come up.

It made me feel as awkward as a child. I rubbed my hands on my linen pants and smiled back.

He scratched at his beard and said, "I think you and I have something to ... talk about."

I nodded, waiting.

"I know what your mother told you back at ... back where you saw her."

Oh god. Don't tell me he *wasn't* my father.

"She said that I'm your dad," he went on. He picked up a chip from the tortilla basket and started spinning it around on the tablecloth. "That we had an affair before you were born." He looked up at me, his eyes sad.

Oh, please no. Please don't take this away from me.

"I loved your mother very much, Ellie," Gus said. "I loved your father too. I never really understood how I could do that to my friend, but I did. And your mother stayed on my mind ever since. I was still allowed to see you from time to time. You remember me around. But I could never be your father. I hope I can be now."

I exhaled, smiling so wide that my face hurt. "You really are my father."

"There was even a paternity test. Your father knew, of course. He was a good man, Ellie, he really was. And I regret what I did, but I don't regret the consequences."

"You sound a lot like Camden there."

He nodded, eyes squinting appreciatively. "Camden

is a good man too. That boy, he's so in love with you that he can't even see straight. I can't even begin to tell you how hard he fought to get you back. He never gave up, even when he was knocked down. You were the most important thing in the world to him. You still are. I hope you can give your heart to him. I know how hard that is for you, to trust, to let go."

I gave him a reassuring smile, his words about Camden inflating me with joy. "He has my heart. He knows it. At least I hope he does. I'll keep giving it anyway. I love him."

I want to spend my whole life with him. I want to marry him, I thought. But of course I didn't say that.

He gave me a quick grin and stuffed a chip in his face, talking with his mouth full. "Good. That's what I wanted to hear. The boy drove me nuts for most of the trip, to be honest. He just wouldn't shut up about you. But he has moxie and I like that. You're both perfect for each other. And if he ever wants to become my son-in-law . . ." He trailed off and looked over my shoulder. "Perhaps I should shut my big mouth now." And in went another chip.

I turned in my seat to see Camden coming toward me. My god, he was absolutely beautiful, knee-length cargo shorts, a wife-beater that showed off his muscles and colorful art, from wrist to collarbone. He still had a bandage over his gunshot wound on the shoulder and his face was marred by a few healing gashes, but that only made him look more manly. That man would kill for me. He would die for me. And he would fuck me to death if I asked him.

I was tempted. What a way to go.

He stopped above us and smiled, dimples and white teeth illuminating his face in the setting sun. "I'm not interrupting anything, am I?"

I shook my head, eager for him to join us, especially after I knew that Gus approved of him. I mean, how couldn't he? This was a man I wanted to spend the rest of my life trying to make happy, trying to give him the life he deserved for the kind of good person he was.

Which is why I had to bring up a more serious topic, one we hadn't discussed yet.

"So, what's the plan after this?" I broached it slowly as Camden sat back down beside me. "How do we get back Ben?"

Camden straightened up at the mention of his son's name, his fingers gripping the end of the armrests. He bit his lip, brows drawn together, and cast a furtive glance at Gus. Then he said, "I don't know yet."

Gus tilted his head sympathetically. "You're still a wanted criminal in the USA. Maybe not as wanted as you were before. It's probably all blown over. But if you're ever caught by the police for something, you'll be in big shit. If you're ever recognized by anyone, you're in big shit. If Sophia ever sees you again…"

"I'm in big shit," Camden filled in.

"Or you're dead." Gus rested his elbows on the table and clasped his hands together. "So we have to do what we can to avoid that. You know this will be the hardest part, even harder than getting Ellie back. Sophia won't give you Ben. You'll never be able to get custody. You'll never be able to see him. You'll never get visitation rights. It's either you take him from her or leave him with her. There is no in between here."

"No gray," I whispered, a sinking feeling in my chest.

"That's right," Gus said. "No gray. These aren't the choices you'll want to make, but you'll have to make them. Can you go on your way and let Sophia have him?"

"No!" Camden cried out, attracting a few looks from the patrons around us. He quickly shot them a sheepish look and then lowered his voice, shaking his head. "No. I can't. She wasn't a very good mother before. That's when all our problems started. When she was on drugs and never at home. Now I know she's involved with her brothers. She's part of that gang. Fuck, she used Ben, her son, *our* son, to lure me in, to get money, to hand me over to her brothers. They were going to kill me, in front of him if they could. It's made me sick every time I think about where he is right now and what he's doing. I can't let him grow up in that life. I won't let that happen."

"Then you've made your choice," Gus told him solemnly. "If you can't let him stay with her, if you can't say goodbye to him, then you must take him. And we will help you. You can't do this on your own."

Camden put his head in his hands, his knee bouncing up and down.

"Baby," I said softly, and put my hand on his jumping knee. "You're not doing this alone. Even if it seems impossible, even if it doesn't feel like a choice you want to make, you have to do this if you want him back. Ben deserves to be with you, Camden. Someone with a big heart, a father who will do anything for his child. That's what you are. You have that in you to give, and Ben is a lucky boy that you're his dad. You're giving him the future he needs."

Camden turned his head to the side, glancing at me with damp eyes. "And you're the future I need."

I leaned over and kissed him, sweetly, slowly, then blushed once Gus cleared his throat, reminding us he was there.

I pulled back, smiling to myself, and had a good long sip of the margarita, gazing out at the ocean. I wondered if Camden still wanted to go to Gualala, that beach town he dreamed of, his personal paradise. I wondered if I was his future, if that's where we could build a home, build a life. Me, him, and Ben. Gus too. And maybe, just maybe, a child of our own.

I was getting ahead of myself—wasn't I?—and Camden sighed, bringing my focus back to the problem at hand. If Ben was in our future, how did we get him?

"It's just that kidnapping a child," Camden murmured, voice barely audible, "I can't imagine how I'd live with that."

"You're doing it for the right reasons," I said. "That's how."

His knee started bouncing again. "But how do we pull it off without hurting Ben?"

That was the problem. I licked the salt off my lips and sat back in my chair, thinking. "Ben knows you're his father. Right?" He nodded. I went on, "He trusts you, then. He's young. Kids are impressionable. I couldn't tell you the things that were probably done to me when I was young, the ways I was used for bait, to con people, to steal, and I don't even remember."

"It won't be easy, but Ellie's right," Gus said. "Obviously we don't want to make a scene or do anything that would endanger or mentally damage the boy. But I think if we take him, in the right way, and if you can find a way to face your guilt that I have no doubt you'll feel for some time, he can grow up with no damage. He'll be resilient. And he'll have the life he needs."

Camden looked up, face newly determined. "So when do we do this?"

Gus scratched at his mustache. "We find Sophia. We stake out her place. We start planning our moves. The three of us, we can do this together. We can do it quickly. No fuss. In and out. It might take a few weeks for everything to roll into place."

"We don't have a few weeks," Camden moaned.

"Camden," Gus said sternly. "You have a few weeks. A few weeks is nothing compared to a lifetime of being together—or not being together. My god, you and Ellie are both as impatient as Chihuahuas. No wonder you belong together."

Camden and I exchanged a coy look. We did belong together. We all did.

*   *   *

Once dinner was over, we made our way back to the small hotel where we were staying, right on the beach. Gus retired to his room, said he wanted to continue watching this Telemundo show he got hooked on when he was being held hostage, and Camden grabbed my hand, leading me to the sand and crashing waves. The moon was in a perfect quarter, its reflection shining on the black-blue water.

He brought me to the ocean's edge and stood behind me, wrapping his warm arms around me.

"I love you," he whispered in my ear. "Every minute that goes by, you fill my heart. I don't know what I'd do without you, Ellie. I've been so close to losing you."

I gripped his hands over my stomach and leaned back into him, my head settling into the crook of his arms, and let that beautifully light feeling sink into me. "I love you. You have me. I think, deep down, you always did, even when I didn't know it."

We stood like that for quite some time, our feet in the cool, soft sand, just watching the waves crash, the stars shining, the moon so far, so close, so constant. Every night it appeared, no matter where in the world we were, even hidden by clouds, it was still there.

"You're my moon," I said quietly.

"Then you're my earth."

He turned me around, ever so mindful of my leg, and kissed me deeply. It was a kiss that reached right into you, stirred you around until you were effervescent and sparkling and deliriously happy. It was soft, warm lips and silken, skilled tongue. It made you hungry and thirsty and longing for more, for it to go on forever, satisfying yet insatiable. It turned me on, flipped the switch, awakened the passion that wouldn't stop until we could fully devour each other. It was a kiss of the earth and the moon, all gravity and pull, a prelude to many forevers.

I don't know how long we made out like that, just feeding from the love and the lust that we could only consume from each other, me surrendering in his arms, his arms that kept me close and kept me safe. Finally he pulled away and rubbed his thumb over my lips.

"I'd suggest sex on the beach," he said, his voice husky, my mouth feeling empty without his. "But I think the two of us deserve a bed for once."

That, and sex on the beach was highly overrated.

He bent down and picked me up in his arms. I let out a small laugh, wrapping my arms around his neck and burying my face below his ear. I breathed in his smell, absolutely intoxicating, and let him carry me all the way to our hotel room, where he laid me down on the white, shabby-chic bedspread.

This was the first time we'd really been alone, been intimate, since we left the compound. I had something to tell him, but I wasn't quite sure how to phrase it. I loved him beyond all doubt, and I knew the man loved me. I knew we were the moon and the earth and each other's future, revolving and evolving. But I was still scared to tell him what I knew, tell him what I wanted.

He bent over me, hands at the drawstring on my pants, but I pushed him back, hand on his chest, and said, "I'm always getting naked first. Drop your clothes."

Camden grinned wickedly and I bit my lip in anticipation, leaning back on my elbows to watch.

He took off his wife-beater first, the tats on his six-pack and chest now on full display, then slowly started to unbutton his shorts.

"Are you doing a striptease?" I asked playfully.

"I'm stripping and I'm teasing," he answered as he very deliberately pulled the zipper down before looping his thumbs around the waistband and inching them off. Bit by bit, until the ink faded into the hard Vs of hip bones, and I saw the hard, glistening tip of his erection appear, flush to his pelvis.

He let the shorts drop and he took my breath away.

"Derek never got me any briefs," he explained, as if I cared that he was going commando. Fuck me, he was a man who would never stop giving me the chills. I'd never seen a cock so large and beautiful as the one on Camden McQueen. My man. My moon. My everything.

He slowly walked toward the bed, growing larger as he came closer, so tall, so strong, so ready for me. His eyes held assurance and lust, drive and desire. He knew what he looked like, he knew what he was offering me, his perfect body and his perfect soul.

"When I saw you I fell in love," he said to me as I lay back against the bed and he crawled on top of me on all fours. "And you smiled because you knew."

I grinned lazily as he bent down and slowly kissed along my neck. "Quoting Shakespeare, now?"

"If only Juliet had been a scowly-faced teenager," he murmured against my neck. "Because while I'm pretty sure you knew I loved you, I don't think it made you smile."

I jerked my head away from him and held his face in my hands. "Camden. You always made me smile, even when I didn't show it. You were my only friend, and I was too young to know what your heart was worth."

"And you know now."

I ran my hands through his thick hair. "I knew then, now and always." I pulled his face to mine and kissed him softly before looking deep and hard into his eyes, trying to figure out how to say this. "Camden... I was on the pill until, well, until we left Veracruz. I've only been with you since."

He frowned, a look of wonderment and fear in his eyes. "Are you pregnant?"

I shook my head. "No. I don't think so. I'm just..." I chewed on my lip. "I'm just thinking... I don't want to go back on them." There. I said it. The weight of it all hung in the room.

He blinked, his dark brow still furrowed, and suddenly I was unbearably frightened that I had scared him off. My heart felt like lead. This was all too fast for us, wasn't it?

"I'm sorry," I said quickly. "I—"

"You want a baby?" he asked gently. His face was softening, his eyes searching mine, pulling truth from me.

"I don't mean right now," I managed to say. "Or maybe I do. But yes. With you. I want a family of my own. To start new. To give us both what we never had."

"Oh, Ellie," he whispered. His face crumpled slightly and he brought it to my neck. He whispered into my ear, "Oh, Ellie. I will give you that. It's all I've ever wanted for us. It's all I've ever wanted."

And suddenly I was all love.

"Really?" I asked.

He looked at me, glassy eyed and grinning so wide, so amazing. "Really. A brother or sister for Ben." He swallowed loudly, taking a moment to contain himself.

"My beautiful Ellie, I want this. I want this. We need this."

He reached down and slowly unbuttoned my blouse until my breasts were bare and spread before him—he wasn't the only one going commando. He trailed his fingers over my flesh, goose bumps rising in his wake, and tugged lightly at my nipple ring. I groaned and arched my back, offering myself to him, needing more.

But he wasn't in a hurry, not tonight. He slowly made his way from my breasts to my abdomen, kissing and licking over my stomach, concentrating his mouth there as if willing his seed to be planted. He finished untying my pants and cautiously pulled them off, taking it slow around my leg.

"Does this hurt?" he whispered as he held my damaged leg in his hand, his eyes roaming all over my naked body.

I shook my head no. "Not right now."

He peered at the bandages. "Once these come off, once it heals, I'll make you beautiful again."

"You already made me beautiful, Camden," I whispered. "Now get your head between my legs."

His dimples appeared. "As you wish."

He parted my legs and started moving his mouth up my inner thigh until he was teasing my lips. Once his tongue found my clit, needy and full, he spent no time getting me off. I grabbed his hair, yanking on it with each wave of orgasm as he moaned into me, the vibrations bringing me to new heights.

When I was coming back down, he looked up at me with his glistening mouth and a devious glint in his eyes. "You know that's not how we're supposed to make a baby."

"Then show me."

He climbed back on top of me and pushed his stiff cock into me, entering slowly, very slowly.

Torturously slow.

"Camden," I whispered, my body bucking for him. "Faster."

"I'm in no rush," he purred. "I want to live in every inch of you."

He pushed in and out, silky smooth with just enough friction. I watched him as his wide chest overshadowed me, straining with each controlled movement. He looked up at the ceiling and groaned loudly as he pushed through, then looked down at me with heavy eyes, his mouth open in lust. His gaze undid me, so much passion and love, now more than ever.

He picked up the pace, wrapping one of his large hands around my waist while the other began stroking at my clit again. Each thrust became harder, deeper, until he was buried far inside of me. His breath hitched as he said, "I want to put a baby in you. I want this. Oh, I want this." He moaned again and I joined in, my nerves white-hot and begging for release. Blood was pooling deep in my core, the pressure building. This was lovemaking, baby-making, an act of creation and pure, raw, primal power.

We lapsed into a steady rhythm, the headboard slamming against the wall, the paintings rattling, sweat streaming off each other's bodies in the hot, tropical night. I was wet, so wet, and blossoming for him, driven by his mass, stretched by his fullness. I was fulfilled and yearning all at once, and I watched as his slick cock slid in and out of me, watched his whole body as he drove in deeper and deeper until I thought I was being staked to the bed.

"Oh fuck!" I cried out, taken by surprise and coming fast and hard. I dug my nails into the back of his shoulders, my hips rocking in unison with his.

He came too, floored by his orgasm, and I felt higher than the clouds as he poured his seed inside of me, my convulsions bringing it out of him and harboring it deep inside. He swore amidst his groans, his thrusts slowing down, until he lay down on top of me and kept himself inside me.

He brushed the hair off my face, gently running his fingers over my cheeks. He cleared his throat and smiled, sated, happy. "You know, if that didn't take, I am game for trying every day. Several times a day. On the hour."

I grinned and pressed him close to me. "Don't think I won't hold you to that. I'm addicted to you. I must have my fix."

"Is fix another term for cock?"

"It is for yours. You should have a warning label on that thing."

He let out a small laugh, his lips tickling my collarbone. "Eh, it'll probably rub off anyway from all the use."

I sighed contentedly and wrapped my arms around him. He made beautiful sense out of all the ugly things I had done.

We fell asleep like that.

CHAPTER SIXTEEN

IT WAS ALMOST sad when we finally bid *adiós* to Mexico. We ended up spending a few more days in the country, just lying on the beach and trying to get our lives back on track, to remember how to be real people in normal situations. The only problem was, the stint in Zihuatanejo was just a vacation, just a blip of normalcy before we had to delve back into things we didn't want to do.

None of us wanted to take Ben like that. If there was any other way, we would have done it. But Gus was right—either Camden would never see his son again or this was his only choice. And in any other mother's arms, Camden would have probably let that happen.

Not with Sophia.

And it was she who was on our lips as we drove up the country and back into California. The border officials were a little suspicious of the three of us, but our passports all went through with flying colors and when they searched our vehicle—thoroughly, I might add—they didn't find anything. We had ditched every weapon from the car in a gully outside of Tijuana. We were clean.

"So where's the first stop for our new lives?" I asked as we drove through San Diego. I felt so much safer being back in America, back on my home turf, but I wouldn't dare let myself relax. Not yet. "Do we need to be close to Sophia?"

"We need to find out if Sophia is still living where she was," Gus said from the front seat. "We can use my place as a home base. I have a friend with a house up the street from me who rents it out on a weekly basis." He looked over his shoulder at me. "Not that I don't want you two in my house, but you know, just having the one bedroom and all it might be a little awkward."

And loud, I thought as I felt the heat creeping on my cheeks. Just the other night someone in an adjacent room complained about how loud our sex had been. Loud *and* frequent. Damn prudes.

Camden winked at me in the mirror, and we drove on until we ended up at the beautiful enclave of Pismo Beach. After Gus set things up with his friend and the house, which was a bit too large for the two of us but at least was available, Camden and I headed to Target to stock up on all things wonderful and American. We had to get through the tough part first, but we were still at the start of our new lives together. I even paused at the baby section, picking up an adorable tiny T-shirt that said *The Cramps* on it.

"Look!" I exclaimed, shoving it in Camden's face. "Your favorite band."

He grinned and raised an eyebrow. "What if she's a girl?"

"Like hell our daughter wouldn't be a fucking rocker chick." I threw it in the basket. "I don't care if I'm jinxing it, we're buying it."

He pushed the cart along gleefully, and I was hit with a sudden wham of pain. Not for my leg—no, that was much better. I remembered what happened the last time I thought I was pregnant, all those years ago with Javier. I jinxed it then.

Even saying his name in my head put shivers down my spine and caused me to look around uneasily. Even though I had gotten prematurely excited with him, it wasn't going to stop me from getting excited with Camden. Camden gave me hope and I was hopeful. He gave me strength and I was strong. We would be together. This all would work out. After everything we'd been through, it had to.

"You okay, baby?" he asked me, putting his arm around my waist.

"I'm good. Just . . . wary, I guess."

He was acting a bit on edge too, constantly worrying that someone was going to recognize him. Ever since we had come back into the country and had done a quick search of papers and the Internet, the whole "Camden McQueen is wanted" thing was pretty much gone. There were far worse people out there to report, including rumors of cartels coming across the borders and the Mexican Drug War flaring up on American soil, fighting for possession of local gangs and marijuana growers. It was only a matter of time before the war would come north, the papers would report after a car exploded in San Diego the previous week. Funny how what we were experiencing south of the border was going on right here in our own backyards. Or at least the ghettos, as it seemed to be.

"I don't think that feeling will be going away anytime soon," he told me with a sigh. "But at least we're working on it, right?"

I nodded and leaned into him and we continued our shopping like any other twenty-something couple who were about to move in together for the first time would do.

When we got back to our furnished house—two stories overlooking the ocean *and* it had a lap pool—Gus came over, and we sat on the upper balcony with two of his computers and started mapping out the plan.

Our first step was to figure out where Sophia lived. The three of us would head into Silver Lake and see if she was still at her old apartment. If she was, that made our plan a lot simpler. If she wasn't, well then we had some digging to do.

"If she's still in the LA area," Gus said, typing in his computer, "we could at least find out where she works. She was still working as an esthetician, right, Camden?"

He shrugged with one shoulder. "As far as I know. She'd definitely have to be working. I think that was part of the reason why they tried to get the money from me. She wouldn't have to work anymore."

"That's if her brothers were even thinking of sharing the money with her." I pointed my pen at him as I jotted things down on my notepad. "You don't know how close she is with them, really, I mean how deep into the gang she goes. Is she just a pawn getting a small cut or does she have a larger stake in these things?"

He sighed and took off his glasses, rubbing the lens against his shoulder. He had found sexy nerd glasses at Target and had the prescription put into them in no time. He still looked hot as fuck to me—the glasses and tats were a delicious combination—but I did miss his eyes a bit.

"I honestly have no idea anymore," he said dejectedly, slipping his glasses back on. "Your guess is as good as mine."

I gave him a wistful look. "It doesn't matter. We'll find her if we can."

"And we just did," Gus announced triumphantly, turning the screen of his laptop to us so we could see. There was a spa in Burbank that said Sophia Madano worked there as one of the skin techs.

Gus picked up his cell phone and handed it to me. "Want to call and make an appointment? What's your name again?"

I took it from him and cleared my throat, not happy about being someone else again. "I can be Elizabeth Waters." I dialed the number on the screen and waited for it to pick up. A woman with a thick Asian accent answered. I asked to make an appointment tomorrow, saying I had a woman give me a facial once, pretty, tiny with long brown hair.

"That's Sophia," the woman on the phone said. "Tomorrow at two okay?"

"Perfect," I said, giving her my fake name. I hung

up, my chest crawling with nerves already. I gave the phone back to Gus and wiggled my hips. "I guess Elizabeth has a meeting with Sophia tomorrow. Hope she doesn't recognize me."

"Red wig, green contacts," Camden suggested. "I doubt she would, she only saw you from afar."

I let out a shaky breath and folded my hands on the table. "All right. Then what?"

"Talk to her, find out where she lives," Gus suggested.

"I might sound like a creeper."

"You're a con artist, Ellie," Gus said.

I frowned at that. "*Was.*"

He rolled his eyes and ran his fingers over the brackets that lined his mouth. "Regardless of whether you were or still are, you know what you're doing. Have some confidence in yourself, and for fuck's sake, stop beating yourself up over this shit. You've done all of this before. It doesn't make you a bad person and it doesn't make you a good person. Act the part, gather the intel, report back to us. We'll tail her, scope out the scene. Then move on to the second part of the plan."

It's too bad the first part of the plan relied entirely upon me. After everything I'd gone through, it was odd that I was suddenly so afraid of having to go through with this, something that was quite simple. I guess after so many close calls and being placed in the line of fire, I was scared to death that something would go wrong again and everything I'd gained would be taken away.

Later that evening we went for a drive, heading into LA and the area of Silver Lake looking for Sophia's old place. The apartment was occupied, and we spent a few hours outside of it doing surveillance. Camden had a hunch that Sophia wasn't there anymore because the window shades were a different color and there was a doormat outside the door that wasn't there before. His suspicion was confirmed when someone stepped outside to have a cigarette; an elderly man, stooped over. Seconds later an old woman came out and yelled at him to come back inside. Definitely not Sophia.

The next morning, I was frazzled, having tossed and turned all night. I wasn't even in the mood for morning sex. At first, anyway, but it's hard to say no to a cock belonging to 6'2" of toned muscle. I honestly didn't know how I was going to pull this off with Sophia. I had no problems lying to her and pretending to be a redhead called Elizabeth, but I knew I'd have problems with trying not to shank her.

We had rented a car for the occasion, under my fake name so it was ironically legit, and I drove out toward Burbank with Gus and Camden in their rental car not too far behind. I had a Mini Cooper because that's just how I rolled, while they opted for a Honda Civic, fast enough but nondescript. I pulled the Mini Cooper into the parking lot of a strip mall with a shitty-looking Chinese buffet next to the "spa," and spent longer than I should have sitting there and trying to control my breathing. I eyed myself in the mirror. The red wig I had on was real hair and fit me like a glove, flowing nicely over my shoulders. It didn't look sex-kitteny, it just looked normal, even up close. It was quite obvious I was wearing contacts though, but the natural green color worked well with my skin tone. I could pass for

Elizabeth, I could pass for Elizabeth, I could pass for Elizabeth.

I wasn't Ellie Watt.

I wouldn't kill Sophia.

I inhaled until my lungs felt like they were going to burst and got out of the car. I was wearing a black pantsuit, sleek and professional. I worked in accounting for an advertising firm. I had my fake business card in my Marc by Marc Jacobs bag we got from Nordstrom Rack. Elizabeth Waters. Single. Twenty-seven years old. Testing out a Mini because I wanted to buy one, but now was afraid the red color clashed with my hair. Loved getting my pores cleaned.

I wouldn't kill Sophia.

I gathered my courage and walked over to the door and strolled inside like this was my weekly treat. The bell rang overhead and I was met with unflattering fluorescent lighting and a woman at the counter who was snapping gum. It was a busy place, with the manicures and pedicures at the front, Vietnamese women attacking feet and hands while chatting with each other. The rest of the treatments seemed to be in the back in dentist-like chairs.

"Can I help you?" the girl at the counter asked, her hair looking like it had been dipped in Pepto-Bismol.

I tried to keep my voice down, not wanting Sophia to hear and see me before I saw her. "I've got a two P.M. appointment with Sophia."

The girl eyed the computer and nodded, snapping her gum again before yelling, "Sophia!" Then she pointed at the end of the room. "She's right there."

I slowly turned and looked. Sophia was walking toward me, a completely blasé look in her eyes. She looked tired but still pretty, a tiny woman with mad curves, her brown hair pulled back off her face so it showed off her aristocratic nose and red pouty lips. She barely smiled, barely acknowledged me.

Which was actually a good thing. But I was so close to grabbing her by the throat and asking if she knew who I was, if she knew what she'd done, if she realized how fucking screwed she was going to get.

I didn't, though. I just gave her a smile and said, "Hi, I'm Elizabeth," and extended my hand.

She looked at it, looked at me, gave me a nod and said, "Right this way."

Bitch.

I followed her over to the station and she instructed me to take off my suit jacket and put my bag on the ground. I lay back in the chair and she asked me what I wanted.

Oh, I had so many answers to that.

None were appropriate.

I told her I wanted my pores squeaky clean and to look fresh. I had a date on the weekend. With a really hot guy.

With glasses, covered in tattoos, I thought, *a real fucking work of art, a tortured soul with a heart of gold, who fucks like an animal and will love me till my dying day.*

I couldn't help but smile at my thoughts, at the truth, and, lo and behold, she smiled back.

"Hot guy?" she asked. "That sounds nice."

"Oh, I bet you have tons of hot guys," I said, my mouth snaking upward.

"Me?" she asked and then quickly rubbed the tip of her nose, sniffing. I bet she didn't have a cold. "No, most of the guys I go out with aren't very hot." She laughed awkwardly.

No, most drug dealers aren't very hot, I thought.

"Maybe it's the area," I tried, fishing for info. "Burbank. Too many actors."

"Oh, no, I live in Pasadena," she said. "Too many married men."

I smiled. "Well, that doesn't help."

"And they never leave their wives for me," she continued with a noncommittal shrug.

I kept smiling, thinking she was kidding. But she wasn't.

I had to play it cool.

I swallowed down my rage and took a deep breath.

"Nervous?" she asked me. She was more astute than I thought.

"Yeah, just thinking about the date," I said, covering up.

"What's the guy's name?"

Camden McQueen. Camden McQueen. Camden McQueen.

The words were dying to come out of my mouth, just to see the look on her face, but I reeled them in and said, "Derek."

Hey, why not.

"Hot name," she said, then she turned her back to me and started making preparations.

The thing I learned about Sophia over the next hour was that she never once mentioned her son, even when I started babbling to her about being single and wanting children and how was I going to balance working at the advertising firm with a child. She didn't offer anything about Ben.

Not until the end.

She was slapping moisturizer on my face, hurrying because I could tell her next client had arrived, and she said, "Well, I hope your date goes well this weekend."

"Thanks," I told her, swinging my legs over the side.

She picked up my bag from the ground and got my jacket from the hook. As I slipped the jacket on over my blouse, she gave me a dry smile and said, "Listen, about the kid thing. Don't bother. They always seem like a good idea at the time, but they'll fuck up your life."

I knew my jaw had dropped open. I couldn't help it.

She smiled coldly. "I'm serious. I wish someone had told me that back in the day. So enjoy your hot man. Just make sure you use a condom."

I closed my mouth and swallowed hard, feeling angry and flustered and shocked all at once.

She motioned for me to go to the counter and then waved over the next woman, someone who was obviously a regular. I walked over to the cashier in a daze.

Had she seriously just told me that?

That definitely didn't help sway my desire to shank her.

And it definitely made me more determined than ever to get Ben far, far away.

I paid for the treatment—leaving her a shitty tip that

had the clerk eyeing me like I was nuts—and then high-tailed it out of there. I got in the Mini Cooper and drove home, my hands kneading the steering wheel through miles and miles of heavy traffic. I knew Camden and Gus were waiting near the salon to tail her when she went home for the evening. I quickly gave them a call, relaying the information that I picked up, but left out that last part. Camden didn't need any more ammo, and if he did, well, then, I would give it to him. For now, he needed to keep his head clear and his emotions under control.

I got home, poured myself a glass of wine, and waited for my men to get home. Then I poured myself another glass of wine and waited some more.

Here's the thing about being alone.

You're not.

You have your demons with you.

Sitting in that house, the house that wasn't mine, with the furniture that wasn't mine, and the red wig splayed across the kitchen table, was the first time I'd been alone in what felt like a long time. There was the time in the jungle before I found Camden, but that was no time to reflect or think.

Now I truly was alone.

And it was terrifying.

Not only being in a large and still unfamiliar house with unfamiliar sounds.

And not only because I still had this undercurrent of paranoia at the back of my head, this feeling of dread that followed me around in this bright Californian sunshine.

But because I was alone with my thoughts.

Alone with my guilt.

Alone with the knowledge of the things I'd done.

The people I'd killed.

So many sins.

I put my head on the table and cried. I cried for my mother, for the father I knew and lost, for Violetta—I even cried for Javier. I cried for the men I shot, in self-defense or self-preservation. I cried for the people I'd stolen from, robbed, conned, lied to. I cried for a lifetime of justifying all my wrongdoings when I never really had an excuse. I cried for being so weak when I should have been strong. I cried for everyone who ever had to meet me.

Everyone except Travis.

For him I felt nothing at all, a stone where my heart should be.

I cried until Camden and Gus eventually came home and found me a blubbering, tear-streaked mess who'd drunk an entire bottle of wine. Camden picked me up in his arms and brought me to bed, where he stayed with me until morning.

Then the sun rose and his lips lightened my soul and his heart set me free.

And I was able to move on.

CHAPTER SEVENTEEN

WHILE I WAS busy having my pity-party at home, Camden and Gus had stayed out until just after Sophia's work closed. She got into a Prelude, newer model, and drove on the 134 until she got to Pasadena, Camden and Gus following her the whole time, two cars behind. From the way Camden described it the next morning, it was like old times with him and Gus in the car, only they weren't chasing me this time.

They said that Sophia lived in a small bungalow on the edge of a golf course, a much easier location to get in and out of than an apartment building, which was good, but she had quite a few neighbors and they were close to her, which could pose a bit of a problem. Camden got choked up when he mentioned Ben. He didn't see him, but he could see a few toys scattered in the front yard, solidifying his existence.

As much as Camden wanted to swoop in there and get his son back, patience was an unfortunate virtue. Gus wanted us to hold off for a few days while they basically stalked Sophia to get an idea of where she went and at what times and who had Ben when she wasn't around. The tighter the operation was, the less traumatic it would be for Ben.

It was on day three of their surveillance that they discovered the neighbor across the street took Ben to her house every other day, while Sophia placed him in daycare during the remaining days. The neighbor was an older woman in her late fifties who didn't appear to have children herself, but would take in a few other kids in the neighborhood, maybe for some extra money. An easier target than a daycare.

When they got home that day and we were lying in bed, I could tell that Camden was beating himself up about it and what they had to do.

"Would it make it easier if you knew that Sophia wasn't a good mother?" I asked, probing him for a hint.

He shook his head and leaned back into the pillows. "No. Not really. Because Ben is just a boy and a boy loves his mom. It doesn't matter how wicked the mother is, that's the only mother he knows. Ben will be crushed when we do this."

"And he'll eventually be crushed if you don't," I reminded him. "As will all of us."

I snuggled into him, kissing down his face, wanting to distract him. "Tell me about our dream life. Where we are. What we're doing. What you will be doing?"

He smiled and sighed and held me close. He knew I was trying to take his mind off of things and he didn't care. "Well, if we could I'd still like to go to Gualala. Though in reality we'd probably end up in Canada or something, because Sophia and her brothers will not take this lying down."

"It's a dream life, Camden. Gualala it is."

"Okay then. Gualala. I don't know if I'd be doing tattoos. Maybe I'd try my hand at painting or sculpture. I've always loved carving things out of driftwood. I could have an art shop. We'd have Ben and a boy or girl of our own, four years younger. Gus would be there too, with some lady love of his."

"And what am I doing?"

"You?" He eyed me appreciatively. "You'd just stand around and look pretty."

"And?"

"Give me blow jobs."

I punched him in the arm.

"What?" He laughed. "I know you love the cock."

"Shut up."

"Well then, you tell me," he said, looking serious and wiping a strand of hair from my face. "What do you want to be doing? If you could do anything."

The thing was, I'd never really thought about that. I was always just trying to survive and keep going, from one place to the next. I never had goals. I never had dreams. Not really.

I thought back to something I did enjoy once. Something that had put a rift between Camden and me all those years ago.

"I think I'd be a photographer," I told him. He raised his brows and I continued. "Of course, you were always better at that than I was." He bit his lip sheepishly and I knew he remembered the photos he had taken of me back in art class, for a project he called "Justification." It had humiliated me at the time, but now I realized that he was only telling the truth. And sometimes the truth fucking hurt.

"I think you would be good at that," he said. "You have a way of seeing people."

I traced my fingers across his chest, making swirls and waves. "I like the idea of giving hope. That you can capture the world in such a way that even the ugly things look beautiful."

The beauty in what was real.

He kissed my head and cleared his throat. "Now. About that blow job?"

I punched him again.

Then I gave him one.

Of course.

*   *   *

I woke up in the middle of the night with a light headache and my stomach grumbling. I hadn't really eaten anything for the last few days. I had been basically fasting when I was in the jungle, only eating when I had the chance and coasting by on adrenaline the rest of the time, so now that I was back in California and still a pile of nerves, my appetite was slow to come back.

But when it did come back, it was back with a vengeance. As I rolled out of bed, careful not to wake Camden, who was snoring lightly, I put my hand to my rumbling stomach and had a silly yet hopeful thought that perhaps I was already pregnant and this was my body telling me so.

I grabbed my robe and slipped it on, a cool ocean breeze coming in through the open windows and smelling of night-blooming jasmine, and made my way downstairs to the kitchen. I popped two pieces of toast in the toaster, poured myself a glass of water, and opened the drawer where I had stashed a bottle of ibuprofen earlier in the day.

I shook two orange pills into my hand and raised it up to my mouth.

My eyes went to the kitchen window.

There was a man in the reflection.

Grinning.

Behind me.

Javier.

I opened my mouth to scream, but he was fast and he grabbed me around the waist with one arm, his hand going over my mouth with the other. I dropped the pills to the floor where they clattered, praying that Camden could hear that, but I didn't think he could from where our bedroom was.

Javier pressed his hand hard into me and started bringing me backward, his hot breath at my neck. There was only one second where I felt a slice of relief that he was still alive. But that quickly vanished. Now I wanted him dead. I wanted Travis to have finished him off. I wanted my gun to have had one more bullet in it. Because no matter what I thought of Javier before, I knew now that he was here for a terrible reason.

All bets were off.

No more promises.

I struggled, trying to kick out with my legs, to knock over a jar full of cooking spoons, hoping to cause more noise, but it was impossible. Javier pulled me out of the kitchen, practically dragging me into the next room, the one-car garage we had.

Dark.

Small.

Practically soundproof.

Not good.

He managed to quietly close the door behind him, shutting us in the garage together, the smell of oil and dust assaulting me as well as Javier's distinctive musk, which made the whole thing that much more terrifying. I breathed hard against his hand, and he leaned back against the door, his arm around my stomach and legs growing tighter and tighter.

"Shhh," he whispered in my ear, lips touching my lobe. "Shhh, angel. Keep quiet. Calm down. I promise I won't hurt you."

That meant nothing anymore.

I could hear his lips against teeth, smiling. "So you think you could just leave me alone to die, yes?"

You left me, you sick son of a bitch. I wished there was light in the garage so I could see the closest weapon, but there was nothing. It was completely pitch black. Dark as sin. And the only sound was my heart pounding and Javier's breathing in my ear.

"This was after, of course, you pulled the trigger." He sucked in his breath. "You know, angel, that really hurt me. That really changed…everything. You were the one person I thought wouldn't betray me. And yet you tried to kill me. How do you think that made me feel? I lost my sister. And then I lost you."

He suddenly took his hand away and put it at my neck, wrapping it around until I could feel the grooves he was creating. I gasped for air, to scream, but only pitiful sounds came out.

"To think I wasted…" I eked out, my breath coming short. "Tears on you."

His grip tightened and he lifted me slightly off the ground, just for a moment, just to let me know he could hang me if he wanted. I couldn't speak anymore. I couldn't even get in one breath.

"And to think I wasted tears on *you*," he snarled, suddenly malicious. He breathed sharply through his nose, and I could tell he was pulling himself together. Trying to be calm. In control. Always in control. "But this is for the best. I can see that. We were never meant to be. You were never as strong as I thought you were. Such a shame though. You had such dirty wings. Such promise. Power makes the world go around, angel. It keeps you alive when you should be dead. Don't you want that immortality? Or are you so happy with a boring, ordinary life? With a boring, ordinary man?"

I felt my heart slowing, the veins in my head about to burst. Then he slowly released his hand and gave me two seconds to wheeze and try to get the air back in before he covered up my mouth with his hand again. I fought against his palm, but he held me hard while his other hand began to ease my robe aside.

I froze like a deer in headlights as his palm slid down my bare middle.

"You know I can give you what you need," he

murmured. "You know I always have. I can make you come just by touching you once, even now."

My eyes widened and his hand moved down between my legs, fingers going over my clit.

"Not very wet," he remarked in a low, careful voice. "You must have missed me. Missed my touch."

And he knew all the right places to touch, the right places to tease. Still, I felt nothing in my heart. And my body, my body only wanted to run and flee. I wanted to tear off my skin and burn it. He felt like a monster, a wicked reptile of cold leathery scales, a creature from my darkest dreams. He would not win me over here.

Perhaps if I let him think he did…

I relaxed into his touch, hoping I could feed his delusion. Not too much that he'd catch on. But just enough. I willed my breathing and my heart to slow and leaned slightly into him.

"That's my angel," he said, and I could feel his erection growing against my ass. His hand loosened on my mouth and I took the opportunity. I bit down hard on his fingers and he yelped, letting go of me. I went for the door, but he was at my side, throwing me hard to the ground, my head banging against the cold concrete, pain flying through me. Everything began to spin, stars and streams went around my head, and I lost precious seconds trying to get up.

By the time I struggled to get to my feet, my bad leg collapsing under me, I heard the shake of metal, the rip of duct tape. I screamed for Camden before Javier grabbed me by the hair at the top of my head and yanked me hard toward him, spinning me around and

slamming my head against the door as if he were trying to knock me out, his fingers finding my mouth. He
stuck the duct tape across my lips.

"Camden can't hear you now," he whispered in the
dark.

My heart sank at that. Had I been a fool to think that
Javier was the only one in the house?

The light in the garage went on. Javier had one hand
against it, the other gripped around my elbow. I eyed
the shelves in the garage, spied a hammer and went for
it, but he dived into me and I went flying into them. Just
before they toppled onto me, he yanked me backward
and out of the way and stuck a handcuff around one
wrist.

"What are you going to do with me?" I tried to say
through the tape, but it came out all garbled.

Javier smiled. He understood perfectly. And I was
able to get my first good look at him. He looked almost
the same, maybe in a more expensive suit, all black,
his hair shorter and neatly trimmed, showing off the
streaks of grey that were threaded through it, and he
had a shiny new gold watch on his wrist. He reeked of
power and deceit. Of confidence.

I could only guess as to what that meant.

"Oh, you poor thing," he said with mock sympathy.
"You really think I came here for you?"

Quick as a whip he spun me around and stuck the
other cuff around the passenger door handle of the
Mini Cooper. I collapsed against the door, slumping to
the ground.

He walked over to a camping cooler in the corner

and pulled it out to me, scraping loudly on the cement. He took a seat on it like we were about to have a little chat and brought out a gun from his inner jacket pocket, looking it over in his hands. My eyes watched it fearfully. I was dumbstruck with complete and utter terror.

He looked up and frowned at me. "I told you, angel, I'm not going to hurt you. I am and always will be a businessman, and I only came here to do a little business transaction."

I stiffened and he grinned at me.

"Oh don't worry," he said. "I'm not after your money. I've never cared much for that. No, what I'm after are men. Manpower. Power. Freedom. The chance to win." He sighed and looked around him with distaste. "You could have been living with me. You could have had it all. Instead you're in a shithole in America. Do you know where I am now? I have the most beautiful house you could ever imagine, with views as far as the eye can see. I have privilege now. More than that, I have...prestige. What Violetta said about me having a cartel nobody cares about? Oh, I wish she could see me now. I took over for Travis. And more than that, I took over from the Morales. I am at the top. Where I always should have been." He leaned forward, elbows on knees, and looked me dead in the eye, face completely serious. "Where you should have been. Angel. Where the fuck did we go wrong?"

Where do I begin? But what was the point. You could tell Javier something a million times, but unless he saw the reason, unless he believed it, it didn't matter. If he thought the sky was red instead of blue, it would be red. Everything I could throw in his face he would justify in some psychopathic way.

"I really did love you," he said softly. Then he straightened up and his eyes were unreadable. Blank. "But there are some things in this world more important than love. Some things that last longer. Empires. You build something great, something large, something that gets people's attention, and you're remembered forever. You love a girl, give her your heart, and you won't be remembered six years later. Love doesn't last. But empires do. They go on. And on. And on. Even if just in history books."

He got up and started deliberately pacing back and forth, toying with the gun. I had to wonder if Camden was okay. Because if he wasn't... God help me.

"Let me tell you a thing about cartels," he said with an air of superiority. "It's all about expansion. And you get to expand by thinking ahead. Mexico is bloody. Mexico is war. But I love it. So what do I do? I go across the border and find the itty-bitty American gangs and their pussy-whipped drug trades and grow-ops and I take over. I get here first, before the Baja cartel. Before the Gulf. I expand. I get more drugs, more people, more money. I only had the tiny asshole opening of Mississippi before. Now I have Southern California. Or, at least I'm trying. There's a rather large operation that needs, um, how do you say, lubrication? Though you never needed that with me, did you, angel?" He stopped right in front of me, his dark, greasy shoes spotless against the dirty concrete floor. "Look at me when I'm talking to you."

I slowly raised my head, not because he told me to, but because if he was going to do anything I wanted to see it.

His lips twisted into a sick smile. "So, I need the grease to get this deal going. Let's call it a peace offering. You see, the Madano brothers were really upset when Camden got away from them, so I figure if I brought him back and handed him over, well, they'd be more likely to do business with me."

My eyes widened, heart hammering with fear until the room started getting fuzzy.

"I know you don't like that," he went on, "and I'm sorry. But I did tell you to never get too close to anything. To anyone. I was just trying to spare your heart from the inevitable. I had my sights on Camden from the moment I saw him in Mexico. Once I found out the lengths you'd go to save your Gus, it all . . . fell into place. I just had to keep you both alive. And I wouldn't be where I am right now if I didn't act on opportunity. I know you knew that once. How important opportunity was to life."

He watched me for a few moments, but I gave him nothing but the horror that was surely on my face. He sighed and threw his arms up. "All right then. I guess we're done here."

He walked to me and put his hand on the side of my cheek and stared me right in the eye. "Take care of yourself, Ellie." He kissed my forehead and started walking toward the door. Then he stopped and brought his fingers to his nose, sniffing them. "Smells like you." He licked his tongue along his index finger. "Still tastes like you, too." He smiled at me, pleased with himself. "I'll make sure to show Camden, see if he agrees with me."

Fucking hell.

Fucking hell!

I started screaming, my cries muffled by the duct tape, and tried to get my hand out of the handcuff. Javier walked to the door, tossing me one last look over his shoulder before he stepped out into the kitchen and disappeared. I stopped struggling and listened, heard Javier going up the stairs and then heard Camden yelling, just once, a swear like "You fuck," something raw and primal, pure rage, and I could only imagine what Javier was telling him, that he did stuff to me.

Tears started flowing down my face, my heart being swallowed by my chest. I heard someone being dragged down the stairs, the low voices of Javier and someone else. Then the front door slammed. A car started down the street and then was gone.

My man was gone.

And I was alone.

I hadn't kept him safe.

I allowed myself to cry for Camden for one full minute, counting down from sixty through the tears, trying to keep breathing properly through my nose. When I hit zero, I got to my feet. I looked around the garage and began to think.

There were the hammer and tools that had been knocked over earlier, only a few feet from the farthest reach of my feet. Maybe I could either hammer off the door handle on the Cooper or hammer my handcuff. But getting to the hammer was a problem.

I took in a deep breath and a tried to wrap both hands around the door handle. I tried to pull the Mini Cooper toward the hammer and struggled stupidly. Of course I couldn't drag it on its own; it weighed like two thousand pounds.

But if it were placed in neutral...

I took off the robe and wrapped part of it around my free elbow. Then I took a step back as far as I could go, steadied my aim, and brought my elbow down into the passenger window with one sharp jab. Glass shattered everywhere and I knew my arm was bleeding even with the thick robe's protection, but at least the window was broken. I quickly used the robe to wipe away the rest of the glass fragments, then draped it over the edge of the door to protect myself when I reached over and jabbed the gearshift into neutral, hard enough that it didn't matter that I couldn't reach the clutch. Then I wrapped my shoulder in the extra fabric and began to push the car forward, the pressure of my whole body on the doorframe.

The Cooper slowly inched forward until the fender was pushing aside the fallen shelves. I was finally close enough. I stretched my bad leg out since it could reach the farthest and pulled the hammer toward me. I let out a giddy little cry once I was able to pick it up in my hands. I had a few jabs at the handcuff, but kept missing and nearly getting my hand, so I went for the door handle instead. Turns out BMW does not construct door handles to withstand blows from a hammer, and after the tenth blow the metal clanged loose to the ground and I was free.

Free.

With no fucking idea of what to do next.

Javier had Camden and was going to do an exchange with the Madano brothers. I had no idea what would happen to Camden after that. But I had a feeling I knew someone who would.

I quickly raced upstairs as fast as I could with my leg, threw on a pair of jeans, my special boots, and a tight T-shirt, then pulled all the guns we had out of the closet. I stuck a revolver in my boots with my knife, then grabbed a pistol with a silencer and stuck that down the back of my jeans. I brought out my lockpicker and quickly undid the handcuff, freeing my captive wrist, and then stuck the cuffs in my back pocket. I went downstairs and grabbed the notepad I'd been writing in, ripping off the top sheet—the one with Sophia's address on it—then ripped out another and scribbled in giant letters a note for Gus, leaving it right on the kitchen table.

Go get Ben! it said.

I didn't want Gus coming after us or involving himself. But with what I was about to do, Ben needed to be kept safe and I didn't have time to do it. I had to go after Camden. He may have been Javier's priority, but he was also mine.

I only hoped it wasn't too late.

I scampered back into the garage, opened the garage door, and revved the battered Mini Cooper. I peeled backward out of the building and ripped down the street.

Heading to Pasadena.

CHAPTER EIGHTEEN

I PULLED THE car up to Sophia's house just before dawn was breaking, face raw and ragged from the wind that blasted through the broken window, my knuckles sore from the sweaty grip on the steering wheel. I prayed that she and Ben both knew how to sleep in, because I wanted as little struggle as possible.

The fact that I was about to do this was nuts.

But with Camden on the line, it didn't really matter. I would do what I had to do. Even the ugly things.

I eased out of the car and managed to sneak around to the back of the house that faced onto the golf course, careful not to trip over Ben's wayward toy dump trucks and his sandbox. The back door was an easier lock to pick with fewer people to spot me. I got the door open in no time and slowly crept inside. The floor was cheap linoleum and silent underneath my feet. There were night-lights lining the hallway, which made it better for me, casting the area in a blue glow. I passed a laundry room and a playroom and a room with the door open.

That had to be Ben's. I swallowed my apprehension and kept going. The room next to that was a bathroom, and then there was another room with the door open only a crack. Beyond that was the living room and dining room and the foyer. I paused at the room with the door slightly ajar and debated how to do this.

There was no rule book.

No plan now.

I had to wing it and hope for the best.

I carefully pushed the door open, crouching low to the ground, figuring mothers were probably light sleepers, and crept inside. Sophia was asleep in her bed and turned over just as I came inside. Faint light spilled in through the window, allowing me to make out everything in fuzzy detail.

There was a lamp by her bed. I went to it, bringing out my gun and pointing it at her.

I flicked on the light.

Waited for that agonizing half second for her eyes to open.

They did. Forehead scrunched. Eyes blinking at the light and at me.

And then at the gun.

Her mouth opened.

"Don't!" I hissed. "Don't you *dare* scream."

I pulled back the hammer on the revolver. The sound that I meant business. Camden did it to me once. Scared the shit out of me.

Gotcha, he'd said.

This time I got her.

I smiled as the realization came into her face,

flooring her with bewilderment. "You were...you had the facial. The redhead with the hot date."

My smile twitched. "I was. I did. Two guesses to who my hot date was." I stared down the barrel of the gun at her. "Where is he?"

"Who?" she asked innocently.

"You know who. Camden. McQueen. Your ex-husband. Where. Is. He?"

She shook her head and I suddenly jammed the gun toward her, the tip just inches from her face.

"Don't you play fucking stupid with me," I whispered harshly.

"Why are you whispering?" she said, her voice growing louder. "Afraid to wake up Ben? You don't want him to see this? Let him. Let him know how psychotic his daddy's new girlfriend is."

She leaned forward and spit in my face. Laughed. Enjoying herself. It was all a game.

I slowly wiped her mucous off my forehead.

She said, "Cunt," under her breath.

That didn't get to me. "You can call me all the names you want, as long as you tell me where your brothers are taking Camden. Where are they meeting Javier?"

She snorted and sat up, all attitude. "I'm not telling you."

I cocked my head in disbelief and tightened my grip on the gun. "I don't think you have any idea of how serious this all is. I will make you tell me."

She gave me a blasé look. "Look, honey. I know all about you. You're some white trash Southern scum chick who pulled a fast one when she shouldn't have and got mixed up with Camden. You're both the same. Good looking, maybe a good fuck in bed, but absolutely inept when it comes to getting anything in life. You can want to find Camden all you want, but really, you're wasting your time. He's as good as dead, and good riddance, and you're not going to get a single thing out of me because you're not built for it. You're a scammer. A con artist. Look at your arms. You couldn't even put a dent in the wall. What the hell are you going to do to me? Shoot me?"

"No," I said through grinding teeth, feeling the rage build up.

"That's what I thought."

I brought my gun across her face in one quick, violent and terrible motion, the end of the pistol smashing into her nose. She cried out and I grabbed her by the jaw, bringing her bleeding face up to mine. "I won't shoot you, not yet anyway. But I will break your nose and your cheekbones and your jaw and every little pretty part of you that can get you a date with hot men. Let's see how they want you after this, huh?"

Finally, I saw it. The fear in her eyes. She got it. She understood that there were some things out there far worse than death. For me, it was a life without Camden McQueen. For her, it was a life with reconstructive surgery.

I grabbed her by her arm and yanked her out of bed. Couldn't put a dent in the wall, huh? She was making me tempted to treat her face like the Cooper's window again, but I didn't want to do anything I didn't have to.

I jabbed the gun into her side. "You're coming with me."

"Just take him," she cried out as I pulled her along.

"Take him?" I asked, pressing the gun into her harder, my fingers gripping her elbow like I was trying to snap it in half. "Take who?"

"Take Ben!" she cried out angrily. "If that's what you want so bad, just take him and leave me the fuck alone."

My head shook ever so slightly, trying to comprehend this woman. "Oh. Believe me. We are taking him. The minute we step out this door, he will be gone. And you won't see him again. Not that you care. But until you tell me where Camden is, until you show me, I'm going to take away all the other things you care about. I forgot to mention how nice your teeth are and how easy they would be to knock out. Think about that for a bit and then tell me where Camden is."

I brought her out into the hallway, back out the door I came in, and around the house. The sky was now violet and gray, the rising sun hidden by the hills and smog. Everything around us was monochrome and I was on autopilot, letting instinct and drive dictate each movement.

I shoved her into the front seat, my gun trained on her as I ran around to the side and hopped in. I held the gun low and instructed her to drive.

"Take me there," I told her. "And if you try to fuck me over in any way, you'll pay for it. But if you do as I say and you get me to Camden, before it's too late, then you live and your pretty little face will remain intact.

Except for maybe your nasal cavities. But your coke addiction and collapsed septum is your problem, not mine. Now drive, bitch."

I forced her leg down, pedal to the floor, and we zipped off.

"Where are we going?" I asked her.

"To the desert," she said, looking annoyed, like my questions were bothering her. Perhaps it was the gun or the threats or the fact that she was driving in her underwear.

"Where in the desert?"

"Look, I don't really know," she said. "I didn't ask." She gave me a sidelong look. "I didn't care."

I jabbed my elbow in her face. She cried out, letting go of the steering wheel as the car wheeled into the opposite lane, the car slowing.

"Keep driving!" I screamed, bringing the car back into our lane again and then pressing her foot down with the hand holding the gun. "And tell me where."

She sobbed, a few tears escaping. It tugged at me a bit, made me question what I was doing. Then I remembered who she was, what she knew, and who she was doing it for.

"Tell me," I repeated more slowly.

"A place with planes. He said it was a place with planes."

"Who said?"

"Vincent. My brother. The one in charge."

I scrunched up my face. A place with planes?

"That's all he said?"

"He said it was abandoned. And that it was easy to hide their men there. It's a setup."

Yeah, of course it fucking was. But now Javier was on the other end of it.

"Where in the desert? What area?" I asked.

She shook her head, trying to stop the bleeding and steer at the same time. "The place that has the milk shakes. Near...Barstow."

That was either Route 66 or Highway 58.

"Turn left onto 15 before San Bernardino," I told her. I think I had an idea where they were going. There was the Edwards Air Force Base out in the desert, but that was highly secure and not a place any cartels would go near. There was also an airplane boneyard on the side of the highway between Bakersfield and Barstow.

The place where old planes go to die.

Shit. This wasn't going to be easy.

But I had to try.

I nudged Sophia with my gun and nodded at the rising sun.

"Keep driving."

*   *   *

The sun was a blinding fist in the sky by the time we passed Barstow and turned onto Highway 58 that would take us through to the airplane graveyard. Bleak, empty desert spread out for miles on all sides of us, ground the color of bleached bones. The Cooper sped along, the air that was blasting in through the broken window still cool at this time of the morning, though I knew it would start baking soon.

I made Sophia drive past the Edwards Air Force Base, the only real pocket of civilization, until we came to what always struck me as one of the eeriest sights in the desert. Off in the distance, shimmering like a ghostly mirage, was plane after plane after plane. Jumbo jets, 747s, commuter planes—every plane you could think of in the commercial aviation industry were all cluttered together like sardines. Part of the yard, which stretched on for miles, was organized, with jets lined up in rows and the other part of the yard was like a dump. The boneyard.

"I'm guessing this is it," I said as we drove closer.

"My brothers can be dramatic," she explained. "This will make the world pay attention."

"Looks like it," I muttered. Cartels, man, always trying to up each other. Well, I guess the Mojave Desert was a good place for a shootout, especially when you had massive airplanes to hide behind.

I asked her to slow the car as we came to the road that led off toward the yard. Dust was flying up as the car went down it, approaching a low building at the front.

"If they're here, they won't be coming through this way," I said, turning to make sure we weren't going to crash into anyone before I ordered her to make a U-turn. "I think the first part of the yard is just airplane storage. The boneyard stretches behind it."

I jerked my head to the desert and pressed the gun into her waist. "Time to go off-roading."

"Here?" she said.

I nodded. "Go straight to that clump of Joshua trees out there. Watch out for tumbleweeds."

She raised her brows and exhaled loudly, but quickly

turned the car off the road and straight into the desert. If we went straight we could go all the way around the boneyard and get in through the back. But the dust cloud that would follow us would be a dead giveaway that we were coming to spoil their party, and alert both the cartels and the authorities who no doubt patrolled at least the airport storage area.

"Park it and get out," I told her.

"I'm in my underwear."

"And your nose is broken. Does it look like I give a fuck?" In my tired, delirious, adrenaline-ravaged state, I had no patience and no time to care. I wanted Camden back. He was the only thing on my mind, the only thing that put one foot in front of the other, the only thing that gave me strength to pull the trigger if I had to. "Now *get out.*"

She opened the door and looked at the hard earth of caked sand and rocks. "I don't have shoes," she said pitifully. She eyed a beach bag I had in the backseat that had a towel and flip-flops spilling out of it. "Can I wear your flip-flops? Otherwise it'll hurt too much to walk."

"Oh for fuck's sake!" I leaned in the back to grab the bag.

Big mistake.

Stupid, foolish, Ellie.

Sophia slammed her arm into my head and I dropped the gun in the backseat. I cried out and quickly grabbed the gun, twisting back in my seat to see her running off into the distance, a small cloud of dust trailing her. Hurts too much to walk, my ass.

I jumped out of the car, my gun trained on her as she went. But I couldn't just shoot her. I needed her. I quickly started booking it after her as fast as I could go. I pressed down on my shot leg, grunting through the pain until I didn't feel anything anymore. I would get her. I would do anything.

Because she was barefoot and the terrain was anything but friendly, she was running slow enough that I was gaining on her. What a sight we would have been for any spectator to see: a girl in a T-shirt and underwear running barefoot through the Mojave Desert followed by a limping chick with a revolver and a psychotic look on her face, dust rising up around us and floating to the blue sky.

It wasn't long before I had her.

I did a running tackle and brought her straight into the dirt, slamming her face into the ground. She cried out in pain, but I did not give a shit anymore. She used the last bit of humanity I had left against me and now I had nothing.

I yanked her up off the ground, so fucking tempted to smash my gun into her temple and drag her to the boneyard. But somehow—I don't know how—I kept it all in and started marching her forward.

"Nice try," I said, my nails digging into her arm until she winced. I looked down at her bleeding feet. "Even a pedicure won't fix that."

She whimpered and I paid no heed. We quickly scuffled ourselves along, trying to disturb as little sand as possible while still moving quickly. The sun hammered down on us, my eyes burning from the glare and dust, my throat raw and dry, but we soldiered on, step after step, until we reached the edge of the perimeter fence. We stopped and looked up. The barbed wire at the top was rusted to shit and tumbleweeds blew past on the other side of the chain links, heading to a scrap pile of jet engine parts. They wouldn't have scaled it, and from the looks of the condition of this part of the yard, there was probably an easier way in.

I brought her around to the back, and we walked down the fence, around Joshua trees, cacti, and wild shrubs and heaps of scrap metal that didn't quite make it inside the boneyard. Finally we spotted an area where the chain links had been cut. Our ticket in. Maybe our only way out.

I took a deep breath and walked us through the opening.

We were inside.

It was fucking eerie.

Up close the planes looked like an armada of plane crashes. Some of them were charred, some were broken into bits. There were flotation devices scattered around, oxygen masks hanging off of shrubs. Many commercial jets were decapitated, their severed heads lying about, stripped inside of all furniture and instruments. Some planes looked like they were about to fly away and some just had the seats left. Broken wings were stacked in piles.

No wonder they picked this place. It scared the shit out of you just being there.

We walked carefully out into the middle, between the giant wheels of a jumbo jet's landing gear standing upright like a giant metal tree and the severed tail end of a Cessna.

I stopped and pulled her back once we were in the open again. Planes surrounded us, each window an eye, watching our every move. I badly wanted to run and hide, to get out of harm's way. But if they didn't see me with Sophia, they wouldn't know how damn serious I was.

"Hello?" I called out, my voice bouncing back from the motionless aircraft. I cleared my throat and yelled, "I have your sister. You know what I want."

I looked around in circles, searching every creepy corner of the boneyard as far as I could see. They could be anywhere.

And nowhere.

I put the gun to Sophia's head. "If you're lying to me..." I ground out.

"I'm not," she moaned, obviously in distress. Good. "I told you the truth. They said planes. *You* brought me here."

Shit. Fuck. Shit.

Was I wrong about this place? Were they somewhere else entirely?

Was Camden already handed over?

Already dead?

I swallowed hard and rubbed my lips together. I couldn't lose it now. Not now. Not until I knew.

"Look," Sophia whispered. I followed her gaze over to one of the airplanes.

There was a face at the window.

I let out a gasp and then started looking closer.

There was someone crouched behind a lone passenger seat. There was another person behind a wing.

We weren't alone.

There was a shuffle by one of the decapitated plane heads and someone that could only be Vincent Madano came out, gun held lazily to his side. Like Javier, he was fond of slick suits and he looked like a complete Mafia stereotype, from the Roman nose to the jutting chin and greasy hair. Another man who thrived on greed and lies and power.

"You must be Ellie Watt," Vincent said as he stopped a few yards away, tumbleweeds rolling between us like we'd been placed in a Western TV show set. "Nice to finally meet you. I've heard many great things, all second-hand information, of course."

"Where's Camden?" I asked, my voice shaking against its will. I would not be afraid. I would not fall apart. I would get him back.

"Camden McQueen," he said, his eyes darkening. "I don't know. I expected to see him here, not you and not my sister."

I pressed the gun into her head. "I don't want to kill her, but I will if I have to."

He nodded as if he were impressed, cool and calm. Nothing ruffled him. "I can see that. Hopefully you won't have to make such…tough decisions." His eyes darted to the side. "And there's the man of the hour."

I whipped my head to look and gasped. Camden was walking toward us with Javier right behind him, his gun aimed at Camden's back. He was wearing a denim shirt, black shorts, hands raised above his head. I took in the details like I'd never see him again. Because maybe I wouldn't.

We locked eyes, and in his beautiful blues he was telling me to stay calm. To stay focused. To not worry.

That made me worry.

Oh, *god* that made me worry.

Because Camden was the kind of person who would give his life for yours if it meant you getting out alive. And I didn't want that. I didn't want life if he wasn't in it. I wanted him and me, with the waves crashing at our feet.

"Here he is," Javier announced, his voice light and masking the gravity of the situation. He pushed Camden forward, just for fun it seemed. Camden stumbled but righted himself, dust and rocks scattering at his feet. The sun continued to sear us, making the whole scene jump in contrast. Surreal.

Yet, this was reality.

Harsh, cold truth.

They stopped a little ways away and looked over at Vincent. "I brought him for you, the peace offering. Now I hope we can do business."

Vincent nodded and wiggled his hand. "Send him over."

"No!" I screamed, losing all control, like the devil was being ripped out of my throat. "Camden stays there. No one fucking hurts him or I will kill Sophia!"

Javier shrugged and pushed Camden forward until he was walking. "I don't care if you kill Sophia."

Sophia stiffened against me, feeling the fear. I stared at him, pleading with his blank, reptilian eyes for an ounce of humanity, of love, of compassion toward me. I'd take anything. Just an inch. Just enough to save Camden. "Please, Javier."

I had no effect on him. "What? I don't care." He motioned to Vincent. "Does he?"

I looked to Vincent. He smiled sympathetically at me and tilted his head downward.

"I'll get over it," he said simply.

My world froze.

Sophia cried out in indignation, anger and betrayal spilling from her lips, and I was too dazed to even hold on to her. She ripped herself out of my grip and ran toward Vincent, fists in the air, screaming her head off, ready to pound on him.

Before I could do anything, Vincent raised his gun and shot her in the chest.

She crumpled to the ground, dust flying around her.

My collateral was dead.

The planet slowed on its axis. Every second stretched longer.

I looked at Camden, who had stopped in the middle of it all, hands still above his head, halfway in between Javier and Vincent. Camden looked back at me.

He smiled sadly.

"Take care of Ben for me," he said.

I blinked, trying to understand the implications of what he was asking while my heart sunk as heavy as rock, falling through me until I knew it wasn't beating anymore.

"Camden!" I screamed, an out-of-body experience.

Vincent aimed the gun at him.

Pulled the trigger.

Shot Camden straight in the chest.

In the heart.

In his beautiful, lovely, endless heart.

He flew backward, all 6'2" of him, tats and muscle and love.

Fell hard to the ground, making it rumble at my feet. Motionless.

A bullet whizzed past my head and I had a split second to react. Not that I wanted to react, not that I was trying, not that I cared.

Because I was already dead. I died out there with Camden.

I didn't even care anymore.

But the body's will to survive is strong. Humanity's instinct to preserve itself lives on. I was acting without knowledge, without thought.

I ducked low to the ground and rolled until I was by the giant landing gear and then popped up behind it, using it as a shield.

I leaned against it, trying to find my heart, but it was gone.

CHAPTER NINETEEN

I SOBBED UNCONTROLLABLY, once, twice, loud, my soul being seared open by the pain, the debilitating pain. I couldn't breathe. I couldn't see. I couldn't even be.

Camden.

My moon.

Shattered.

Lifeless on the floor of the Mojave Desert.

Another bullet rocketed off the landing gear, making me snap to attention. To the reality that was going on. There was a firefight. I was in the middle of it.

I peered around the gear, my eyes straying to Camden, who was still lying there on his back, head facing straight up. Vincent was shooting at me. Javier was retreating behind a wing and shooting at Vincent. Este was suddenly there, jumping off the top of a plane and onto one of Vincent's men, taking him out. Guns were going off in all directions.

Vincent started running toward me and I fumbled for my gun, ready to finish off the man who had killed the love of my life.

But Javier popped up, aimed, fired, and shot Vincent in the side. He fell to the ground and Javier took off running behind the body of a 737.

I quickly got up and walked straight to Vincent, feeling mechanical: no thoughts, no mercy. I turned him over with my boot so he was looking up at me, barely alive, and stepped on his chest.

I didn't even have words. I just pulled the trigger. Aimed at his head.

Done.

Then I looked around me. The fighting seemed to have moved and was going on behind the jetliners, giving me a moment of clarity. A moment of quiet. I may have still been an easy target, but I had to take it. I had to take this moment and make it mine. We deserved that.

I staggered over to Camden, my legs growing weaker and weaker with every step I took, until I finally collapsed to my knees and crawled the rest of the way, dragging myself over the coarse sand.

I grabbed for his hand, his still-warm hand, and held on to it as the tears unleashed. I sobbed, beside myself in the agony, in the grief, knowing I had to somehow pull through in life without him to take care of Ben. But it shouldn't have been this way.

The hero doesn't die.

And Camden McQueen was a hero unlike any other.

Selfless, brave, protective.

Good.

So fucking *good*.

I ignored the sounds of gunshots in the distance,

knowing I was so close to death in so many ways. I moved another inch and tried to see through my tears to his flawless face, to take it in one last time. I placed my shaking hand to his lips.

He kissed it.

His eyes flew open and he looked at me.

I almost screamed. I jerked, startled, scared.

"Hey," he said, voice hoarse.

I couldn't even form words. My chest was about to explode from sheer and utter joy. How could this be?

I looked down at his wound. He was shot, wasn't he? I put my hand there, feeling along the denim, expecting it to come away with blood. There was nothing. His chest was stiff, harder than normal. With my mouth agape, I unbuttoned the first few buttons of his shirt and saw the bulletproof vest underneath.

"What the..." I was unable to finish the sentence.

I laughed, confused, elated and looked at him, my hands flying for his face. "You're not dead."

He smiled and kissed my palm. "No, thankfully. Feels like I got slammed with a brick though." He tried to sit up and looked around him. A bullet pinged off something in the distance, though I had no idea where it had come from. "I think we need to get out of here."

I put my hand behind his back and helped him sit straight. "I still don't understand. Why do you have a vest? Who gave you a bulletproof vest?"

He cocked his head to the side, dust falling off his black hair. "Javier."

I shook my head, unable to comprehend any of this.

He was alive!

He was alive!

"Why would Javier give you a bulletproof vest?" I asked incredulously as the gunfire continued behind us.

"I smooth-talked him."

I raised my brows and got to my feet, helping him up. "How the hell did you smooth talk Javier?"

He shook out his arms and ripped open the rest of his shirt to get a better look at the vest. The crunched bullet fell to the ground. "Well, I didn't know if it would work, but I used you as leverage. I told him the truth, that you might be pregnant with my child, and that if he really, truly cared about you, he wouldn't take me away from you. So he had a change of heart and gave me the vest. He's wearing one too. He did when he got shot at Travis's as well. Playing dead worked well for him, so I thought I'd try it too."

"A change of heart?" I exclaimed, my brows furrowed. That was barely a change of heart. "He assaulted me, kidnapped you. He still handed you over to Vincent! What if Vincent shot you in the head instead of the chest? What would have happened when he eventually discovered you were wearing a vest? What then?"

"Ellie, he doesn't have a very big heart." He gave me a pointed look. "But I'm sure in his fucked-up mind, he was being noble. I'm at least grateful for that."

"I'm going to fucking kill him," I sneered. I got my other gun out of my boot and started looking around wildly, wanting to find him and get rid of him for good. The firefight had stopped. There were no more sounds coming out from behind the planes. We were alone. Javier was gone. Escaped into the desert like the rat he was.

I didn't want to live in fear anymore.

"I have to find him," I growled and started running toward the way we came in, my eyes searching high and low for him and only seeing other bodies instead, spread among the airplane carcasses and dry terrain. Camden ran after me, our footsteps echoing in the boneyard.

Suddenly Javier stepped out from behind a jet engine.

A tense look on his face.

His hands above his head.

And Gus behind him, a gun in each hand, aimed at Javier's head.

Just as I was doing.

Like father, like daughter.

I had no idea how Gus found us, but I was sure as hell glad he did.

Javier, to his credit, did seem scared as he looked between the two of us, four guns trained on him. And this time my hands were as steady as the rocks around us.

Still, Javier nodded at Camden and said, "You made it. That was lucky."

"Shut up," I sneered. "Give me a good reason why I shouldn't kill you for good."

"Or why I shouldn't," Gus spoke up.

Javier eyed Camden, who only crossed his arms on his chest and shrugged. "A fifth gun would be overkill," Camden remarked.

"Speaking of," I said, looking over Javier's shoulder at Gus, "shoot for the head. He's wearing a vest."

Javier looked at me in shock.

I waved my guns at him and in the direction of the fence. "Walk," I commanded. "Keep your hands above your head."

I nodded for Gus to lower his weapons, to leave us alone. This was between Javier and me.

Javier slowly turned around, his brow furrowed in confusion, and now I got to jab my gun into his back.

"Keep going," I said. "All the way to the fence. Stay turned around."

"Angel," Javier said, fear breaking in his voice. "I saved your Camden for you. I did it for you."

I walked over to him until I was right behind him. I could sense Gus and Camden hovering nervously in the distance, but to their credit they didn't say anything and they stayed where they were.

"I know you did," I told him, right into his ear, the back of his hair tickling my face. "And that's what makes you and me so tragic. Don't you think?"

"Angel," he pleaded.

I pressed the gun into the back of his neck.

"You won't ever call me angel again. Because I am not your angel. And my wings aren't dirty."

I pulled my mouth away from his ear. "And I don't have your soul. But if it's out there, you might want to find it, before it's too late for you."

I quickly bent down and pulled the pair of handcuffs out of my back pocket, the same ones he'd used on me last night. I flicked a cuff open, his eyes widening in surprise, his body shaking slightly.

"Don't get any wrong ideas," I said. "That kinky shit is over."

I snapped one cuff over his wrist and snapped the other to the chain-link fence, his hand held slightly above his head. He turned and stared at me, absolutely flabbergasted.

I stepped back and grinned happily at him. "I really hope you've been bribing the DEA agents well, Javier Bernal. Because you are going to need a lot of help to get out of this one."

He shook his head. "You can't leave me here."

"Just be glad you're intact enough to leave behind," I said. *"Puta, cabrón,"* I swore in Spanish, spitting at his feet.

Then I turned to look at Camden and Gus, who were staring at me with a mix of awe and surprise. My men. My wonderful men. I blinked back a few tears, over-whelmed by even the sun in the sky, then walked over to them.

"Time to get the hell out of here?" I asked.

They nodded in unison. Camden grabbed my hand. And together we ran out through the hole in the fence and across the desert floor.

I didn't look back at Javier.

*   *   *

Gus had parked his car right where I had left the Mini.

"How did you find us?" I asked, wiping the dust and sweat off my brow. In the distance I could hear heli-copters, hopefully the DEA and the feds, maybe called by Gus. They were going to have a field day once they got their hands on Javier. The new leader of Los Zetas, caught right in their own backyard.

Gus looked at me like I was an idiot. "Tracking device. Haven't you learned anything, Ellie girl?"

Camden's head snapped up. "Where's Ben?"

"He's fine," Gus said quickly. "He's safe. My friend has him and he's waiting for us back at home. You guys get in and follow me." He eyed the sky, hearing the choppers too. "We're going to have to be quick about this."

Camden got behind the steering wheel and I climbed in the passenger side as Gus got into his car and roared out of the desert.

"You okay to drive?" I asked him, knowing he could have a cracked rib even if the bullet didn't go through.

He gave me a cocky smile. "Baby, I'm Camden McQueen."

I laughed, for the first time in what felt like ages, and grinned back. "Okay, then let's make this fast."

"I'm good at that," he said, winking at me as he floored the Cooper forward, growling after Gus's trail. "Remember? Best five minutes of your life?"

I put my hand over his. "Let's make it the best fifty years of my life. And then some."

"It'll be the best of everything."

Calexico's "Fortune Teller" came on the radio, bringing back a million memories, all of them rising up with the sand around us, flying forever into the atmosphere. I looked though the sunroof up at the impossibly blue sky, the color of Camden's eyes, and smiled to myself.

He was alive.

I was alive.

We had our lives left to live.

New paths.

New journeys.

New hope.

"Let's go say hi to Ben," I whispered.

We left the desert behind us in a cloud of dust.

EPILOGUE

"That's a beautiful tattoo," the barista behind the counter said, looking down at the woman's leg.

The woman looked down at herself. She'd taken to wearing shorter skirts lately, even though the wind off the Pacific was known to flip them up at a moment's notice and flash the world your underwear. The woman didn't care though. Her legs were now a work of art.

"Thank you," the woman said with a gracious smile. She was a stunning woman in her early thirties, high cheekbones, dark brown eyes, and long blond hair that cascaded down her back. Her face was tanned from days spent outside, sunscreen no match for the Californian sun.

"I love cherry blossoms," the barista commented, handing the woman her massive café mocha. "And I love that moon in the middle of it all."

The woman smiled to herself, not wanting to share the whole story with the barista. There weren't many people she could tell the truth to, that the tattoo of the moon was not only for the man who inked it there, but also to cover up the scars of a bullet wound. The coast north of San Francisco wasn't exactly known for high crime, unless you counted Eureka, but no one ever counted that.

"Where did you get the tattoos done?"

"I know a guy," she said slyly. "Has a shop in Gualala. Only works part time though."

"I love Gualala," the barista exclaimed. "They have an amazing barbeque joint there. Really quiet town though. You live near there?"

The woman nodded, eager to get away from the Chatty Cathy. "I do. But I work up and down the coast. Makes driving down to Bodega Bay worth it just to get Starbucks."

She then thanked the barista and left before she had to start talking about her job. Not that she minded, but it always made her feel a bit edgy when people asked too many questions about her.

She got in her car, a sexy black 1973 Dodge Challenger that she drove way too fast up and down Highway 1, and looked over her shoulder to the backseat to make sure her photography equipment was still there. Satisfied, she gunned the car, taking it north. Today's photography session was a pretty simple one, engagement photos on the beach, a happy young couple in love.

The woman felt a bit sad at the fact that she never got to have engagement photos. But then again, no one could do a better job than she could. She would have never been satisfied with them, and besides there was no point in photos when her wedding had been such a simple one. Just her, her husband, and her father on the beach at Gualala State Park.

And their son and dog, of course, two unreliable ring bearers.

She flipped through the radio stations, pausing when she heard Guano Padano over the air, and grinned to herself. The little-known Italian band was finally getting some airplay in the States. She rolled down her window and stuck her head out, smiling like a fool into the waning sun.

When she finally reached the house, the sun was close to setting. She had to hurry. She hated missing sunsets.

She parked in the gravel driveway and grabbed her camera. She looked over the edge of the dunes in front of her house and saw two children chasing each other on the sand, a dog darting between them.

Gus was sitting down on a beach blanket, having a beer and trying to throw the ball for the dog. Sammy wasn't having any of it, preferring to run down the kids instead, barking and wagging her tail.

In front of them, out in the surf, stood her husband and his strong, solid silhouette, ankle-deep in the waves, watching the sun begin its descent.

Her heart bloomed and she ran down the wooden steps to the beach, her feet running through the warm sand, one of her most favorite feelings in the world.

She waved at her father as she passed him, and then prepared for the onslaught of the dog as Sammy jumped up at her. The woman raised her camera in the air, knowing the dog's tendency to slobber all over it, and scratched her quickly behind the ears.

"Hey, Mom!" yelled Ben, a spritely eight-year-old with dark hair and a tall build. A short attention span too. He looked to Gus. "Grandpa, throw me the ball."

Gus threw it underhand and Ben caught it, just as Violet came screeching toward the woman's legs.

"Mommy!" Violet cried out, wrapping her tiny arms around her cherry blossom tattoo. "You almost missed sunset." She was four years old and into keeping track of routine. If the slightest thing was out of place, everyone would hear about it.

"But I didn't," the woman explained happily, crouching low. She smoothed the fine blond hair off of Violet's head and peered at her. "How are you, baby? Almost bedtime soon."

"No!" Violet screeched.

The woman laughed, used to this. "Yes. Now go say hi to Grandpa. I'm going to go take a few pictures and then we'll put you to bed and read you a story."

"No," the girl still said, but she giggled and ran away to Gus, flopping onto the towel beside him.

The woman watched her go, then straightened up and looked to the ocean.

Camden was staring at her, a big smile on his face.

She grinned right back and trotted up to him.

"Hey, sweetheart," he said to her, opening his arms for her. She snuggled right into it, not even feeling the sharp cold of the Pacific Ocean as it crashed around their feet, then raised her head for a kiss. Camden kissed her deep and long before pulling away.

He was all dimples and blue eyes. He still took her breath away.

"How was work?" he asked, putting his arms around her waist and holding her close.

She rested her head on his shoulder. "Good. Couple in love. You know how that goes."

"Uh-huh," he said. "Lots of blow jobs."

She laughed and elbowed him. She looked over her shoulder at Ben throwing the ball for the dog, at Violet chatting Gus's ear off. He was listening with utmost patience to whatever crazy story she was concocting next.

"How did Dad's date go with the woman from the bar?"

Camden grinned and looked at the sunset. "He won't tell me. Which I think means it went well. I decided not to push it."

"Good plan."

"You going to take some photos?" he asked.

She gripped her camera, about to raise it up and capture the last sliver of sun before it disappeared, then hesitated and decided against it.

"Nah," she said. "I'll commit it to memory this time."

They watched as the sun sank into the sea, as the waves crashed around them.

He squeezed her tight. She kissed his hand.

"You happy?" she asked him quietly.

"I am. Are you happy, Ellie?"

She nodded. "Yeah."

She was happy.

Don't miss Book One in

The Artists Trilogy

Read on for an electrifying extract ...

PROLOGUE

This will be the last time.

I've said that before. I've said it a lot. I've said it while talking to myself in a mirror like some Tarantino cliché. But I've never said it while having a pool cue pressed against my throat by a crazed Ukrainian man who was hell bent on making me his wife.

It's nice to know there's still a first time for everything.

Luckily, as the edges of my vision turned a sick shade of grey and my feet dangled from the floor, I had enough fight left in me to get out of this alive. Though it meant a few seconds of agony as the cue pressed into my windpipe, I pried my hands off of it and reached out. Sergei, my future fake husband, wasn't short, but I had long arms and as I pushed aside his gut, I found his balls.

With one swift movement, I made a tight, nails-first fist around them and tugged.

Hard.

Sergei screamed, dropping me and the pool cue to the sticky floor. I hopped up to my feet, grabbed the stick, and swung it against the side of his head as he was doubled over. When I was a child, I was never in a town long enough to get enrolled in the softball team, which was a shame because as the cue cracked against the side of his bald head, I realized it could have been a second career.

Hell, it could even be a first career. I was quitting the grifting game anyway.

Sergei made some grumbling, moaning noise like a disgruntled cow giving birth, and though I had done some damage, I only bought myself a few seconds. I grabbed the eight ball from the pool table and chucked it at his head where it bounced off his forehead with a thwack that made my toes curl.

For all the games I played, I'd always been a bit squeamish with violence. That said, I'd never been busted by one of the men I'd conned with my virgin bride scam. I chalked this up to "kill or be killed." Self defense. Hopefully it would be the last time for that, too.

Not that I was doing any killing here. After the pool ball made contact with his head and caused him to drop to his knees with a screech, I turned on my heels and booked it into the ladies' washroom. I knew there were two angry-looking men stationed outside of the door to the pool room, and they definitely wouldn't let me pass while their friend was on the floor hoping his testicles were still attached.

The ladies' room smelled rank, like mold and cold pipes, and I wondered how long it had been since it was cleaned. The Frontier wasn't the sort of bar that women hung out at, and that should have been my first tip that something was awry. The second was that no one even looked my way when I walked in the place. It's like they were expecting me, and when a dodgy bar in Cincinnati is expecting you, you know you're on someone else's turf. Third thing that should have tipped me off was the pool room was in a basement and there were an awful lot of locks on that door.

But, as I balanced my boots on the rust-stained sink, I found there were no locks on the rectangular window. I slammed it open and stuck my arms out into the warm August air, finding soggy dirt under my hands as the rain came down in heavy sheets. Just perfect. I was going to become Mud Woman in a few seconds.

Mud Woman was still preferable to Dead Woman, however, and I pulled myself through the narrow window and onto the muddy ground, the cold, wet dirt seeping into my shirt and down the front of my jeans. I heard Sergei yelling his head off and pounding on the bathroom door.

This had been a close one. Way too close.

I scrambled to my feet and quickly looked around to see if anyone had noticed. So far the bar looked quiet, the red lights from inside spilling through the falling rain. The street was equally quiet and lined with Audis and Mercedes that stuck out like gaudy jewelry among the decrepit meat-packing buildings. My own car, which I reluctantly called Jóse, was parked two blocks away. I may have underestimated the situation but I was glad I still had my wits about me. When an old friend emails you out of the blue and asks you to meet him at a sketchy bar late at night, you do take some precautions. It's too bad I hadn't clued in that it wasn't an old lover of mine but Sergei, out for revenge.

I took advantage of not being seen and ran as fast as I could down the street, my footsteps echoing coldly. By the time I rounded the corner and saw the dark green 1970 GTO sitting on the empty street, the rain had washed the mud clean off of me.

I wiped my wet hair from my eyes and stared at the glistening Ohio license plate. It was time for that to come off, and I mentally flipped through the spare plates I had inside. I knew I'd never set foot in Cincinnati again after this, and now that I knew this had been a set-up, I couldn't be sure they hadn't noticed my car. I had a wad of Sergei's money—which I'd been keeping strapped to the bottom of the driver's seat—and apparently he was the type who'd follow up on that kind of thing. He was the type that would hunt me down. I should have figured that from our email exchanges. This wouldn't even be about the money anymore, but the fact that I pulled a fast one on him. But what do you expect when you're trolling for virgin brides on OKCupid?

Men and their stupid pride.

I supposed he could try and hunt me down. He could try and follow me from state to state. But I knew as soon as I got in Jóse, he wouldn't be able to find me. I'd been hunted before and for a lot more than money.

And they still hadn't found me.

Yet.

Hearing distant but irate voices filling the air, I quickly opened the door and hopped in. My instincts told me to just drive and never look back, and unfortunately I knew I had to listen. I had to leave my pretty apartment, my safe coffee shop job, and my yoga-infused roommate Carlee behind. It was a shame, too. After living with Carlee for six months, the flexible little thing had actually grown on me.

I'll mail her something nice, I told myself and gunned the engine. Jóse purred to life and we shot down the street, away from the bar and from Sergei and his buddies who were now probably scouring the streets looking for me.

It didn't matter. I was used to running and always kept a spare life in the trunk. Spare clothes, spare driver's licenses, spare Social Security Numbers, and a spare tire. As soon as I felt like I was a comfortable distance away, I'd pull into a motel under a new name. I'd change the plates on my car. Yes, Jóse wasn't the most inconspicuous of vehicles, but I was sentimental about the car. After all, it wasn't even mine.

Then tomorrow, I'd figure out my budget. Figure out how long I could go before I'd need a legitimate job. Figure out that moment when I'd have to stay true to my word and make sure that this truly *was* the last time.

I careened around a corner then slowed as the car disappeared into traffic heading across the Ohio River. With my free hand I opened my wallet and went through my spare IDs. Now that I was going to go legit, I didn't have much of a choice.

I took out the California license that said Ellie Watt. I'd need to change the expiration date and photo since the last time I set foot in the state was seven years ago, just after I turned nineteen. But it would do. I was Ellie Watt again.

I was finally me.

Oh joy.

Ex-con artist Ellie must find a way
to stay ahead of the game ... before
it destroys her and the only man she
ever loved.

Shooting Scars

CHAPTER ONE

Ellie

"You wanted me to catch you, didn't you?" Javier's voice cut into my thoughts like a drill. I blinked at the dry, rough desert of Arizona as it flew past my window, trying to remember what was happening. This wasn't a dream, this wasn't a scenario; this was real. I was in the back of an SUV driven by a thuggish man, and the ex-boyfriend of my nightmares was right beside me. I had given Camden a second chance at life, at love, at everything by taking a step backward with me. I was Javier's prisoner now, his six years of chasing after me having finally come to a close.

I was trapped with a man who would either love me or kill me. There was no middle ground with Javier Bernal.

"Didn't you?" he repeated. Out of the corner of my eye I caught him as he waved his hand dismissively, his watch catching the sun that streamed in through the tinted windows. "Oh, it doesn't matter. I know."

I didn't want to take the bait. I wanted to keep looking out the window, pretending this didn't exist. I wanted to ignore the anger that started to prick at my toes, rising up my limbs, and the disgust and defeat that was about to sink in my chest.

He had found me.

"You tracked my cell phone," I said, my tongue sticking to the roof of my dry mouth.

He chuckled. The hair on my arms stood up.

"Seriously? Your cell phone. Angel, you aren't Jason Bourne."

I wanted to laugh derisively at the way he pronounced *Jason* and sneer at the use of my old pet name, angel. I had been angel six years ago. That angel had died on broken wings and with a broken heart.

He continued, "I can't track your phone unless I have physical access to it."

"Then you were tracking the car," I said, still to the window.

Another chilling laugh. "Tracking that car all this time? I had people looking out for it—you took quite a big chance driving around in a flashing find-me sign. But no, there was no tracking device in the car. Why would I plant one in my own car?"

"Someone might steal it."

"Only you, my dear."

His voice lowered over that last phrase, twisting in a curiously compassionate way. I brought my eyes over to look at him and immediately regretted it. I realized that up until that moment, I'd been trying to see through him, as if he were a hologram.

Javier's hair was longer now, but just as thick and dark. His face had thinned out a bit over the years and his build was somehow wider, stronger. He looked like a citron-eyed lion in a white linen suit, a creature larger than the sum of his parts. The more I stared at him, the more the space around me became smaller.

He smiled at me, his eyes glinting. It wasn't a kind smile, and I quickly cast my eyes downward, feeling that the less eye contact we made, the better it was for me. I caught a glimpse of his *Wish* tattoo on his wrist, partially covered up by his watch.

"Ellie Watt," he said smoothly. "It didn't take me long to figure out your real name. In fact, it was almost like your name came floating in my window one day. So, you must realize that when you're on the run and using your real name, well, any fucking idiot can track you down."

I blinked hard and turned my head to the window again. I'd been so careful with Camden's name, going through all the steps to make sure he could never be found as Connor Malloy. I didn't do the same for myself. The minute we knew that Javier and his men were after me in Palm Valley, the minute we headed for Nevada, I should have been more cautious. I should have concentrated more on myself than on Camden. Javier had tracked me to the resort in Laughlin, and after that I thought I was playing it smart by taking on an old persona.

I hadn't been smart enough.

"I had people waiting in Las Vegas, you know," he said, and I could see him examining his fingernails. "It wasn't hard to figure out that's where you'd be going next, that you needed to keep laundering your money. You were cocky enough to stay on the Strip. One of my men saw your car—*my* car—driving through. Followed you to your hotel, where you went through a halfhearted attempt to hide it."

I swallowed hard. Disgust was beating out defeat at the moment.

"I realize now, angel, that I didn't know you very well at all. I don't know who I knew. But I do know you're not an idiot. You wanted me to find you. Perhaps you've been asking for it since you ran away."

"Where are we going?" I said, trying to keep my breath from shaking.

He sighed. "I told you. To the past."

"I have many pasts. Pick one."

He leaned back in his seat, his legs splayed, the tip of his knee touching my leg for a brief second. Just a tap. His way of reminding me where I was. I eyed the rocky landscape flying past and wondered when jumping out of a moving vehicle could be considered too reckless.

"Child safety locks," he whispered, and I wished he'd get the fuck out of my head. "And *our* past. Do you remember it?"

"No." It wasn't that much of a lie. I'd had so many pasts that it was easy to bury them all with each other. After I'd left Javier all those years ago, I remembered the pain he brought me, the humiliation and deceit, only for as long as I needed to. For as long as I needed to become someone else, to never make the same mistakes again. Then I let it go.

"Now you're just trying to hurt me." His voice couldn't have sounded less sincere.

I cleared my throat. "I'm thirsty. Do you have any water?"

"Later. First we have something to discuss."

I turned my head and shot him a deadly look. "We have nothing to discuss."

The corner of his wide mouth twitched up into a smile. I wondered how I ever found this man charming. I must have been out of my mind.

My phone rang, jarring me. I reached for my jeans pocket but Javier was quicker. His fingers wrapped around my wrist, twisting it painfully away from me while he deftly got the phone out with his other hand. He held my arms down, pinning me against my door, and checked the screen. His eyes blazed for an instant before he punched the button for the window to go down and then chucked my cell out of it.

In a second, the window was back up and he was sitting in his seat like he'd never moved and my wrist was left aching in my lap. He smoothed his hair back behind his ears and grinned to himself. "Don't worry. We'll get you a new phone."

I looked down at my wrist, the red marks from his fingers quickly fading. He'd never used force on me before, at least not in a nonsexual way, and to tell you the truth, it was sobering. For the first time since I'd gotten in the car, I was actually afraid.

What had I gotten myself into?

"So, tell me about this Camden McQueen."

My heart rattled in my chest. "I'm sure you know more about him than I do."

"I found out a lot, yes. But you...you seemed to be *intimate*."

Acid burned along his words, seeping through his smooth facade. I really didn't want to discuss my relationship with Camden, although I felt like doing so out of spite. It bothered him, somehow, after all this time, that I had been with another man. And I guess somewhere, somehow, I still held a grudge.

"I fucked him, if that's what you mean," I said bluntly. *I told Camden I loved him too*, I thought to myself, playing with the sentence like a hand grenade but deciding it was safer keeping it inside.

Javier stiffened beside me for an instant. "So crude."

"Yeah, well," I said. "It is what it is."

"Nothing more?"

Against my better judgment I glared at him. "What is it that you want, Javier? I'm sure it can't be whether I got nailed by Camden or not, because you have your answer."

"I want," he said slowly, drawing it out. He licked his lips. "I want you and me to work together."

I nearly laughed. In fact, a small snort escaped from my lips.

He raised one perfect brow and tilted his head toward me. "You find this funny?"

My fingers were splayed against my collarbone. "I find this horrifying."

"Eden," he said, then squeezed his eyes shut and shook his head. "Ellie. You don't think you're here just for the sake of being here, do you?"

"You tell me. You fucking kidnapped a mother and child in order to get me. You paid I don't know how much money. You have me now. For whatever you want. And you're telling me, after all these years, you found me because you want us to *work* together?"

His eyes were on me, growing more golden in the light. Steady. Not blinking. Unnerving if I wasn't so sure this was a test. He who looks away first loses. I wasn't losing yet, not when I was unaware of the prize.

I stared right back.

"Yes," he said after a few beats. He licked his lips again, and it made me realize how thirsty I was. "I could have found you long ago, if I really wanted to. I would have let you go. The car, the money, the lack of answers—"

"The lack of answers?" I repeated.

"You just left. No note, no phone call. No answers." He slowly broke into a grin and then turned his attention to the window where a truck was thundering down the highway, dirty exhaust in its wake. "You know I love my answers, angel. You left me as high and dry as my mother's bed sheets."

My mouth gaped, tongue fumbling for something concrete. "What the fuck are you talking about? I left you high and dry..."

He shrugged. "No matter, it's the past."

It *was* the past. The past he was totally wrong about.

"You cheated on me!" I spat out, instantly ashamed at how much passion there was in my voice.

"Right," he said. He raised his hand in the air as if to shut me up. "I did. I forget that sometimes, that what I did was wrong on some accounts. But that's nothing."

It wasn't nothing. What he did, me finding him in bed with some ginger-haired bitch, it shaped who I was. It ruined my heart, my ability to love, to trust, to... live. He scarred me just as much as Travis had done. It wasn't nothing. Maybe, maybe it should have been.

I took in a deep breath, knowing he probably loved the fact that I was getting so riled up. "Okay, so it was nothing. You could have found me years ago, so you say. Why now? You're lonely, is that it? Having a lot of money not getting your dick up enough?"

His eyes closed into slits. "I'm not the person I was six years ago, my dear. And, I can see, neither are you."

He was right about that. Javier had obviously changed for the worse. Had I?

Stupid question.

"I can understand why you think I'd pursue you for, uh, delicate reasons," he continued. "But that's not the case. We both want the same thing. And for once, I think you have the upper hand in getting it."

My forehead scrunched. "Don't tell me you need lessons in being a con artist."

I saw the first genuine smile yet stretched briefly across his face. "You're a lot better at other things, Ellie. You have something that I don't. You have access, contacts, and in some cases... womanly charms. Jesus knows how I fell for them once."

His eyes glided up my body from my jeans-clad legs to my bare arms. To where the tattoo, his tattoo, wrapped around my bicep like an anaconda, squeezing the life out of me.

"And what if I won't help you?" I said, rubbing at

my parched throat. I was thirsty, and thoughts about what Javier might do if I ever refused him dried me out even more.

"I don't think you'll refuse," he said with total confidence. He leaned forward and tapped on the tinted glass that separated the driver from us. "*Agua, dos,*" he said, and the bald driver leaned down and brought out two water bottles. Javier handed one to me and the window went back up.

I quickly unscrewed the cap and took a large swig. It was cool and strangely sweet and did a lot to quench my thirst.

"And if I refuse?" I repeated, wiping my mouth.

He slowly sipped his water, his eyes on me, far too intimate, far too observant. "I have ways of making you see the bigger picture. Now, drink up."

At that, I immediately brought the bottle away from my lips.

"So suspicious, Ellie," he crooned. I felt the bottle slipping out of my hands as I tried to grasp it. He plucked it from me and pressed down on my shoulder so I was back against the seat. His fingers were rougher than I remembered but hot, as if fueled by a radiator. Everything was starting to go loose and numb. The interior of the car swirled.

"Naturally," he went on, leaning forward and peering into my eyes, "you have a right to be so. Eden White was far too trusting."

My head had lolled back onto the seat. I could see the lightning jags of gold and green meeting his pupils, the tiny lines that formed at the corners of his eyes, the one strand of salt-colored hair that dared to show its face at his widow's peak. Javier had aged. There was nothing scarier.

"Sleep well, my angel." His voice came to me on a wave of vibration. There were swirls of light and then everything went black.

Find out where Ellie and Javier's dark, breathtakingly sexy
and dangerously toxic love story began. . .

On Every Street

The Artists Trilogy – Prequel to Book One

A beautiful, damaged con artist after the drug lord
who was her ruin.

A dangerous and seductive henchman for the enemy,
who she can't help but fall for.

With body and heart battling with the deepest desire for
revenge, no one will walk away from this con a winner.

*'At that moment, this man saw me.
The real me underneath the bombshell mask.
I felt like he must have seen everything.'*

Utterly explosive and shockingly sexy, join
Ellie and Camden on their addictive journey. . .

The Artists Trilogy – Book One

A con artist escaping to her hometown to leave her
grifting life behind.

A figure from her past who's bigger, badder and sexier than
before, and with a thriving tattoo business.

The two come head to head and enter a dangerous bargain.
The wild ride has only just begun. . .

'He filled me with light. With effervescence. With hope . . .
"I love you," he whispered.
"From now until the end, under any name you choose."'

The Artists Trilogy continues with an unforgettable,
electrifying journey of love and revenge. . .

Shooting Scars

The Artists Trilogy - Book Two

A con artist trapped by her former lover in his dark,
twisted game.

A dangerous, heinous crime must be committed to save
the only man she's ever loved.

In the name of revenge and to honour his heart, the love of
her life is forced to unleash his darkest, deadliest side.

'I had given Camden a second chance at life, at love . . .
I was Javier's prisoner now . . .
I was trapped with a man who would either
love me or kill me.'

headline
ETERNAL

FIND YOUR HEART'S DESIRE...

VISIT OUR WEBSITE: www.headlineeternal.com

FIND US ON FACEBOOK: facebook.com/eternalromance

FOLLOW US ON TWITTER: @eternal_books

EMAIL US: eternalromance@headline.co.uk